In The

Dark

of a

Dream

L.E. DeLano

IN THE DARK OF A DREAM

gaze publishing

ISBN 978-1-7364731-2-2

DEDICATION

For Elizabeth, John, Rodney, Teyla, Carson, and Ronan,

who kept me company on many a long and lonely night.

1

"Let's begin with your death."

"Last night?"

Dr. Grady nods as my fingers curl into a fist. I take a deep breath and force them to relax.

"Okay," I begin hesitantly. "Last night."

My mind goes back to the memory, and I rub my palms against my knees, unsure of just how much I want to share.

"Take your time," she says quietly.

I do take my time, reliving every horrible moment of last night's dream. The point of the arrow tore through me in a searing burst, but rather than feel my chest explode, it was more like an implosion. The air sucked in through my split and bloodied lips, and the burning, oh God, the burning, pulling into the hole in my chest before it sharpened into cold that became a slow, spreading ache. My body went numb as my sluggish mind tried to grapple with the all-encompassing truth that I was dying. My rapid, shallow breaths lifted and lowered my abdomen and I wondered how many more breaths I had until it was over. I wondered if I was only imagining my hand moving and I was already gone. They say your brain can live for minutes after your heart stops beating.

"The arrow hit me here." I point at the center of my chest and give her the condensed version of my dream. "And I knew I was dying."

"Were any of your family with you?"

I shake my head and my fingers trace the exact spot where the arrow penetrated. I can still feel the dull, lingering ache of it.

"Was there anything else?"

Someone nearby was crying, the sound raw and ugly, like an animal—something between a shriek and a moan. Then the horrible sound turned into a low gurgle, and I realized it was coming from me. I was choking on my own blood. I held my breath to make it stop, but the noise echoed and echoed until my foggy brain understood that I wasn't alone.

"There were other people," I go on. Their faces are a murky tease of a memory now. "Some of them were screaming. Some were trying to talk to me, I think. I don't remember what they said." I pull in a shaky breath. "We all died."

Every single time I die, it feels real.

Dozens—maybe hundreds? I don't know how many deaths I've experienced, there have been so many now. The night terrors have been life-long and have now escalated to the point where they've become my nightly personal hell. So here I sit, trying to sift through nightmares and reality with my new personal therapist.

"Is there usually this much detail?" Dr. Grady asks. "When you dream like this?"

"I don't know. I don't think so. Maybe." I shrug helplessly. "I mean—that's the problem. I don't usually remember my night terrors. But lately, I have been. More and more every night."

She clicks her ballpoint pen and writes something in her notebook.

"Lately, as in 'since your father died and you were brought to the island?'"

I give her another shaky nod. "Yeah."

"To live with your mother?" She clicks the pen again.

I nod. We stare at each other for a moment, like she's expecting me to say more about that, but I don't want to.

"Do you think that's related?" she asks.

Of course, she's not going to let me off that easy. She's a therapist. She's here to get inside my head. That's why my mother made me come to this appointment.

"I don't know," I tell her honestly. "It's a big change. I mean—a lot is different now."

Dr. Grady gives me what I call *the terribly sympathetic but encouraging smile.* That's what adults do when they know you lost your dad and your whole damn life, but they want you to be okay eventually. The sooner the better, too. She must notice me noticing because she clicks her pen again and writes another note.

"We're not going to get into that just now," she says, finishing her scribbling. "Let's go back to the night terrors. Your mother tells me they started when you were a child?"

"Yeah. Since I was two, I think." There's a fray in the fabric of the couch I'm sitting on, and my fingers fidget with it, pushing the edge back and forth. "I had them a lot when I was little, but I grew out of them, mostly. I still get them, but I'll go months without any and then get a couple of weeks of them in a row."

"That's quite normal for night terrors," she assures me. "And if it's any consolation, early-onset night terrors are usually the mark of a very bright child."

"No, it's not really any consolation."

She waves her hand. "Back to last night. What happened when you woke up?"

I rub my chest again. "I just laid there in my bed and couldn't move for a while. That usually happens."

Dr. Grady taps her pen on her chin. "Sleep paralysis," she says, making a notation. "That can go hand-in-hand with this kind of intense dreaming. A stress trigger can bring on clusters of these sorts of dreams if you're susceptible to them. I know it's frightening for you at the time, but it's just your subconscious telling you it doesn't like where you're at."

That's obvious, I think. But I say, "I guess."

"Having to move, losing your parent, it's a lot for anyone to live through," she tells me. "You need to give yourself permission to grieve—and not just for your father, but for your way of life before now. No one expects you to be okay with any of this, J.J., especially your mother. But she loves you and she grieves along with you."

My head snaps up from where I was watching my finger play with the upholstery on the couch. "I'm supposed to believe that she grieves for my father?"

I probably shouldn't spout off this way because she's a therapist and she'll read all kinds of stuff into it, but I have to say something about this.

"Like I said, it's okay to be angry—" she begins.

"My *mother?*" I spit the word like it's a curse word. "My mother walked out on us to be with the man she was having an affair with. Before I came here, I'd seen her twice in the last five years. If she didn't have to pay child support, she wouldn't have contacted my father ever again."

"You don't know that. And none of that means she doesn't have feelings about him, or you," she assures me. "Guilt can be a powerful thing, especially if you're trying to pretend it isn't there."

"It isn't there."

Dr. Grady gives me the sympathetic, stupid, encouraging smile again. "Regardless of her feelings for your father—or lack thereof," she amends, putting up a hand as she sees me start to protest. "Her feelings for you are very real. And she grieves the fact that you grieve. She knows how close you and your father were. You may not see it now, but you and your mother need each other. You're more alike than you think."

"I'm nothing like her." I snap, ripping at the stupid fray until it becomes a full-on hole in the couch. Good. I feel like destroying something.

"I'm only saying that maybe her fiery red-headed temper is in your shared DNA." She glances disapprovingly at the anger chasm I ripped into her couch. "You were only twelve when your parents divorced and I'm sure they shielded you from a lot of the conflict that went on between them. Your mother dealt with the aftermath by distancing herself—which she may regret now."

I answer her with raised brows, tight lips, and a blank stare. She obviously doesn't know my mother well. There is no 'red-headed temper' in her share of our DNA. My mother is cool to the point of emotionless. At least, with me, anyway.

"J.J.—"

"I thought you said we weren't talking about this stuff. Just the dreams." I cross my arms and glare at her. This was a stupid idea. It's not like she can cure night terrors. I've had them practically my whole damn life.

"If we're going to get to the root of what's triggering these dreams, we need to put them into perspective with everything that's affecting you. But I think we've talked ourselves into a corner on this subject for now." She scratches out a few more notes. "Let's talk about school. How are you acclimating?"

I relax a little now that we've left that line of questioning. "It's okay. Different."

She reaches for her cup of coffee and leans back in her chair. "Yes, I imagine it is. Public school in Chicago is a far cry from a private high school of seventy students with a view of the beach."

I smile a little at that. "That's one of the good parts."

"Have you made friends?"

"A few. It's small enough that everybody knows everybody. So far, they're all okay.

"Classes?"

"Fine."

Dr. Grady opens a folder and pages through, finds a sheet and gives it a quick scan. "Three AP-level classes? I know you're a senior, but don't you think you need to give yourself some breathing room? Remember, we're a lot more flexible here since we're essentially an online school with guided facilitators."

"I can handle it." I shrug. "I think it helps, having a challenging course load. It takes my mind off things."

She looks at me thoughtfully. "And we're back to my earlier point: give yourself space to grieve, J.J. Ignoring what you're feeling won't make it go away."

I'm not getting into this again. I look away as the heaviness settles inside me. She clicks her pen writes again.

"Your mother says you've been having the night terrors almost non-stop since you got to the island. That was three weeks ago. You really should have come to see me earlier—we can find something that might help you get a better quality of sleep." She turns to the computer on her desk and starts clicking the mouse, scrolling through to find what she's looking for.

"There has been some research that suggests benzodiazepines—that's an anxiety medication—can be effective in treating night terrors. I'll start you on a low dose, and we'll see how that goes." She clicks the mouse again. "I've emailed the prescription over to the dispensary at the company infirmary. They should have it on-site and if not, they can order it from the mainland and have it here within a few days. Your mother can pick it up for you."

What kind of company keeps a stock of anti-anxiety medicine? I can't help but wonder. This whole island complex with its security gates and armed guards gives me the creeps.

"Thanks," I make myself say.

"I want to see you next week. Is Thursday after school okay again?"

"It's fine. Can I go now?"

"Do you want to go? You still have ten minutes left on the appointment."

"I want to go." I grab my backpack and stand up.

She tears off the sheet of paper she's been writing on and tucks it into a folder on her desk. "Take it easy this week," she says, walking me to the door. "You've got a lot on your plate. Self-care is an important coping skill and we're going to work on that. The dreams will likely let up on you when you decide to let up on yourself."

I nod, but I don't believe her. These dreams are different because my whole life is different now. *I'm* different.

I don't want to be here. And at night, I don't want to be there, wherever *there* is.

Comfort is a luxury I don't get to have anywhere.

2

My mother is waiting for me when I get home. Normally, she's at work until six or later, but I guess she feels like she's doing her motherly duty by coming home early to make sure her daughter isn't losing her mind on this isolated hunk of dirt, hundreds of miles from civilization.

"You're back," she says, looking me over. "How was your visit with Dr. Grady?"

"Fine. She called the infirmary and set up a prescription to help me sleep. I guess I'll try it."

"Dr. Grady is very good."

"I'm sure she is," I agree, just so she'll stop talking. "She'll have me cured in no time." My lips stretch into a deliberately forced smile that brings a frown of irritation to my mother's face.

"Don't forget you're on your own for dinner tonight," she reminds me. "Evan and I have an important meeting."

I shoot her a frosty look. "If you want to get laid, I can find somewhere else to be."

"J.J.!"

I imagine a door flying open on the top of her head, revealing a secret anti-aircraft gun blasting me to pieces. Blasting me back out of her life. I turn and walk away, the invisible mortars falling all around me. She won't bother to call me back or even follow. She never does.

Once inside my room I turn to swiftly close the door, simultaneously tossing my backpack onto the bed. A voice goes *oof!* and the backpack lands on the floor, shoved there by the sixteen-year-old girl sitting cross-legged on my bed. I jump, startled.

"Rio! You gave me a heart attack! How long have you been sitting there?"

"I just got here," she said. "I thought we could work on our biology homework. Your mom said to wait since you'd be back soon."

"I was at the stupid therapist."

"Dr. Grady?" Rio tilts her head to the side. "Is it because of your gory, bloody nightmares or something?"

"Yeah. You know her?"

Rio shrugs. "My parents sent me to her when we first moved here. They were worried about me becoming a rebellious teen or something. I was just mad that we had to leave Tokyo and all my friends. When they consolidated all the global offices and brought everybody to the island, it screwed over a lot of people."

I suppress a smile. The idea of Rio Nakamura being a rebellious teen is hilarious. Her dark hair sits in two high ponytails with fluffy pink feathered scrunchies decorating them at the base. Her glittery green eyeshadow and dark liner stretch out into cat-like proportions from the corners of her eyes. Her bubblegum-pink lipstick matches the bubblegum-pink on her fingernails. She's wearing a t-shirt with a sloth, dragon scale leggings, and red high-top Chuck Taylors. She looks about as harmless as a baby bunny, and generally has the energy level of one.

"So, what's the ultra-important meeting tonight?" I ask, sorting through my backpack. Rio's dad works in security, so he knows everyone who comes in here.

"They're hoping to land a big military contract or something," Rio says. "My dad let that slip. People are grumbling because we're hosting the investors for the next few weeks so they can get a better look at our research facilities. Dad says their people look like terrorists—but don't repeat that."

"I wouldn't," I assure her. "They never let anybody into the compound. I'm surprised they let me in," I say half-jokingly.

"If your mother wasn't who she is I doubt they would have," Rio says. "Dad says Dr. Walters is still manic about keeping everything as secret-secret here as he can, but if he wants research money, he has to bend." Rio holds up a hand, waggling her fingers. "Should I get rid of the pink? I'm thinking dark and sparkly." She holds up a bottle of nail polish in glittering navy blue. "It would look great on you, too."

"Okay, but only one coat—glitter polish is such a pain to take off your nails."

"Nails first, then dinner, then homework," she says, ticking the list off on her fingers.

I pull a bag from the bottom of my backpack, tossing it to her.

"Here, I've got dessert."

"Kit Kats! O-M-G, where did you get these?"

"It's the last bag I brought from home. They're only the mini size but there's six or seven left."

"And you're sharing them with me? Are you mental, or something? You could make bank selling these at school."

"You're my only friend in this god-forsaken place," I tell her. "Even with a therapist in my face I think I would seriously go crazy here without you."

"It'll get better," Rio promises. "Dad says once they get this contract signed, Dr. Walters might open things up again. And you're graduating this year."

"Five months." I let out a sigh of relief. "Then I'm going to college. I still have a few more places to apply to, but it really screws things up that I can't make any in-person college visits." I make a disgusted sound. "I hate this place."

"You've got the nicest house on the island." Rio shrugs, like that makes up for everything. But I don't belong here. I belong at home. With my Dad. A blanket of grief wraps around me, and it weighs a thousand pounds. I slump down on the bed next to Rio.

"I don't feel like Biology right now. I feel like eating and binge-watching something."

"Thounds goodth." Rio's voice is garbled. She gives a guilty start as I catch her shoving a Kit Kat in her mouth.

"Those are for dessert!"

"I'm a rebellious teen!" She reminds me. "Join the revolution" She extends her hand with a Kit Kat resting in her palm. I snatch it away from her, rip it open and shove it in my mouth, grateful at least, for chocolate and a friend that can share it with me.

3

 and the air feels heavy. The smell of something burning floats on air filled with fine particles that rain down from the sky, leaving a powdery coating on everything, including my uniform. I am in full military gear—nondescript green fatigues, complete with a rifle on a strap over one shoulder, and a satchel on the other.

Something flashes in my mind—a tendril of reality seeping in at the ludicrous sight of me in an army uniform. I am dreaming. I know that, even though I know this is also real, somehow.

It takes a moment for me to acclimate, then I jump as a bullet ricochets off what's left of a nearby building and a fist-sized chunk of concrete strikes my hip, sending me stumbling.

I crouch behind the remains of a tank, burned black and half crushed in by what must have been a very large explosion.

A sudden volley of gunshots makes me flinch, sounding in rapid succession further down the street. The scream of another shell goes off and it hits closer this time, knocking me off my feet and leaving my ears ringing. My knees rip open on the rubble as I go down and roll to the side, covering my head with my hands.

I have to get out of here! I have no idea where safety could be, but it's definitely not here in the middle of the street. I push up to my feet, limping from the pain in my knee. Another blast goes off and my hands fly up to shield my head. They're getting closer—possibly even targeting me—and there isn't a lot of cover around. Further down the street there are a few buildings left somewhat intact, including a clocktower. It's the tallest standing structure around, and if it withstood all of this shelling, it must be engineered to take it.

It's my safest bet. I run, crouching low and doing my best to hug the walls of the few remaining bits of building I can find. As I cross an alley a hand reaches out, roughly grabbing my jacket at the shoulder and yanking me nearly off my feet.

I let out a shriek and immediately start thrashing, but another hand claps over my mouth and a voice growls low in my ear.

"Shut the hell up. Are you trying get us killed?"

I look over my shoulder into the face of a young man wearing the same military uniform that I am wearing. He's grimy and his dark hair is streaked gray with sweat and dust. Whoever he is, it looks like we might be on the same side.

I am dreaming, I tell myself. *Wake up. Wake up now, before you die.*

I hold up both my hands to let him know I'm not fighting him anymore. He releases me, and then his gaze drops down.

"You're that medic!" He exclaims.

My eyes follow his down to my satchel and sure enough, you can't miss the white circle with the bright red cross.

"I—I'm not sure what's going on, here," I stammer.

He makes a sound of exasperation. "Welcome to the club. Now get down to the end of the alley and make yourself useful."

His push is more like a throw. I stumble over the rubble down towards the other end of a narrow alley where a group of soldiers huddle. Their heads all turn in my direction as I make my way toward them.

"Could she be any louder?" snaps one soldier—an Asian woman with a clipped British accent.

"Sorry," I whisper, wincing as another shell explodes somewhere nearby.

"You're new." A middle-aged man—who looks to be in charge judging from the stripes on his shoulder—eyes me carefully. "Who sent you?"

"I'm not sure." I flinch hard as an explosion rocks the street behind me. "I just showed up here. I don't know why."

"Just like the rest of us," says the British girl.

The man with the stripes runs a hand through his dusty hair and tilts his head to my satchel. "You're a medic? We've seen you before, but every time we've gotten close to you, it's been too late."

"Are you all—are you in my dream, or am I in yours?" I ask.

The British girl makes a scoffing sound. "This isn't a dream."

I look back to the man in charge. "Where are we?"

"Hell." A low, growling voice, accompanied by a groan of pain comes from somewhere behind me.

"Beast ripped his leg open," the man in charge says, and he jerks a thumb toward one of the biggest men I've ever seen in my life. His long black hair is pulled back in a ponytail—definitely not a military cut, despite his uniform. Through the tattered remnants of a sleeve his arm is covered with intricate tattoos in swirling patterns.

"Sarge," he complains, making a face. "I'm not even bleeding anymore, hardly."

"We all know you're indestructible, Beast," Sarge replies. "But let the nice medic clean it out for you, okay?"

My head is shaking before he finishes talking. "I'm not a doctor. I'm in high school."

Sarge stares at me. "You know who you are?"

"Yeah. I think so." Honestly, I'm not sure what to think right now. I'm in a war. I'm in a dream. This can't be real, but it feels that way. "Wait—you don't know who you are? You—"

The scream of a shell cuts me off and I hug the nearest piece of a wall.

"Do you have any first aid training?" Sarge asks quickly, his eyes scanning the end of the alley.

"I—yeah. Some."

"Then get over there and help Beast," Sarge orders. "We'll talk more when we get clear of this."

I give him a shaky nod. "Okay. I'll do what I can."

"Aww, Sarge." Beast's exaggerated sigh lets me know that despite his blood-soaked pant leg, he feels like this is nothing. I cautiously step over bits of fallen building to get to him and he tries to push to his feet. I wave him back down.

"No—don't get up. Stay seated."

He responds by dropping his pants and then sits back down. I gape at him open-mouthed and hear a snicker behind me.

"I believe she may faint," says the British girl, with a smirk.

Who are these soldiers? None of them seem to fit with each other, but familiarity and trust is obvious between them. And I have a vague sense, almost like déjà vu, of having seen them before. Maybe in another dream? What did Sarge mean when he said they tried to get close to me? My mind is whirling with questions, but first, I need to help Beast.

I swallow hard, trying to keep my eyes only on the wound near his knee as I open up my bag and look inside. I know what all of these instruments are and how they are used, but I also know somehow that I've never actually used a single one of them before. Two more mortars go off nearby, shaking the ground. Dust and debris fall from the buildings on the other side of us.

One of the soldiers—a young Black man with kind eyes—throws his body and arms over me and protects my head as chips of building rain down on us.

"Thank you," I say shakily, once the shelling stops. "Isn't there somewhere safer we can go? I need to treat this wound without dirt getting in it." I brush the latest layer of dust and grime off my arms and shoulders.

"If there were somewhere safer," he says, "do you not think we would be there?" His voice has a rhythmic accent I can't quite place.

"Just get it done!" Sarge barks over his shoulder.

Responding instantly to the tone of command, I reach inside the satchel and pull out the iodine swabs, ripping one open and shaking it out before wiping a brown trail of disinfectant across the wound. Beast doesn't even flinch at the sting. I stare at the ragged ridge of flesh revealed once the dirt and blood are cleaned off the leg. It doesn't seem deep enough to require stitches, but the wound covers a lot of area. For a brief moment, my trembling hand frames the edges of the ruined flesh, and I'm still wearing the glittery blue nail polish I put on after school today.

Part of me still recognizes that I am dreaming, but all of me knows this is real. The dirt, the bullets, the explosions. All real.

"Is that nail polish regulation?" Beast asks with a poke to my arm. I think he's trying to distract me because my hands are shaking badly.

"I'll loan it to you if we get out of here," I tell him.

He gives an appreciative chuckle and makes a motion for me to get on with it. "Do your worst, Sparkles."

I bandage him up, tearing off the adhesive tape with my teeth to secure it and then give Beast a nod, turning away as he pulls his pants back up. I just finish stuffing everything back in my bag when the guy who grabbed me earlier runs down from the other end of the alley.

"What's the sitch, Rookie?" Sarge asks him.

"Clocktower," Rookie pants. "He's moved to the clocktower. I couldn't see him directly, but I caught a glimpse of his shadow when I changed my viewpoint."

"Do you think you can see enough of him to take him down?" Sarge asks.

"Take who down?" I look from Sarge to Rookie and back again.

"The sniper." A tall blond soldier with a deep southern accent says. "He's had us pinned down here for hours. Every time we try to get closer, he tries to pick us off. It's a miracle you weren't hit."

"She's got a Red Cross," the British girl points out.

"If he saw it," Sarge reminds her. "He can always ignore it—they've all done that often enough."

"I can take out the sniper," Rookie assures them all. "But I'll need cover fire."

Sarge points at the tall blond soldier. "Gears, you and Shadow see if there's a higher area for recon. Find out who else is out there. We don't need Rookie being drawn into an ambush."

Then he turns to me. "Grab your rifle."

I put up my hands and back up, wildly shaking my head. "I don't know the first thing about guns."

The British girl makes a rude sound. "Where did they get her? A nail salon?" She looks pointedly at my still-shaking hands.

"Zip it," Sarge says, turning back to me. "This is what we call field training," he explains in a calm voice that completely belies all the explosions going off around us.

"If you're going to be a part of my unit, you're going to learn how to fire a gun and you're going to keep firing a gun until you get really good at firing a gun—got it, Sparkles?"

I guess he heard Beast's nickname. The British girl makes a huffing sound that's clearly a covered laugh.

Sarge yanks the rifle off my shoulder and rams it into my hands. "This is the trigger," he explains, "And this is the safety. Take it off, brace this end against your shoulder, point the other end where you're supposed to point it and shoot up high. You don't need to be accurate—it's just cover fire. That's all the training I've got for you right now. Now get down to the end of the alley and stay out of sight. Wait for your signal and shoot like all hell when and where Rookie tells you to shoot. Got it?"

Rookie gives me a slow once over that makes it very clear that like me, he thinks this is a bad idea. Still, he motions me to follow.

I need to stop dreaming. I have to wake up. *Wake up. Wake up!* I whisper, and I pinch myself, hard. Nothing happens.

"Sparkles!" Rookie snaps his fingers in front of my face. "Come on!"

I give him a shaky nod and we quickly pick our way over the rubble to the other end of the alley. He pulls out a long mirror that looks like a dental mirror only it's bent near the end so that he can use it around corners. He carefully extends it a few inches out of the alley.

"See the clocktower?" he asks me.

"That's where I was headed when you grabbed me," I tell him.

"Then, it's a damn good thing I saved your life because the sniper would have picked you off," he says. "What I need you to do is make him think that we're all coming for him. I need you to fire at the top of that tower and just keep firing. Stick that gun out, point it up there and light it up. And whatever you do, keep it aimed high and over to that side. Don't hit me."

"Wait—where are you going to be?"

"I'm going to get a little closer, but I need him distracted so he doesn't see me until it's too late."

"How long do you need me to—"

He's off before I can even finish my question. I've never fired a gun in my life, and he expects me to do this without hitting him! I slide off the safety like Sarge showed me and put my finger to the trigger. It's incredibly sensitive because the gun blasts off a stream of bullets that sends me backwards. My backside hits the ground, and despite my ears ringing I can hear snickers from the other end of the alley. Keeping my finger away from the trigger, I get back up to my knees and crawl forward to lean my head out around the corner, fearful I may have hit Rookie.

The bullet hits the upper left side of my forehead, tearing a stream of fire through my scalp and into the bone. My brains splatter down my face and blood pours down my neck as I lose sight in one eye. My face hits the ground. Warm blood seeps down into the dirt and spreads until it touches my nose. I am aware that I'm not breathing. Part of me feels like I really ought to be. What is breathing? I don't even know, but the pain is gone. I'm very warm and heavy and I cannot hear anymore.

The sudden sound of a door opening jolts me awake, and a shaft of light illuminates my mother's silhouette from behind in the doorway.

"J.J.?"

I manage to groan in reply.

She pushes a hand through her hair. "Are you all right now?"

A hitching sound comes out of me—not quite a laugh, but the best I can manage at the absurdity of the question. I am most definitely not all right at the moment, but she wants to go back to bed, and I don't need her standing over me. It's not going to make anything better.

"Yeah. I'm okay."

She sighs loudly. "You were screaming."

"Sorry."

"Is it the dreams again?" She mumbles as she covers a yawn.

At last, the paralysis eases and I pull myself to the side, curling into the fetal position with a death grip on my pillow.

"Yeah."

"Did you take the medication that Dr. Grady gave you?" Mom asks sharply.

"I took it. It didn't work."

She sighs. "Then you go back to her tomorrow and try something different. Maybe a larger dose."

And with that, she closes the door behind her.

Looking up at the ceiling, I struggle to make sense of things that are perfectly senseless. Why is this happening to me? My personal life is eating away at my brain, pulling me into war every night. And how long can I go on like this? That was entirely too real.

I rub my chest and try to remember the breathing exercises Dr. Grady gave me. In and out. In and out, counting to five on each breath. It's a long, long time before exhaustion pulls me back into sleep.

4

IN THE WARM PATCH of sunlight coming in through the classroom window, my eyes begin to droop as my body tries to make up for the sleep I didn't get the night before.

Then I jerk awake with a start, staring blearily at nothing in particular. It takes a few seconds to focus my eyes. A sharp sting lingers on my arm just above the elbow.

My head whips to the right as I glare at Rio. She is blowing on the point of her rainbow prism pencil, having successfully wielded it as a weapon in her quest to keep me from falling asleep in class.

Up at the front of the room, Mr. Silva is detailing the last of the lab work required on our project involving polymerase chain reactions in DNA, but I have no idea what those are because I have been zoning out. I blink owlishly as he dismisses class, hoping my brain has somehow pulled the lesson from the air through osmosis and transmitted it to my subconscious while I was out of it. No such luck.

Maybe I can get Dr. Grady to prescribe me a massive dose of caffeine the next time I see her. If I can't get the rest I need at night, I can at least get something to keep me awake during the day. And if I'm going to be pre-med in college, I can't be flunking AP biology in high school.

"You were falling asleep or something," Rio informs me—as if it's news to me.

"Tell me you were taking notes on all of this," I beg, gesturing to the whiteboard.

"I got you covered." She waves a careless hand. "We just have to pick what kind of fruit we're studying for the GMO project—which is a total waste of time if you ask me. It's not like we have giant supermarkets on this island. Just about everything is fresh off a tree or dug out of the ground. We're not going to find many GMOs."

"I know, right?"

She swings her backpack over her shoulder as a young man in a janitor's uniform enters the room. He gives us a nod and walks over to collect the trashcan from the corner by Mr. Silva's desk. We just step out into the hallway when I remember I wanted to take a picture of the whiteboard.

"Hold on a sec," I tell Rio. She follows me back in and we both come to an abrupt stop at the sight of the janitor rifling through the drawers of the teacher's desk. He has a stack of files in his arms, and he jumps a good six inches off the ground when he notices us.

"Sorry," he says, "I was only curious. I always wanted to study—" He looks around the room, taking in the posters featuring diagrams of cells and the two microscopes on the counter. "Science," he finishes.

"There's a lot of science going on around here," Rio tells him, raising her brows to make it clear that she thinks he's a little unbalanced.

I'm staring at him for a different reason. He reminds me of someone. I can't put my finger on who, but I swear I know that accent from somewhere.

"You're not from the island, are you?" I ask him.

His dark eyes go wide. "No," he says carefully. "Originally, I am from Nigeria, but my family settled in Chile a few years ago. Chile is not so good for jobs, though. I heard there were jobs on the island, so I applied."

"Did you go to school in Chile?" Rio asks. "Because I know they do internships here. Maybe you could apply, since you like science."

He's been fiddling with the folders the entire time we've been chatting and for a moment, his hands hesitate. Then he opens the file drawer and places them carefully back inside.

"I will look into that. Thank you," he says hastily. I know I'm still staring at him, which is probably isn't helping his nervousness.

"Please—do not tell the teacher," he pleads. "I need this job. I was only curious."

"Don't sweat it," Rio reassures him. "There's nothing exciting in there anyway, unless you're interested in modified food products, and mitochondria, the powerhouse of the cell."

I snicker at that, and he laughs along with us, but I get the feeling he has no idea what's funny.

"I'm Rio Nakamura." She steps forward sticking her hand out. Rio has no less than fourteen brightly woven bracelets on her arm in a variety of colors, bought from local street vendors in the nearby village.

"Akoni Bolaji," he tells her, shaking the hand.

"J.J. Ashford." I step forward to shake his hand, too. His eyes widen at my last name. I wonder if he's encountered the razor edge of my mother's tongue at some time in the past. He doesn't seem like he's much older than we are, and if he's trying to make a good impression, she's not someone you want to piss off, being Dr. Evan Walter's second in command.

"How long have you been on the island?" I ask.

"A few months." He shrugs. "It seems like a good place."

"Seems like a boring place," Rio says, twirling her rainbow pencil.

"It's a good job," he says, eyeing us warily. The silence between us stretches, growing awkward.

"We'd better let you get back to work." I nudge Rio to the door.

"See you around," Rio calls back.

"See you," he replies, but his eyes are on me, and my eyes are still on him. It's not just the accent—there's something about the almond shape of his eyes, something in his face. There's no way he and I could have met before, but I can't shake the feeling that I know him.

"So, I'm thinking we should start a club or something," Rio says as we walk down the hall.

"Might alleviate some of the boredom."

She stops in front of the glass case in the hallway that bears a handful of trophies, a few decorative plaques, and several group pictures.

"Maybe we can attend a conference on the mainland someday or something," she says. "Then we can at least put a certificate in with this pathetic collection."

I look at the scant markers of a painfully small and isolated school. One small soccer trophy, set carefully in front of a team picture, one certificate of participation in a virtual

STEM-related conference, one small robot built by the Engineering Club, and an odd little bonsai tree courtesy of the Gardening Club. I guess for a small school, it's not a bad collection. Just as I'm about to turn away, my eyes slide across one group picture near the back of the case and jolt to a stop.

"What club is that?" I gesture to the picture as I try to remember how to breathe.

Rio leans in to look. "That's the archery team. You're not thinking of joining, are you? They only had a few members anyway, and since the team captain left the island, I don't even think they even meet anymore."

I move my hand to point directly at the handsome, dark-haired young man in the center of the picture, sporting a sly grin and clutching a bow.

"The team captain— is that him?" I ask, my mouth as dry as paper.

Rio nods. "That's Mateo Ruiz. He graduated early and went to college somewhere in the U.S.—Stanford or something. He was hot. Don't you think?"

"Yes," I say faintly as she turns and walks away. "That's a face you wouldn't forget."

I should know. I saw him in my dreams last night.

His name was Rookie.

5

"**THEY'VE MOBILIZED TO THE** north of us," says Sarge. He's nearly shouting so he can be heard over the rushing sound of the river directly behind him. I have a moment of fuzzy acclimating confusion while he drones on before I notice the squad of soldiers before me, the scratchiness of the woolen uniform I'm wearing, the musket strapped to my right shoulder, and the leather satchel with a caduceus burned into it slung over my left shoulder.

Here we go again, riding the nightmare rollercoaster.

"That you back there, Sparkles?" Sarge calls out. "Move up here and pay attention. The objective is to capture the plantation house on the other side of these trees, then locate and seize the correspondence that was delivered there earlier today," he continues.

"Why didn't we just get the messenger?" Beast asks.

"Intelligence reports were inaccurate as to transmission time," Sarge replies.

"Selective intelligence," the British girl says with a disgusted sound.

They continue discussing the mission as I move out of the trees to stand next to Rookie. My mind flashes to the picture in the trophy case of those dark eyes, of that crooked smile.

The young man in the archery club photo was Rookie. I'm sure of it.

No, I'm not. That's ridiculous. How could it be?

I shift my gaze, trying not to look like I'm staring at him, even though I am. He has dark eyes, a straight nose, and high cheekbones. He's actually handsome, and I might have noticed before if his face hadn't been so dirty and people weren't trying to kill me. Was his nose a little bigger? And his hair—it's not really the same as in the picture. Of course, in the picture it was neatly combed with only a slight tousle up front, probably very deliberate but meant to look casual. Here, it's messier, thick and shining in the bright sunlight. He has extraordinarily long eyelashes, and a small scar near the corner of his mouth. Was that in the picture? I don't remember. That mouth lifts into a smile now as he stares down at me.

"You falling in love with me, Sparkles?" He drawls. "We don't have time for that."

"Don't flatter yourself." My face burns with embarrassment, and Sarge's eyes fix on us both.

"Sorry to interrupt you two," he snaps, "But I've got a mission to run."

I give him an apologetic nod. This time, I'm going to get some answers. "I was just wondering—"

"Wonder later," Sarge says. "Move out! Shadow, Gears, Chef—you circle the perimeter. Rookie, you're on point. Beast, you've got our six. Sparkles, with me."

He motions for me with a wave of his hand, but I hesitate, fighting to keep my expression neutral while my mind continues to whirl.

Rookie moves to push past me, and I reach out and grab his arm.

"Wait!" I say to him. "I need to ask you—"

He gives me an impatient look. "We'll answer your questions later. Where did you go, anyway? Pay attention to the briefing next time." He shakes off my hand and keeps walking.

"Wait!" I call out to Rookie again, but he doesn't turn around.

Suddenly, hoofbeats thunder out of nowhere. Shots crack in the air around us, and a musket ball ricochets off a nearby tree.

"Move! Move! Move!" Sarge shouts. "Defensive positions!"

I run behind a large tree, but I have no idea how to use a musket. I have a vague memory from history class about bags of gunpowder and musket balls, but I'm far more likely to have a musket explode in my face than to get it loaded. And they're coming. I toss my satchel down on the ground and forage through it until I find a knife. It's a surgical knife, but it's better than nothing.

Wake up. Wake up, J.J. Wake up, you psychotic idiot!

Useless, as usual.

One of the enemy soldiers—who looks barely my age—has spotted me. He fires his gun in the moment I freeze like a deer in headlights and I wait to die all over again. But his musket jams. He looks as surprised as I do and I take advantage of the moment and run.

And then he's chasing me and we're running and running, my lungs are burning. He tackles me near the bank of the river. His fist grabs my hair and he tries to bend my neck back like he plans to slit my throat, but I turn my head and bite down hard on his wrist. He releases his grip and jerks back, giving me enough room to push up and roll on over, raising my knife. When he throws himself on me again, the blade goes straight into the middle of his chest. The sound he makes is terrible and my heart twists with remorse while nausea floods me. I manage to push him up and off me, then lurch to my feet as a flash of burning pain erupts in my ribs.

I stare down at the spreading red across my side, and the handle of the soldier's knife buried there. Disbelief sends me staggering backwards and the ground falls out beneath my feet. The British girl—Shadow—lunges for me but gets knocked aside by an enemy soldier. I hit the roiling river water and immediately get sucked under, spinning and flailing and I can't see the surface. Hands make contact with my shoulders, and relief makes me go limp—until the hands push me down, down, down. I try to fight but I'm getting weaker, and I can't breathe, can't breathe, can't—

"J.J." My mother's voice startles me, too close to my ear. "J.J.!"

I open my eyes, still panting from exertion, still feeling the water as it rushes into my nose and down my throat.

"You were having a nightmare," she says.

"I know." My chest expands under my fingers as I pull in a full breath, welcome and long.

"It's time to get up," she says, shaking my arm. "Evan's going to be here in just a few minutes."

When I blink at her in confusion, she reminds me. "Don't forget Evan is driving you to school today."

I groan loudly and my mother looks down her thin, pointed nose at me. At least I wasn't stuck with that bit of DNA. I have my dad's nose, shorter and slightly upturned. Perky, he used to call it, usually just before he tapped it with a finger. My hand moves up to rub it as she rants on.

"Honestly, J.J.," she fumes, picking up the clothes I left lying on the floor and cramming them into the laundry hamper in my closet. "Whether you like it or not, Evan is a part of my life, and I am a part of his. You're going to have to get used to each other and I think when you do, you're going to get along fine."

"Doubtful," I mumble as I roll out of bed. I pull in a few deep breaths, still trying to clear the feel of the water from my lungs and ground myself in reality. Then I shuffle into the bathroom and take a layer of enamel off my teeth, brushing them furiously as she storms out of the room.

Why am I being bullied into this? When she suggested it last night, I only agreed just to get her off my back. Any reasonable person could see that this isn't the way to forge a relationship. You can't force people to like each other. I don't like Evan, and even though he oozes charm and fake friendliness, I'd be willing to bet cash money that he doesn't like me either. I am not in the mood to put up with one-on-one time with Evan, particularly after another rough night.

My mind goes back to my dream—and to Mateo Ruiz. I had to be imagining the resemblance to Rookie. Maybe I was subconsciously inserting him into my dreams. That's plausible enough. After all, I pass that picture every day on my way in and out of school. I'm sure I've glanced at it before.

But what about all these other soldiers? Why would I be dreaming about them in particular, over and over? The enemy seems to vary from dream to dream, or at least there are no memorable features. Why do I keep seeing this squad?

They're also completely unsurprised at the sight of a seventeen-year-old girl dropping into the middle of their battle scenarios. What had Shadow said when I told them I had no idea why I was there? *Just like the rest of us.* Something about that statement makes my stomach clench. My logical mind says these are just a bunch of repetitive, crazy dreams featuring a guy from a picture I pass every day. Yeah, it's weird, but maybe not *that* weird.

It certainly feels that weird.

I yank a plain blue sundress out of my closet, slide my feet into some sandals, and cram my hair up into a ponytail. I'm not even going to bother with makeup. I definitely don't want it to seem like I'm putting any effort into this.

The front door opens, and I hear my mother offering Evan coffee. Then their voices drop to a low murmur so that they can talk about me and not be overheard.

Evan has kept away from me so far, sleeping at the visitor quarters since I arrived. Dr. Grady told my mother it would probably be best to let me get acclimated first before having Evan in my life every day. I know it's wearing thin for them both, and tonight he's moving back in for good. It's his home too, after all. I'm just an unwanted houseguest, on this island that is home to the company that began the downfall of my parent's marriage.

Codonexus is a biotechnology company and the brainchild of a brilliant group of scientists who thought nanotechnology was the next new and exciting frontier in medicine. My parents co-founded the company along with a few others. Then Dr. Evan Walters joined the group, and they worked side-by-side in the lab, all of them. Evan was hired more for his business sense than his research or code-writing skills. When they elevated him to CEO of the company, it was because he'd managed to secure all of the major grants and funding they needed to get to where they are now. Codonexus had offices in four countries, but a little over two years ago they began consolidating.

They bought a large chunk of undeveloped land on Isla Avenzoar—this small island off the coast of Chile. They built a state-of-the-art complex so that they can work without the threat of trade secrets being easily leaked or stolen, and from the rumors Rio's managed to share with me—also free of any government regulatory body looking too closely over their shoulder. There isn't even any kind of a police force on the island other than company security, which I'm sure suits Evan just fine.

He's a slimy, money-grabbing charismatic con man—and no, I'm not just saying that because he had an affair with my mother and broke up my parent's marriage.

There's just something about Evan that I instinctively do not trust. His graying blond hair is too expertly arranged, his smile too polished, his words too perfectly padded with buzzwords and double-speak. Before I moved here, I hadn't seen him since I was twelve years old, and even then, it was only a handful of times—company picnics and the occasional visit to our home. He was always trying to butter me up by giving me stupid presents, generic things you'd give to a little girl, like plastic princess tiaras and cheap costume jewelry.

I was too busy hunting bugs in my backyard and putting them into discarded Petri dishes from my dad's lab. I grew mold on bread, hiding it on my closet shelf, then looked at it under the microscope Dad gave me for my seventh birthday.

Even though I was young when they all still worked together, I could see my dad's frustration growing on a daily basis and the stress it put on my mom, too. She was working later and later at the office and even going in on weekends. I could hear my parents fighting about it sometimes after I was in bed, when they thought I was sleeping.

And then suddenly my dad didn't work there anymore. He took a job at another research firm. A week later, I came home from school and Mom had moved out, without even letting me know. She hadn't let dad know either. He did his best to shield me from a lot of what was going on, but I'm not stupid. I knew she'd left with Evan, and there would be no more plastic tiaras and no more reason to pretend that I liked him, for her sake.

I still see no reason to pretend.

A glance at my phone tells me I've run out of time. I need to leave for school. Might as well get it over with. Stepping out of my bedroom, I shake my head no at my mother's offer of breakfast. She and Evan share a look, and it makes me want to flip them both off.

"You ready to hit the road?" Evan asks, as he grabs his computer bag and opens the front door.

Mom gives me a forced smile and a pleading look as she tips her head toward the door.

"I'm ready," I say, resigned to my fate.

We walk out to Evan's sports car—the one he had shipped to the island—and he opens the door for me, making a grand, sweeping gesture with his hand, like he's some kind of knight and I'm climbing into a carriage. I don't bother acknowledging that as I slide in and let him shut the door.

"I could have walked to school," I grumble as he slides into the driver's seat.

"But then you would miss having everyone watch you pull up in a sweet ride like this," he says, patting the dashboard.

We drive past the farm co-op area, turn at the transportation depot, and make our way past the larger complex that contains the research labs, dormitory, and the community of small, thatched houses for most of the families that work here—the ones who aren't executives, anyway. The execs get nicer homes near the beach like ours.

Just inside the gate, Evan slows the car, and we pull up next to three men dressed all in black, and each has a gun and a knife on their belt. Evan pins on that smarmy smile.

"*Buenos Dias,* Armando," he calls out. "I was not expecting you so early."

Armando turns slowly and I try not to stare. He has a wicked scar that runs from his ear to his mouth, the knotted, red tissue twisting his upper lip into a permanent sneer. He's the smallest of the three men—the other two are big and well-muscled. Despite that, there's a wiry strength in his lean frame, and the predatory look in his eyes freezes Evan in place for a charged moment before he answers.

"Are we not free to look around?" His voice is low, steady, and his English is clear, with only the slightest hint of a

Spanish accent. "We are making a significant investment. And we've all signed your non-disclosure agreement."

Evan recovers his charm and waves a casual hand. "Of course. Absolutely. But I wanted to accompany you personally so that I may answer any questions or clarify some of the more complex research data that we've compiled for you."

"I'm sure you would." There is a pause as Evan waits for him to expand on that, but he doesn't. Armando's eyes shift to me. "Your daughter?"

"No." Evan and I both answer at the same time, though my answer is a lot more emphatic.

"She's a student here," Evan clarifies, and I get the feeling he's uncomfortable telling Armando this. "I need to drop her at the school and then perhaps we can have breakfast together before going over the latest projections?"

Armando gives a nod. "We will meet at your office."

"Outstanding." Evan's smile is so wide and the tone of his voice so fake I nearly laugh—until Armando stares right at me, and his twisted lip curves into a smile that sends a chill skittering down my spine.

"Be careful with your precious cargo," he says to Evan. Then he strides away, his shadows falling into step behind him. Evan drives off, a bit too fast.

"So—J.J.," he suddenly says, obviously changing the subject to alleviate the tension. "I'm just a clueless male, here.

You have to help me out. Your birthday is coming up soon, right? What do you want?"

My life back, I think. *I want to go back to Chicago. I want to be on a different hemisphere from you and this creepy place and your even creepier business associates.*

"You don't have to get me anything," I tell him instead.

"Of course, I do, but it's liable to be something that's not useful to you if I don't get a rough guideline, here."

He looks at my locket as I absently slide it around on its chain. "There are a couple of tradesmen in the village that make beautiful pieces. I could commission something to your taste—give you a little variety in your jewelry wardrobe."

"That's okay. I'm not a jewelry wardrobe sort of person." Is this how he won my mother over? Ugh.

"Gift cards are so impersonal—and with shipping costs added in they don't get you much," he muses. "The nearest shopping mall is two hours by boat and another hour from there by car. How about an experience? There are a few activities and excursions we can buy here on the island. What sort of things did you like to do back at home?"

The question makes my stomach clench. I don't want to talk about all the things I used to do with my dad. Or any of the things I miss from my old life. From when I had a life.

"You don't need to get me anything," I tell him around the tightness in my throat. "It's just another day."

"That's not true," he protests. "Your birthday was one of the greatest days of your mother's life—next to meeting me of course."

He gives a forced chuckle that sets my teeth on edge. I don't dignify that with a response, turning my face away until we finally pull up in front of the school.

"How about I take us all out for a really good dinner at that nice place in the village—the one on the beach?" He offers.

"Fine." I say, exiting the car. I don't look at him as I shut the door, and I don't bother saying goodbye.

I know I'm going to hear about this conversation from my mother later at the house. My mouth twists into a bitter line. My house, but not my home. I lost that the day my father's car went into the north branch of the Chicago River.

6

"**HOW MUCH LONGER, DADDY?**" My nine-year-old voice rings out in the quiet of the lab. Dad looks up from the microscope. He's been channeling all of his attention to his slides and his computer screen for what feels like an hour to me but was probably in reality only several minutes. He blinks his eyes a couple of times before they focus on me.

"Not too much longer, Bug," he promises. "I just have to get this last bit of data recorded. These experiments are time-sensitive, so we had to come back to the lab tonight."

"What are you studying anyway?"

"This particular experiment," he says, carefully swapping out one Petri dish for another, "is about molecular recognition."

"What's that?" I ask, wrinkling my nose.

"It means that fabricated molecules can be designed so that a specific arrangement is favored due to non-covalent intermolecular forces. In other words," he says, adjusting the focus on the microscope, "we're looking at the electromagnetic reactions between the molecules and the nanites to see if we can get those reactions to repeat themselves. Then we'll have more control over the process and we can duplicate favorable experiments more easily. If my adjustments to this batch of nanites work, it'll be great." He sighs, rubbing his neck. "Really great."

I yawn. "It's kind of interesting, but I'm tired of sitting around."

"Well, Bug," he uses his favorite nickname for me. "If I had known your mom was going to a dinner meeting, I could have arranged for Miss Michelle to stay with you for a while tonight. But it came up on short notice, so you're stuck with me."

"I've looked at all these slides already." I gesture at the stack of old specimen slides he'd pulled out to keep me amused. "Do you have other stuff I can look at?"

"I know!" he says, holding up a finger. "How about you run out to the vending machine and get us both a couple of Cokes?"

"Mom doesn't like me drinking Coke," I remind him.

He looks at the door and gives me an exaggerated waggle of his brows. "Mom's not here, is she? I won't tell if you won't."

I break into a wide grin. "Can I have a Snickers, too?"

He chews his lower lip as if truly mulling over his decision. "I suppose just this once. And don't you tell on me!" He wags a finger in my direction, making me giggle.

I slide off the chair and skip happily over to him, holding out my hand for the money. He digs a few crumpled dollar bills out of his pocket, along with the heavy handful of loose change he always has—change that often leaked out of his pockets into the folds of his recliner in the living room at home. He fell asleep in that recliner some nights, and after he'd get up and go to bed, I'd sneak back downstairs and dig the change out of the chair.

"I want a Reese's!" He calls after me as I skip over to the door.

"I know!" I call back, pulling the door wide and then running down the hall. There's almost no one else here this late at night, and it doesn't take me long to run back with our contraband soda and snacks stuffed into my arms. I manage to get the door to the lab open and rush inside, running over to the counter where my father was working. Somehow, I don't see the cord that stretches from his laptop and snakes across the floor to the electrical outlet on the wall.

My toe catches the edge of the cord and snacks and sodas fly out of my hands, slamming into the plexiglass case of experiments on the counter, and sending it and my father's empty coffee mug crashing to the floor. The mug breaks apart, scattering pottery shards along with a half-dozen Petri dishes.

"Shit!" My father swears. "Shit shit shit!"

"I'm sorry!" I cry. "Oh Daddy, I'm so sorry!"

I drop to my knees, reaching for the pieces of the mug.

"Ow!"

The sharp shard drops from my hand and a fat, red drop of blood wells up, dripping down the side of my finger.

"Bug!" Dad exclaims. "Hold on honey, let me grab some paper towels. I think we have a first aid kit in here somewhere."

I shove my finger in my mouth, sucking the blood clean, staring at the Petri dishes littering the floor and hoping I haven't wrecked his experiment too badly. Carefully, I begin picking them up and setting them on the counter, but my finger is still bleeding. I've gotten blood into one of the specimen dishes. I look over my shoulder and Dad is rummaging through a cabinet.

"Hold that finger up," he calls out. "And whatever you do don't put it in your mouth. It's not sanitary."

I hastily use a clean finger to swipe the blood out of the Petri dish and then I rub my hands together to remove the remnants of the gel that held the nanites my father was studying.

He hurries back over with a wad of paper towels in one hand and a box of Band-Aids in the other.

"Here we go, Bug. Let's wrap this around you." He carefully winds the paper towel around my finger and then he tears open an alcohol swab. "Is it deep?"

"I don't think so." I scrunch up my nose as I stare at the blood drops on the floor.

He peels the paper towel off to look at the wound and we bonk heads as I lean in to look at it as well. Dad laughs.

"You want to see it under a microscope?" he asks.

"Nah, I've seen my blood before," I remind him. He very gently swabs the cut with an alcohol wipe.

"Not too deep at all,' he says. I make a face because it stings a little.

"There's my brave girl." He kisses my forehead before he wraps the Band-Aid around my finger and then kisses it.

"I'm sorry, Daddy," I say again. "Did I ruin your experiment?"

He looks down at the Petri dishes, and then he picks up the garbage can and begins to drop them into it.

"It's been compromised," he says. "I can't use data unless it's accurate and if the experiment has been compromised—"

"The data can't be defended." I finish for him. "I'm so sorry."

"It was an accident, Bug. And it was only a twelve-hour experiment. I can repeat it again tomorrow."

"Really?"

"Really. Not a big deal. And hey, at least I get a Reese's and a Coke with my best girl."

I giggle again and we carefully pop our Cokes open, laughing as they foam over from being dropped. We clean up the mess, then clink them together before we drink.

"Ahhh. I didn't realize how much I needed that break," he says, leaning back in his chair. "In fact, I think I need a *dance* break. How about you, Jenny-Jenny?" His face splits into a grin as he jumps to his feet.

I thrust out a hand, shaking my head violently. "Don't! Don't do it!"

Right over the top of my objections, he breaks into his best dad moves, belting out *"Eight-six-seven-five-three-oh-ni-ee-iine!"* Which of course, I echo until the song is over, even though I mostly hate the song. It always makes him happy, though. I often wonder if he didn't name me Jennifer after my grandmother and instead set me up for this song. I'm the perfect dad joke.

"Lay it on me," he says, holding out his hand for our special shake, consisting of hand slaps, fist pumps with both arms, bumping hips and all in rhythm. This is accompanied by our own special chant:

"You and me

Me and you

Nobody rocks it

Like we do

Just us two!"

We gleefully finish with two fingers raised to the sky.

"You know what, Bug?" He asks. "I think—"

The slamming of the front door wakes me from my dream and for a change, I'm devastated to be woken up. For once I had a nice dream—a warm and wonderful memory from a time when I had a family—and it's snatched away too soon. My hand moves unconsciously to my chest, rubbing at the hollow place inside it, feeling an ache that goes all the way down into my bones. Tears well and run down the sides of my face and onto my hair and pillow. I would give anything, *anything* in this moment to be hugging my dad again. Anything.

Evan's voice carries from the hallway in a low, hushed tone.

"She goes to bed early," I hear him say.

"It's nearly midnight," my mother answers.

"Is it? The night is still young!" I hear her high-pitched laugh, a silly, girlish sound that feels entirely wrong as I listen to it—especially since it's punctuated by the sound of big, smacking kisses.

"And it's a school night," she goes on.

"Ah, yes. School. How much longer has she got?"

"Five months," she says. "Then she graduates."

"Where do you suppose she'll go?" Evan says. "If she's not ready to leave the nest, she could do an internship here—didn't you say she's interested in medicine?"

"That's what she tells me," Mother replies. "If you can believe she's interested in anything anymore."

"If she has half the brains of her father and half the brains of her mother, she's entirely brilliant. We can always use more brilliant."

"I'll suggest it but don't hold your breath," Mother says. "She still hasn't unpacked all of her things yet and I can't help but feel that's for a reason."

Damn right. Once I graduate and have a college acceptance in hand, I'm out the door and on a plane. There's nothing for me here with either of you.

"You looked through her stuff, didn't you?"

I sit up because Evan lowered his voice even more to say that. Pushing myself slowly out of bed, I walk quietly to the door, putting my ear up against the crack to hear more clearly.

"I went through every bit of it," Mother says. "Twice. There's no key, no passcode, nothing."

"Armando was pressing for answers again today."

"It's research. Research takes time." My mother snaps. "I've told him that."

"We can't stall him forever."

She sighs. "No, I suppose we can't. And I get the feeling it will be very unpleasant for us if we don't resolve this soon. I'll look through her things again—maybe I missed something."

"I'll have them sift through the storage unit in Chicago again, as well." Evan says. "We'll find something. Now—where was I?"

His words grow muffled, like he's burying his face in her neck or her hair. I feel clammy and slimy all over as my mother laughs again and their bedroom door shuts. The nausea churns in my stomach, but my mind is racing.

They're searching my storage unit? And who are the *them* they have searching it? Why are they searching my stuff? What does this have to do with Armando? And what are they looking for—a key or a passcode? To what? It's not like Dad had money stashed away in a safe somewhere.

Did he?

Unless—maybe it's not money they're after. Then what? My Dad left the company five years ago, but he left in a hurry when he went. Maybe he knew something. Some corporate secret they don't want to come out. You don't move your company to an island and behind a guarded electric fence if you're not into some shady stuff.

My stomach clenches hard as a thought slithers into my brain: was my father's death really an accident? It was a rainy night, and he'd been coming around a curve and the car supposedly hydroplaned, but still—

Oh, God.

I drop down onto my bed, my mind racing, bile rising in my throat.

Evan knows a lot of powerful people. He brags about his connections all the time. Is he connected enough to cover up a murder? I wrap my arms around my waist, rocking.

No. Why would my mother allow that? She didn't want to be stuck with me anymore than I want to be stuck with her. She and Dad divorced, but she didn't want him dead. Did she?

I run my fingers through my hair, strong enough to yank it hard and make me wince, then get to my feet and pace.

This is crazy talk. It's probably money. Dad had life insurance money, and there was money from the sale of our house. I don't get any of it until I'm eighteen—it's held in trust until then, so they can't touch it, but what if Dad had other money somewhere—hidden investments or something like that?

Maybe the company is in trouble. They did close their offices around the globe and buy space on this island instead. Is it all to keep his investors from knowing how bad things are? After all, they're looking for people like Armando to invest, and he's definitely giving off dirty money vibes.

The earlier thoughts are still oozing through my mind, despite this new line of thinking. My mother was actually stateside—in New York, she'd said—the night of my father's death. I never asked her why.

Pressing my palms into my eyes, I try to get a grip. Try to not hyperventilate until I pass out.

I need to figure out how to get a message off the island, to my dad's lawyer. All communication and internet activity is monitored on Evan's orders. That's part of what Rio's dad does in the security office, scanning emails and websites on network computers and devices accessing the company Wi-Fi.

Rio! She hangs out and even does work for her dad a few days a week. Maybe she—

That thought is discarded immediately. Who knows what kind of trouble I could get her into if she gets caught? Her dad could be fired. I need to think of another way. I sit back down on my bed, strumming my fingers against my leg.

There are ships that go back and forth from the mainland bringing supplies. I wonder if I could get a message through someone on board to my father's lawyer. But who would help me here? It's not like I know any of the working staff.

My thoughts go back to Akoni. He's only a custodian, but maybe he knows someone who works the supply run, or even better—maybe runs the tourist ferry from the mainland to the wildlife preserve on the other side of the island. If he's willing to risk his job going through the file drawers in a teacher's desk, maybe he's willing to do something for me—if only to keep me from telling anyone about his snooping. I really don't give a rat's ass about whatever he's looking for, but I'm not above hinting at blackmail if it'll get me the connections I need. In return, I could talk to Evan about an internship for him. I'm not sure what he could do exactly, but if Evan thinks Akoni is my friend, he will probably agree to make me happy and maybe win brownie points with my mother.

It's the start of a plan and the most I've done to move forward with my life in months. With a sigh, I take one of the new sleeping pills Dr. Grady prescribed and crawl back between my covers, mind racing and hoping to return to my father's warmth and love.

Instead, I land in a brand-new level of hell.

7

IT TAKES A FEW moments for my eyes to adjust so that I can make sense of what I'm seeing and recognize that it's a dream once again. Above me in the sky hang not one, but three moons. One is very large and dark orange, swirling with white clouds and darker banded areas. The other two are much smaller and yellow, but overly bright, shedding the majority of the light upon us.

I'm aware of the entire squad around me now, all of them blinking as their eyes adjust, too. Someone sucks in a breath and off to my left Gears says succinctly:

"Shit."

His southern drawl makes it sound like two syllables. Shadow is standing next to me, and I look at her in question.

"The Citadel," she says, pointing up above what I thought was the horizon to a giant, gleaming black pyramid off in the distance. It's huge, standing as tall as a skyscraper. Its four corners take up what would easily be a city block.

And that horizon? It's actually the top of the obsidian walls before us, and we are at the entrance to a maze. The pyramid sits in the middle of this enormous labyrinth.

My body is encased in a tight black jacket and pants made of sturdy material. There are stretch panels at all the joints on my arms and legs. No boots, but I'm wearing flexible shoes clearly built for running, with soles that grip, and toes reinforced with metal. My medic bag still bears its red cross, but the bag is now tightly woven black metallic mesh.

A rifle is on my shoulder, and it's far more advanced than anything I've held before. Rookie steps closer to my side and gives me a crash course on how to use the laser sight, and how to engage and disengage the safety mechanism.

"Can I test it out?" I ask. "Or do we need to be careful of making noise?"

"It's the Citadel," Shadow says, running a hand through her short dark hair and rolling her shoulders. Next to her, Beast, Chef and Gears are stretching their legs and shaking their arms as though preparing for a marathon run.

"You don't have to worry about being quiet," Rookie says grimly. "They already know we're here."

"But be careful where you fire," Chef breaks in. "Bullets can ricochet off the walls."

"All right, circle up!" Sarge calls out. "You know the drill. Command says we have to get into that pyramid. We need to disable the defensive measures, then we break the passcode to their classified tech."

"And we have to do it all before they kill us," Beast adds.

"And we have to do it all before they kill us," Sarge echoes. "Use your wits. Stay focused and keep pushing forward. Team up!"

He points as he calls out assignments. "Shadow, you go with Gears. He's on point. Rookie and Chef—you've got Sparkles. She'll take the wall and you watch her front and back. Beast, you're with me."

He pauses a moment, reaching out a hand to touch my shoulder. "Sparkles, I'm counting on you to be a fresh set of eyes, here. Be creative—but be careful. Try to figure out the best way through. Everybody ready?"

They all nod but I'm thoroughly confused. Be creative? What the hell does that mean? Sarge and Beast walk straight down the passage in front of us. Shadow and Gears head off to the left, leaving me, Chef, and Rookie with the passage on the right.

"Wait—I don't know what I'm doing!" I say to them as panic begins to set in.

"We use the right hand method," Chef says. "Normally when you make your way through a maze, you use one hand as a guide." He holds up his right hand.

"You stick your right hand to the wall," Rookie clarifies, "and you don't lift it. Just keep following it around and around until you come out the other side. Most mazes can be solved that way."

"And this is one of them?" I ask. "It seems a little too easy."

"That is the easy part," Chef agrees. "The only easy part."

"What you need to know is everything in this maze is trying to kill you." Rookie gestures with the barrel of his rifle. "There are booby traps all over the place—all sorts of crazy stuff."

"And drones overhead—they will start flying any second now," Chef says. "They fire lasers that will burn a hole right through you."

"What was Sarge saying about us using our lasers?" I glance up at the sky and look for flying death drones.

"The laser sight on your gun," Rookie says pointing toward it. "You can't put your hand on the wall—something might electrocute it, burn it, or rip it off. Use the laser sight on your gun to track the wall to your right for us. Chef will watch ahead for any upcoming traps. I've got the drones."

"What about when we get into the pyramid?"

"Don't know." Rookie shrugs. "Nobody's ever made it that far. Let's go." He starts moving.

"Wait—Rookie!" He looks at me impatiently, and I force a joking tone, hoping he can't see how badly I want to throw up. "If we're facing certain death, shouldn't I at least know your real name?"

"No time for that." He points his rifle up to the sky and lets out a burst of gunfire as a half-dozen drones swoop down, lasers blasting the ground and walls around us. "Move!"

I flip on the laser sight of my rifle just like Rookie showed me, aiming it on the wall to the right and just ahead of us as I run behind Chef down the corridor. My hands shake so badly my light flickers all over the place. Rookie is behind me with his gun trained on the sky. I look back over my shoulder and somehow, he can sense it without even turning his head to look at me.

"Keep your eyes forward!" He snaps. "I've got your six. We need you focused on what we're walking into."

"Fibonacci!" Chef calls out, stopping in his tracks.

"Dammit." Rookie swears softly.

"Is that bad?" I ask frantically. "Fibonacci?"

Chef points down at the floor, which is sectioned off into a series of tiles. Seven up, five across.

"We have to step on them in exactly the right order," he says, "or they blow up. It's called the Fibonacci sequence."

"I know what that is."

He's dealing with a girl raised by science geeks. Ironically, Dad and I sometimes played Fibonacci hopscotch when I was a kid. The Fibonacci sequence means you add the current and previous number with every iteration. So you start with one hop in the first square, then two hops in the second, three hops in the third, five hops in the fourth, eight hops in the fifth, and so on. I tried to explain it to my elementary school friends at the time but I gave up explaining after a few failed attempts.

Chef points to the tiles. "Left to right, closest to farthest."

"And you can't do it without looking," Rookie adds, shouldering his rifle after he fires off another round that dispatches the last of the drones. "Let's do this. Quick."

"Just stay behind me and step where I step," Chef says.

"Not you," Rookie says, pulling me behind him. "You stay behind me. The faster I get through, the faster you've got a gun covering you."

I look back over my shoulder. Still clear.

"Let's go!" Chef counts aloud and steps. "One. Two. Three. Five."

Our reprieve ends as a drone zips over the wall and chunk of floor explodes to my left.

"Faster!" Rookie shouts.

Chef picks up the pace, raising his voice, the numbers coming one on top of the other as Rookie and I frantically dodge and return fire as we try to keep up.

"Eight! Thirteen!" Chef shouts.

Rookie throws himself into me, balancing precariously on one foot and leaning across two squares as he tilts sideways to avoid a drone blast.

"Twenty-one! Thirty-five!" Chef leaps from the last square, rolling into the wall of the next passageway. Rookie makes the leap right behind him and I moved to follow but I'm not fast enough. Pain sears into my leg like someone set it on fire as I'm grazed by a laser and a chunk of wall explodes next to me.

I go down, clawing at my calf. Rookie already has the drone in sight, and with a few shots, he takes it down. It falls to the tiles, and the resulting explosion when it hits sends shards flying and creates a shockwave that vibrates the ground and sets my ears ringing.

"Up!" Rookie shouts. He starts to haul me to my feet but I get there on my own. Like hell I'm getting blasted or blown up like a rat in a maze.

From somewhere else within the maze, comes the sound of gunfire, drone fire, and explosions. Someone screams for Shadow, and Chef and Rookie turn their heads in that direction, but with solid walls between us there's nothing we can do except keep moving.

I glance back at the section we came from, mentally marking which wall was the right wall and I train my laser sight back on it again as we move forward. I'm limping badly, every step sending deep, radiating pain up my leg.

Rookie sees another drone coming, and takes it down.

"Keep a few paces between us," Chef cautions as we round a corner. "Just in case."

I cling tightly to my rifle, which is sweaty in my grip. My medical bag is cutting into my shoulder, so I readjust it, wondering if I shouldn't just ditch the thing. I don't think I have time to take it off or look inside for anything to treat my wound—and I definitely don't want to put my gun down in order to do so. My leg is in agony, and I'm running on pure adrenalin.

I look up from my bag to see Chef just . . . standing there. He's looking at his badly shaking hands like he's never seen them before, and his face is slack, like he's in a stupor. His gun is discarded on the ground. Did something happen? Just as I start forward, his head snaps up and he charges, his face morphing into a look of pure, furious rage directed solely at me. He slams me into the wall, and the shock stuns me for a split second before I scramble away.

The sound was a bare whisper, so quiet I wasn't even sure what I'd heard. A second later Rookie opens fire again and another drone shot blasts a hole near my feet as I dive to avoid it. I turn to look at Chef.

He's down. But it's not from the drone. His neck and face are covered with tiny, needle-sharp darts. His eyes are open wide, and he's not breathing.

"Chef's down!" I call to Rookie. "Something—something happened to him and he was—he was—" I don't even know how to explain what he was. How he went from normal to utterly blank, then homicidal in seconds.

"Keep moving!" Rookie shouts over his shoulder as several drone hits in a row slam into the floor and walls around me. My leg buckles as I try to jump out of the way and I go down to one knee.

"Get up!" He screams. "Get up and run!"

"But the darts!"

"They're done! It only fires one round!"

"Help Chef!" I shout as he keeps shooting. "I don't think I carry him—my leg." My laser sight moves off the wall so I can fire up at the drones.

I give one last burst of gunfire from behind the corner of the nearest wall, and somehow, I manage to wing a drone. It spins wildly, still firing, and shots are ricocheting all over the place.

Rookie dives and rolls to avoid one, coming up to his knees before he finishes it off. In one smooth movement he's up and running again, grabbing me by the hand and pulling me along. I look back at Chef.

"He's gone!" Rookie yells. "Leave him!"

He yanks my arm, throwing me forward as we barrel down the passageway, turning right. I get my laser sight back on the wall as we endlessly turn and turn and turn, always right even if it's three rights to make a left. There's a scorch mark on my leg. I suppose I should be grateful the drones fire lasers. If that had been a bullet, I'd be bleeding out.

Two more turns, and two more drones. I can hear Beast shouting through the mayhem somewhere and then his voice cuts off abruptly at the sound of an explosion.

Keep going, I tell myself. *Keep going keep going keep going.*

Rookie takes down another drone and I turn to join him in firing.

"Leave them to me," he says. "You watch for what's in front of us."

"Sorry!" I turn my laser sight back on the wall. I'm trying my best to run forward when suddenly my legs slide out from under me, and Rookie goes down too.

Whatever we've slid into, whatever substance this is, it is beyond slippery. Somewhere between a grease and a goo, and no amount of scrambling will find purchase for my feet or hands. I fall forward, slamming my chin hard. My teeth cut through my lip and blood fills my mouth as I slide even more.

"Roll!" Rookie shouts as he angles his rifle up and takes down the last drone. "You have to roll!"

I don't question him. Holding onto my rifle tightly I roll, awkwardly trying to get over my med bag with every revolution. I should have taken it off.

He clears the area before I do and rolls over, sitting on his behind as he wipes his hands and shoes on the ground, careful to set his feet down in a clean spot.

I can't lift my injured leg and I don't want to let go of my gun. Rookie grabs my pant leg, forcing my foot to his thigh. I give a stifled moan of pain as he wipes the goo from the bottom of my shoes on his pants. Then he hauls me to my feet again and off we go. My chin throbs, and my leg is one unending, screaming mass of agony, blinding my eyes with tears.

The laser sight on my rifle wobbles as I try to keep it trained on the wall. A loud bellow of pain and rage echoes from somewhere else in the maze. More explosions. Silence. More gunfire.

"Down!" Rookie shouts as a drone suddenly comes around the corner. It must have been another section of the maze and came after us once it completed its mission—its mission of killing someone else in the squad. We both duck, and the drone hits directly behind Rookie, blasting him forward.

The scream that tears from his throat when he hits the ground is raw and ugly. My mind can barely wrap around the horror that my eyes are taking in. The section of floor he landed on has a thin sheen of water on it. The smell hits my nostrils at the same time his screams hit my ears.

Not water. Acid. Sulfurous, corrosive acid. His uniform disintegrates in wisps of acrid smoke as the acid goes to work, eating away the flesh of his hands and knees, peeling them down to bone in seconds as he tries in vain to crawl out of it. He falls forward, face contorted in agony as the acid melts through it, and his dying, raspy moans echo around me as his body twitches uncontrollably.

I take a compulsive step forward, then my survival instinct kicks in, and I stop.

Screaming his name over and over, I watch as he dies slowly and in unendurable pain. Bile fills my mouth and I retch, unable to watch anymore, only to come face-to-face with another drone. The blast to the center of my chest throws me backward to land next to what's left of Rookie.

Then I don't feel anything at all.

8

"J.J.? Hello? J.J.?"

More knocking. I look away from the TV screen and debate whether I want to answer or not. On any given day, I'd love to have a visit from Rio, but right now? Right now, I just want to be alone in the cocoon of my bed, mindlessly watching movies while my brain tries to process everything it went through on the overnight.

When I came back into myself last night it took a very long time before I could move again. I huddled in my bed, shaking, tears running helplessly down the sides of my face, my breath a hollow rasp in the quiet of my room.

And as much as I have tried today, I still can't un-see the melted skin and the smoking bones beneath it, I can't remove the memory of Chef's sightless eyes, the smell of Rookie's burning flesh, or the sounds of the others as they were mowed down or ripped apart echoing through the walls of the maze.

My biology project is due today, and I'm still in bed, still shaken. There is no way I would be able to make a presentation in front of the class, even with Rio there to chatter through her half of it. They'll all see my shaking hands, my pale skin, and the dryness of my mouth won't permit me to speak easily.

How do soldiers do this? Real soldiers, I mean. How do they watch someone get blown apart, or burned alive, or tortured and keep on going? I can't even get out of bed and go to school. I am not all right. I am really, *really* not all right.

The knock sounds again, more insistent this time. Then I hear the front door open.

"Dude are you awake? Are you? Seriously, are you awake?"

Rio's voice is right outside my bedroom door. My mother is at work, but I guess she didn't lock the front door when she left.

"J.J.?" she persists. "I'm only going to stay another fifteen minutes or something just in case you do wake up from the sound of my voice because I don't want you wondering what woke you up."

I let out a sigh, clear my throat and answer her.

"I'm awake."

"Finally!" She sighs with exaggerated relief as she flings the bedroom door open. "I was actually getting scared that you were laying here dead. Like, totally dead or something. You didn't come to school today and the project was due, and I know you die in your dreams and some people say when you die in your dreams you die from a heart attack because of the stress of dying in your dream or something, and O-M-G, if you were dead I was going to be *so* freaked out."

She drops her backpack, kicks off her shoes then climbs up on the bed next to me through that whole tirade and makes herself comfortable, grabbing at pillows and rearranging them to support her.

"Can I just say—" she yanks the pillow out from under my arm that I was partially laying on. "That I love this pillow. Seriously love it. You have to get me one."

"That's my favorite Pegasus pillow." I reach out to stroke its softness. The pillow is shaped like the side view of a Pegasus horse, complete with fluffy, glittering wings.

"Your *favorite* Pegasus pillow?" she questions. "You have more than one?"

"I had a real thing for Pegasus growing up," I confess. "My dad bought me Pegasus everything. I had pillows, blankets, mugs, sneakers, tee shirts, hoodies, socks, pajamas, jewelry." I hold up the large silver locket around my neck so she can see the engraved Pegasus on the front of it. "I even had sunglasses with a holographic horse head in the center of each lens and the sides were shaped like wings."

"Wicked!" Rio breathes. "So does that mean I can have the extra pillow?"

"I had to leave a lot of it behind when I came here. My mother put it all in storage back in Chicago and someday when I get my own place after college, I'll decide what I want to keep. I promise you I'll set a Pegasus pillow aside for you."

Rio smiles happily. "How are you feeling? I was freaked that you missed school. You didn't eat the meat on the stick from that guy in the village with the furry brown mole on his ear, did you? I warned you about that place."

"No, I didn't even go to the village yesterday. I just—had a rough night," I say tiredly. "Dr. Grady thinks once I adjust, maybe the night terrors will stop."

"Are they getting worse?"

"Some nights are bad. Some nights are horrible." I give an involuntary shudder at the memories. "These dreams— they're so real. And the soldiers are real people to me. They get afraid and they get hurt and they die and—and I think it's because my mind is torturing them. I made them up, and I'm torturing them. What does that say about me?"

"I had a dream once that I dissected a live dolphin with a pair of chopsticks and when I reached in to pull out the brain,

I found the head of a creepy doll that my aunt once gave me." She shrugs. "What does that say about me?"

I arch a brow. "Maybe you need to stop eating nachos before bed?"

"Not likely." She shrugs. "Dreams are just dreams."

"But they're becoming sort-of friends," I tell her. "The soldiers.

And it's true.

These last few weeks I've been remembering my dream time more and more. I've been climbing in and out of trenches, running from pursuers, and learning to use a gun, or a knife, or just my fists. I feel like I'm living an entire other life on the other side.

"So, you stayed home because you think you're cuckoo-bananas?" Rio asks.

"I kind of needed a mental health day. My mother tried to fight me on it at first, but I promised her I'd see Dr. Grady for an extra session this week and she agreed. I think she's afraid I'm losing my marbles."

"Your marbles are fine," she assures me.

I bite my lip, turning to look at her. "I'm really sorry I bagged out today. Was Mr. Silva pissed? Did we flunk?"

"Chill. He's letting us do the presentation when you get back. He knows your situation. All the teachers do."

My stomach tightens. "They all know I'm going crazy?"

"No," she says, squeezing my hand. "They know about your father dying. I can't even imagine how hard all of this has been for you," Rio says. "If anything happened to my parents, or my little brother . . ." her voice trails off. "Seriously, you're doing okay."

"Yeah, that's why I have to see a shrink once a week—or more," I cross my arms over my chest and lay back on the pillows, feeling the tears sting my eyes.

"You don't owe anyone an explanation," she says firmly. "You're not on anybody's schedule but your own for getting through this. Or deciding *how* you're getting through this. It's your life."

"Terms and conditions apply," I say, making a *poof* gesture with my fingers.

Rio scrunches up her nose in confusion. "Huh?"

"It's something my dad used to say." I smile a little at the memory. "You know how at the bottom of an advertisement there's an asterisk? And it says *terms and conditions apply?* Dad used to say that life was that way. There's always an asterisk so you need to be ready for it."

Like I could have ever anticipated going into battle every night. Or that I'd be living a life without my dad. I breathe in sharply, pushing the words past the lump in my throat.

"Thanks for coming over, Rio. Really."

"No big deal," she says reaching for the remote. "So—what are we watching?"

I take the remote back from her to shut it off. "It's just an old show that my dad and I used to watch together called Stargate. It was sort of our go-to for vegging out. They also had a spinoff called Stargate Atlantis—and that was set in the Pegasus galaxy." I waggle my brows at that.

Rio laughs and looks at the screen, which is frozen on the shot of a space ship in ancient Egypt.

"Sci-Fi Works for me," she says, clicking play. "You want me to make some popcorn?"

I give her a sheepish look and reach down beside the bed to pick up the bowl I had on the floor.

"Excellent," she says as she settles the bowl next to her on the bed.

I start the show and we watch and munch in silence for a while.

"Rio—" I chew my lip, trying to organize my thoughts. "Do you think I'm mentally unbalanced?"

"Didn't we just finish a pep talk or something? I'm pretty sure I just cheered you up already. I thought I recognized my voice." She scratches her head comically.

My finger toys with the edge of the blanket. "I feel like I'm living more in my dreams than I am in reality now. The lines are getting blurry. Every day I wake up feeling like I just survived a brutal, bloody battle. It stays with me, and I can't shake it." I hate that my voice cracks on the last few words.

"Do you want to talk about it? All of it?" Her hand reaches across the covers to hold mine.

"No. I don't think I can. Not right now."

She looks thoughtful. "Then tell me about your dad," she says. "Tell me about the fun stuff you used to do. Tell me about the bad meals he cooked for you. Tell me about the stuff that would have made me love him as much as you did. You do that, and maybe he's not as far away as he feels sometimes."

"My Dad?" I look at her warily.

"When my grandmother died, it was like no one even wanted to say her name. I guess it made them sad or something. But I hated that. I missed her. I wanted to be reminded of her."

I blink hard and then actually huff out a tiny laugh.

"Okay first of all—he had the worst dad jokes. I mean the *worst*. Like if he was eating a cookie and it was the last cookie and I wanted it, I'd ask him for it and he tell me it was a cheesy cookie."

Rio stares at me, not understanding.

"Is this a language thing? My English is pretty fluent but I don't get it."

"Your English is outstanding," I assure her. "But clearly you don't speak dad. It's a set-up so you'll ask what he means. Then he'd tell you a cheesy cookie is a nacho cookie. Get it? You can't have it because it's *na-cho* cookie."

"Wow. That really is bad." She shoves a fistful of popcorn into her mouth. "Tell me more."

So, I do. The weight of last night lightens. I don't know if it will ever entirely leave—if any of this will—but having a friend who doesn't judge helps a lot. And as I talk, it feels like my dad is sitting on the bed with us, for just a little while.

9

I AM FLOATING THROUGH the air. Wind rushes by me and the sound of something loudly flapping causes me to look up. That's when I see the parachute.

I'm in a parachute!

My body sways back and forth, buffeted on the wind. It's bone-chilling cold, and the only light comes from occasional flashing off in the distance, followed by a boom of thunder. Being up in the sky with a lightning storm coming at you is no place to be, even if you wanted to be hanging in the sky in the first place. And I most definitely do not want that, especially in another damn dream.

I release the death grip of one of my hands on the straps and feel around for a handle. I have a vague memory of there being steering handles on ropes for parachutes, but there's nothing for me to find except my medic bag slung across my body. In the dim light, I can see that my uniform is different. Camouflage this time, but in varying shades of white and gray. Does that mean I'm coming down into snow? Trees?

My eyes adjust to the darkness enough to make out craggy shapes off to my left. A mountain! I'm going to hit a mountain! I yank the straps and lean hard to the right. The parachute shifts.

The ground rushes up at me with alarming speed. I'm coming down into a clearing and there are tall pine trees in front of me on the other side. *Come on . . . come on . . .* I plead, pulling hard on both straps as I lean back, hoping the shift will send the parachute behind me to create some drag. It helps, but not enough.

My feet hit hard, sending me stumbling, jumping and dragging along the ground. There's too much momentum and not enough time to stop. The trees are right in front of me— way too close, and I am about to slam into them at what feels like fifty miles an hour.

Suddenly, I'm pulled violently from behind. All the air punches out of my lungs as my momentum is abruptly halted by a hard yank on my harness.

I slam into the ground on my behind, rolling onto my hip. My fingers dig into the dirt and grass, ripping off one glove. I spasm, trying desperately to recover the air that was just knocked out of me. Once my lungs start working again, I sit up to look at the boulder my parachute is wrapped around. With a groan of pain, the impact to my butt and hip becomes apparent. That is going to be one ugly bruise.

A sudden gust of freezing wind pulls the parachute, making it ripple and tug at my straps. I feel the harness up and down until I find the latches, and with numb fingers, it takes an inordinately long amount of time for me to get free.

Rolling to my knees, I push awkwardly to my feet to walk into the howling wind. Thunder rumbles off in the distance. Occasional slight scuttling sounds that could be leaves or small animals—please let them be small animals—startle me as I walk.

I try to remember any landmarks I saw when I was coming down. The squad could be close, hiding in a town or the woods nearby. It may be crazy to depend on dream strangers, but I need my squad.

Do I even have a weapon? I stop for a moment to pat myself down. Something is strapped to my calf and a quick examination with my fingers tells me it's a knife, and a good-sized one too. So, I have a knife and my med kit. That's what I have to rely on.

I palm the knife. My boots are sturdy, and my jacket keeps out some of the chill, but it's not nearly heavy-duty enough to weather a mountain storm. At least it doesn't feel like it to me.

Something scurries across my path, and I leap back, managing to stifle my startled shriek. Whatever it was, it was small and probably just as scared of me as I was of it. I give a tiny laugh of relief and lift my foot to take another step when a hand reaches out and grabs my ankle. This time, the scream rips out, tearing through the quiet of the forest.

"Hush!" A male voice says harshly. "You're going to get us both killed again!"

Rookie's head pokes out from what I thought was a pile of branches and brush.

"Nice of you to join the party, Sparkles," he drawls. "I figured that was you coming down. You're shit with a parachute."

"I've never been in one before. I'm not a soldier."

"You didn't have to tell me." He gestures. "Come on inside."

"Where are the others?"

"That's a very good question," he says. "Looks like we've got a U.S.S."

"What's a U.S.S.?"

"Unscheduled Survival Scenario," he explains. "We were dropped west of here and nobody noticed the storm coming in behind us. The wind picked up and scattered us all to hell. So, we're in a survival situation. We need to shelter here until morning then rendezvous in daylight and reassess. Now get in here before someone or something spots you."

"Someone?"

"We're near a heavily guarded supply hub. Our mission objective is to break in and steal a coded manifest, but that isn't happening with just the two of us."

"Are they patrolling the forest?" I ask in a whisper.

"They might be, if any of them saw us come down," he says. "But the more immediate danger is wolves."

"Can't we light a fire to keep them away?" I can't help the way my voice squeaks.

He snorts. "And they call me Rookie."

I immediately realized my mistake. "We'll be seen if we have a fire."

"Keep it up, Sparkles." Somehow, the name sounds like a slur when he says it. "You're learning. Slowly. Now get in here."

"There are probably spiders in there," I grumble, wishing instantly I didn't sound like such a wimp.

"Probably."

I get on my hands and knees and slide in, wondering how in the world we're going to fit two of us into this space.

Rookie shifts to make room in the shelter, which is just a stack of branches layered together and resting against a tree. The branches snap and crackle in protest, and part of me worries that the whole thing is going to come slamming down on us. I put a hand up to keep my face from getting scratched as Rookie pulls another branch in behind me to seal us off.

"How will we know if the wolves come?" I ask.

"We should hear them," he assures me. "They usually run in a pack, so they make some noise."

"Maybe the smell from the pine sap and pine needles will disguise us."

"Not a prayer." He sounds almost cheerful as he lays his rifle down on the other side of him. "Big spoon or little spoon?"

I turn my head, barely able to make out his face in the enclosed darkness. "Excuse me?"

"It's freezing. And even with the branches, some condensation is definitely filtering in through the tree cover. We're going to need to conserve our body heat."

"So, you want to—spoon me?"

"Or you can spoon me, I don't really care. I just want to be warm."

"Oh." I'm grateful it's dark and he can't see the redness of my face. "I guess that makes sense."

Rookie makes a sound through his teeth that tells me he's still pretty tired of having to deal with me. I roll on my side and scoot back, and his arm comes around my waist, pulling me closer as he settles himself in. I'm warmer all right, but sleep? Not going to happen.

"Close your eyes," he says as if reading my mind. "I'll take first watch."

"I don't think I can sleep."

"Just because you've got a crush on me, Sparkles, doesn't mean I'm up for anything."

"I do *not* have a crush on you," I retort. "And that isn't my name."

"Sure thing, Sparkles." He shrugs and I grit my teeth in irritation. "It fits you."

"What's that supposed to mean?" I glare at him over my shoulder.

"It means you're about as far from a soldier as a person could be."

I start to roll over and face him but his arm tightens and makes me acutely aware of every single inch of his warm body against mine.

"What have you got against me anyway?" I ask.

"Take it easy," he says. "I'm just saying that we've finally got our rhythm down, we're working really well as a unit, and now you get thrown into the mix—someone with no combat skills or experience. Why?"

"I don't know." I am so tired, and still cold, despite his body heat. I just want to wake up in my bed already. "I'm doing the best I can and not a damn one of you has explained much of anything to me."

His cheek settles against the back of my head, and his breath tickles my ear as he speaks.

"I forget what it's like," he says. "Being new. We haven't had anybody new since I joined the squad."

It isn't much of an apology, but I'll take it. I'm not going to lay here pretending to sleep. There's no way I'll be able to with him wrapped around me. I'm going to use this precious time when no one is shooting or stabbing me to get some answers.

"So, what's your name—really?" I try to sound like I'm just making conversation. "And why do they call you Rookie, and not something like Matt? Or maybe—Mateo?" The name has zero effect on him.

"I'm Rookie because until you showed up, that's what I was. The new guy on the squad." He shifts, trying to get more comfortable and I try to calm my suddenly ragged breathing. "None of us remembers much about our lives. Practical knowledge is still there, and specialized training, as far as we can tell. But no one remembers how they acquired it or when.

Or who we were before we started the scenarios." His fingers are cold on my cheek as he moves my hair out of his face. I shiver at the touch.

"Scenarios? Like what you said earlier about this being an unscheduled survival scenario?" I say slowly as the words return to my mind. "Like the Citadel? Or the street with the sniper?"

"All scenarios. We've done the clocktower scenario dozens of times," he explains. "They change the location of the sniper, but the town is generally the same. He's managed to kill me most times, but I'm getting better. I've disabled or killed him the last three or four runs of that scenario. Once we get past the sniper, the objective is to get into the enemy encampment on the other side of town and get our hands on their most recent coded dispatch—the codes change all the time, and we have to keep on top of it."

"You mean to tell me that all of you have been fighting and reliving this stuff over and over again?" I can't seem to lower the pitch of my voice. "All these scenarios end up that way?"

"Not all. Sometimes we accomplish the objective and we get a breather for a little while. Then we change scenarios when we sleep," he yawns, as if he's trying to reinforce the word.

"Are all the scenarios like this? Like war?"

"Wait till you hit Paleo Planet," he says. "I'd tell you that you get used to it after a while, but you don't. Most times, you come back to life for the next scenario. But sometimes . . ." his voice trails off.

"Sometimes?"

"Sometimes you die and don't come back. There were nine on the squad originally. Now we're down to six—well, seven, I guess, since you showed up."

You can die and not come back? That sounds decidedly ominous. And what about going a little crazy? Like what Chef did at the Citadel?

"How long ago have you all been doing this?" I ask.

"Months? Years, maybe? Who knows? The scenarios start to run into each other. You never know if you're going to land in day or night, winter, summer, spring or fall." He shrugs. "It's hard to keep track of time."

I'm afraid to ask it, but I have to. "And you all wake up to your normal lives in the morning like I do?"

He shifts up on his elbow and peers down at me. "You wake up? What's that supposed to mean?"

"I mean, this isn't my whole life. I wake up and go back to my normal life. And I remember my name and all of that while I'm here."

"This is all a dream to you? That is—" He falls back, slaps a hand to his forehead. "I don't know what that is. So you shift into a non-combat scenario?"

"Not a scenario. My real life."

"Huh." He says it like he finds that hard to believe.

"It's true," I assure him. "None of you leave here?"

"Never. Just change scenarios."

"That's freaky."

He huffs a laugh. "Not the F word we use to describe it."

Despite the horror of the situation, that makes me smile. "You really have no memories of who you were before this?"

"Nope. And you retained everything?"

"I remember my name, my life, my family—"

I think about my family the way it is now, about how I'm going to wake up in a little while and still be stranded on that godforsaken island.

"Well, I don't really have a family anymore," I tell him softly. "Or a real home."

"Guess you'll fit right in, then."

"Guess so."

We're silent for a minute, listening to the sound of the wind in the trees.

"Why can't you get out?" I ask. "Wake up?"

The branches shift as he shrugs. "We've had all sorts of theories. Mass hallucination. Space aliens. Nobody knows."

"I'm sorry." I mean it. This is my psychotic imagination they're trapped in, after all. I shift, trying to find a comfortable position, but there's a branch poking down right into my face.

"C'mere," Rookie says. He rolls me over and pulls me into his chest, away from the branch, and wraps his arms around me. "Get your beauty sleep, Sparkles. I've got your six."

And despite the cold seeping through from the ground, I'm warmer now. The sound of his heartbeat under my ear is strangely soothing. I begin to relax.

What seems like just minutes later I'm jolted as Rookie pushes me off him and reaches for his rifle. He clamps a hand over my mouth before I can ask what's wrong. I nod, letting him know I understand. A low sound of scratching is all that carries over the rustling of the wind. Just as Rookie starts to slide out the back of our shelter, the branches are ripped away and a body slams into him.

"Beast! Dammit!"

Rookie shoves him off, and Beast rolls to his feet. He offers a hand and pulls me up.

"Sorry," he says apologetically. "Didn't realize you were in there together. You okay, Sparkles?"

"Other than the heart failure, I'm fine," I say, brushing snow off my clothing and pulling twigs from my hair.

"Asshole," Rookie grumbles as he gets to his feet. "Did you find the others?"

"We were never lost," Beast says. "You were."

"Finally!" Sarge's voice comes from behind us. "Where you been, Rookie?"

"Snug as a bug cuddling all night with Sparkles," Beast smirks.

"We—we were just keeping warm," I stammer, and my cheeks flush as I realize that makes it even more awkward. "And it wasn't all night."

Sarge waves an indifferent hand. "Shadow got into the bunker—"

"And barely got out," she finishes as the rest of the squad joins us. She looks like hell, covered in dirt and scratches. A large gash over her eye drips blood.

"What happened?" Rookie asks. "Did we get the coded manifest?"

"We got booby-trapped instead," says Chef.

"The whole bunker was rigged," Gears adds. "Shadow damn near got her head cut clean off."

"You weren't followed?" Rookie's eyes scan the trees.

"The place was empty," Shadow says, swatting my hand away as I try to dab antiseptic from my med bag on her cuts. "Looks like they set us up and then pulled out."

"After they planted false intel," Sarge says with a good deal of disgust. "Another wild goose chase. They're not going to make it easy."

"Who's *they?*"

The group looks at me, then looks to Sarge. He rubs the back of his neck, then shrugs.

"We don't know, entirely," Shadow says. "Every scenario, Sarge receives our orders."

"It always involves getting some kind of information from the enemy," Beast adds. "Sometimes we succeed and get to take a little vacation and sometimes things go south."

"Most times," Gears adds glumly.

Sarge acknowledges that with a grim nod of his head. "I don't know where you came from, Sparkles, but having a fresh set of eyes could be good for us."

"Have you tried talking to the enemy?" I suggest. "Trying to find out if they're trapped here, too?"

Beast makes a rude noise, and Chef shakes his head.

"They do not make conversation," he says wryly.

"Shoot first, ask questions later." Gears mimes shooting me with his fingers. Strangely, an actual bullet hits the tree right next to me, and I jump. My mind barely has time to register the impact when Beast shouts, "They found us!"

We all drop, some from gunshots, and some trying to crawl to cover. Bullets tear through the air, winging off trees and rocks or striking flesh with a sickening, ripping sound as screams and moans follow. I'm shoved to the ground hard as Sarge throws himself over me, but it does no good. I feel him jerk as the bullets rip into his back, feel the rush of cold air as his body is kicked off mine and I'm flipped over, my terrified eyes locking on the grinning faces of my murderers.

Then I'm in my own bed, clutching my throat, where the first bullet tore through. The rest hit all over my body. It was the one through my heart that ended me, which feels impossible since my heart is currently pounding out of my chest. Every muscle is rigid and unable to move.

A sudden, blinding light strikes my eyes and I squeeze them shut.

"J.J.?"

It's several seconds before I can form an answer. My lips soundlessly form the letter M, but that's the best I can do.

Footsteps. Then a hand on my shoulder, shaking me roughly.

"J.J.!"

This time, I can form the entire word.

"Mom."

Barely a whisper, but she heard me.

"Are you awake?" She's not angry, but there's no warmth in the voice. I'm sure she was sound asleep before I pulled her out of bed.

"Uh-huh."

"Are you okay?"

"Yeah," I croak through dry lips. "Sorry I woke you up."

"Do you want me to—" Now that my eyes have adjusted, I can see her glancing around the room. "Do you want me to bring you a glass of water?"

"No. I just want to go back to sleep."

I can tell from her face that she doesn't believe my lie, but she's not going to argue with me. She's tired. Tired of dealing with this every single night. Tired of me. With a nod, she walks out, turning off the light before she pulls the door closed behind her.

Eventually, the sleep paralysis loosens its grip and I roll to my side, curling into a fetal position.

What sort of sick creature am I, dreaming about this stuff? I bury my face in my hands. I need to talk to Dr. Grady again soon. Something is very wrong with me. I can't seem to stop saying it to myself. Then my body goes cold all over as a frightening, intrusive thought worms its way in.

What if Dr. Grady is working with Evan and my mom to get whatever it is they're searching for? I see the self-hypnosis exercises she's been giving me in an entirely different light. What if she's using my night terrors—my trauma—against me? Could she be trying to—I don't know—crack into my mind on some level? She might try to get me to think of Rookie as someone I can form a relationship with, maybe even confide in. Then she puts me under again and sifts through my grey matter until she finds what Evan is looking for. Or worse, they won't find anything because there's nothing to find. How much sifting will Evan push her to do then? Will I end up stuck permanently in these nightmare scenarios? They could hide me here on the island indefinitely, laying in a bed somewhere, glassy-eyed and drooling as my mind turns to mush.

I force myself to breath, to calm the hell down.

That entire theory is ridiculous. Dr. Grady didn't really put me under, anyway.

At least, I don't think she did.

I am freaking out over paranoid, delusional, psychological scenarios now. Just another sign that something is very wrong with me.

Something is very, *very* wrong with me.

10

"**Well**," **says Rio, tapping** her foot as she gestures to the empty classroom. "This has been a fabulous beginning to our climate-changing crusade."

"Just because nobody showed up this time doesn't mean they won't for the next one," I protest. "Lots of people are concerned about climate change, and if they're not, we just have to convince them to be."

"With less than a hundred kids in school the odds aren't so good," she reminds me.

"Even if it's just you and me, we can still get things done. We'll be the tiny drops that fuel the waterfall."

Rio looks at me doubtfully. "We need a better name or something," she says, holding up her iridescent glittering pen with the hot pink troll doll on top.

"Instead of Climate Club?"

She crinkles up her nose. "How about Climate Champions?" she counters.

"That's good!"

"It so is!"

"Should we change it to Spanish, since that's native here?" She types into her phone, then holds it up to me. "Google says *Campeones Climáticos.*"

"Yeah, but classes are taught in English since the students are from all over." I remind her.

"No matter where we come from," Rio says. "We're all stuck on this boring-ass island."

I looked over at her. "Really? You feel that way?"

"Who doesn't feel that way?" She snorts.

"I thought you liked it here. You're always at the beach. You always seem happy."

"I'm always at the beach because there's nothing else to do in this place outside of an Xbox and food," she grumbles. "And I only recently got happy when I finally met a cool friend."

My smile is genuine—and grateful. "You've helped me a lot too," I tell her, and mean it. "These last couple of months have been pretty awful otherwise."

Rio puts her pen down and comes to sit next to me on the teacher's desk, legs dangling, kicking out her hot pink combat boots with the fuzzy purple laces.

"It'll get easier once you stop dreaming yourself to death. Literally."

"Dr. Grady says having friends and developing a new hobby like Climate Club—"

"Climate Champions," she corrects.

"Climate Champions," I amend. "Having a hobby or a club will help me acclimate. It'll get my mind off my dreams and my grisly, torturous deaths."

Rio flips open her notebook and jumps down to slide into a desk. "I've been hit by inspiration. What about a series of graphic novellas about a group of soldiers who battle for climate change?"

I rub my forehead and make myself smile. "That could work—as long as you leave out the grisly death part."

Rio scribbles furiously. "We can get that seventh-grade kid to illustrate—the one who walks funny. He draws all that Manga stuff on the backs of his notebooks."

"He walks funny?"

"He's bow-legged. Don't say anything, though. He's probably sensitive."

"I wouldn't," I say, taken aback. "I swear, you notice the weirdest things about people."

"I'm observant. And you should be, too." Rio flips the page over to a clean sheet. "Now use those observational skills and tell me about your dream squad."

I raise a brow. "You are entirely too fixated on my dreams."

"Come on," she whines. "Your dreams are the most exciting thing that's happened to me since I moved here."

"Okay," I finally relent. "Guess I'll start from the top. Sarge is our leader and I swear he was born in uniform. A career military man. And a good guy. He tried to save my life."

I remember how he threw himself over me, literally taking bullets for me. I can't imagine Evan ever taking a bullet for anyone, and I've known him longer.

"Fearless leader, defender of the Earth," Rio intones. "We'll need a catchier name than Sarge, though." She waves her pen, gesturing for me to go on.

"Gears is an engineer. I watched him build a gun from discarded parts and redirect an aqueduct to drown an enemy combat unit."

"He can design green buildings and electric vehicles." Rio notes. "Next?"

"The guy they call Chef is a master chemist who creates homemade grenades and bombs from fuel, baking supplies, paint, and whatever we can rummage around and find. He's seriously smart, and not just about that stuff. A total science guy."

Rio waves her pen again. "He's self-explanatory. But we'll give him a good nerd name like Nigel or Dieter."

"Beast is unsurprisingly well-named and lethal," I go on. "And Rookie is a sharpshooter and close to my age."

"Maybe we make Beast a shifter and he can turn into endangered animals," Rio muses. "And Rookie—I don't think we can have him picking off people who litter with a high-powered rifle or something."

"I'm behind the idea, but I don't think Mr. Silva will approve."

"We'll get back to Rookie. Your character will be the medic. They can heal everyone who's sick from polluted air or contaminated water. They'll use herbal remedies, yoga, and meditation."

"Um—okay."

"What about the bad-ass girl? Not that you're not—" she starts to amend. I put up a hand.

"No, it's okay. She is a bad-ass. I'm just a normal ass most of the time. Sarge has me practice sparring with Shadow—who knows enough martial arts to headline her own action movie franchise. She wipes the floor with me, and I never even manage to land a blow."

"Training new warriors. Check." Rio makes a notation. "You've got a dream posse. That's awesome!"

I wouldn't call my nighttime adventures awesome, but I find I want to tell her about all of them.

"We look out for each other," I share. "Sarge is like a second dad to everyone. He's strict, but he watches out for all of us. Beast is a tattooed teddy bear that can snap you in half. Chef taught me to make a fire and he's got to be the nicest person on the planet. Shadow can sneak up on you like a ninja and kick your ass before you'd ever see it coming. Gears can tell you in a few seconds if a building is about to cave in or fall over. And Rookie—"

I don't really know what I want to say about Rookie. "He's—well, he's amazing. With a bow or a gun, I mean." I flush a little at having revealed too much.

"Amazing." Rio gives me a knowing look. "So, what does Rookie look like?"

I wrap my fingers around the edge of the desk and swing my legs in time with hers. "Okay. You're going to think this is completely crazy—"

We're interrupted as the classroom door opens and Akoni—the janitor we met last week—peeks his head through.

"I did not realize there was someone in here," he says hastily backing out. "I will come back later."

Rio looks over her shoulder. "Chill," she says. "We were just finishing up." She picks up her notebook and shoves it and the troll pen down into her backpack.

"You go on ahead," I tell her. "I'll be right there."

"What? You want to stare out the window some more or something?"

"I uh—I need to ask him a question," I stammer.

"So, ask," she shrugs. "I can wait."

"Nevermind," I backtrack, giving Akoni an apologetic wave of my hand. "I'll get you next time."

He gives me a confused look as Rio lets out an exasperated sigh.

"O-M-G, just ask him," she exclaims. "Unless you're buying meth or something. What's the big secret?"

"I don't want to get you in trouble." I say quickly.

"But you want *me* to get in trouble?" Akoni asks, raising his eyebrows.

"I'm not getting you in trouble," I tell him. "And I may not even be doing this at all. I just—I *might* need to do something at some point." Now they're both looking at me like my brains are scrambled. Which they are.

"Okay, so here's the deal," I take in a breath and continue. "I was wondering if you know anybody on the supply boats, or maybe the tourist ferry. Somebody who's a friend that would be willing to carry a letter off the island for me. I can pay them—" I pause to think about my very limited bank account. "I mean, I could pay a little bit."

"Are you selling company secrets or something?" Rio asks in a hushed tone. "That's so cool!"

I wave my hands quickly in front of me as Akoni's expression turns to dismay.

"No!" I shoot Rio an incredulous look. "No company secrets. Nothing like that. This is personal."

I'm not sure where to take this. I don't want to say that my dad might have hidden money because I don't really know Akoni well. What if I end up kidnapped and ransomed?

"I think there may be something I need to see in my father's will, and I don't have a copy," I say, keeping it vague. "I overheard my mom and Evan talking about it. They don't want me to know. I need to get a message to his lawyer so I can find out more about it."

"You could have just asked me," Rio says. "I do work in the security and communications office two days a week."

"I'm not going to have you sending messages and then deleting them for me. I'm sure the company keeps backup servers and you and your dad could get in a lot of trouble. This is about me, so let's just keep it with me."

Akoni finally speaks. "I do not want to get in trouble," he says. "I just started here."

"I wouldn't ask you to do anything more than introduce me to the person I would ask to carry the message," I reassure him. "In return, I might be able to talk to Dr. Walters about some kind of internship for you. It may not pay much, but it might lead to a better job, eventually."

"You would do that for me?" He looks at me in disbelief.

"Her mom is banging Dr. Walters," Rio says, jamming her thumb in my direction. "He's practically her stepdad."

I glare at Rio, then turn back to Akoni. "Evan is trying to win me over," I explain. "He'd probably hire you just to make me happy if he thought we were friends. What sort of career are you interested in? Medical research? Or technology?"

He nods enthusiastically. "I have a certificate in journalism that I completed in secondary school, and I also ran the social media accounts for a few local businesses. I'm saving money to attend university."

"If Codonexus gets that big contract, they're going to need more people in marketing and public relations," Rio interjects.

"She's right," I tell Akoni. "I'll talk to Evan, and you let me know who I can trust on that boat to mail a letter for me once they hit the mainland."

Akoni sticks out his hand. "*No Wahala*. We say this in my country. It means you don't need to worry. You help me, I help you."

"And I'll watch from the sidelines as international intrigue and clandestine meetings swirl around me or something," Rio chirps, rubbing her hands together.

I grab her by the strap of her backpack and propel her out the door.

"See you, Akoni!" I call back.

"We will speak later," he promises.

"You don't have to manhandle me," Rio says as we walk down the hallway. "I just think it's really freaky that your mom and Evan are plotting against you or something."

"I think they are. Then again, it was late at night, they weren't talking very loudly, and I'd just woken up from a dream. I might have hallucinated the whole thing."

"Dude. You live on a secluded island and your mom's banging the president of a secretive corporation. There's all sorts of Netflix movie-level stuff going down. You know it."

She gives an affirmative nod that shakes the glittery pom-poms on her ponytails. I glance at the photo in the trophy case as we pass by, and the feeling in the pit of my stomach tells me she's right.

11

Dr. Grady is waiting for me with a pitcher of lemonade as she gestures to the couch.

"Shall we get started?" she asks. "It's such a warm day I thought the lemonade might be nice."

I take the drink and pretend to sip just in case my conspiracy theories aren't delusional. She smiles at me as though we've already made a breakthrough in my psychiatric care. Then she opens her notebook and clicks her pen.

"Now," she says. "Where did we leave off?"

You're the one with all the notes, I want to say to her. *You tell me.*

"Um—we were talking about my acclimating," I remind her.

"And?"

"I'm in a new club."

"Terrific! Which one?"

"I mean, I created a new club along with Rio—that's my friend," I explain. "We're both concerned about climate change, so we started a club for that."

She sets her pen down and claps her hands together, her face practically glowing with happiness. "That's wonderful!" she exclaims. "You're making friends, you started a club, and you found something you're passionate about. Great strides." She beams at me. "And how are things with your mother?"

I can feel myself shutting down, pulling in. Like my body is folding up into itself. I take another pretend sip of lemonade so I don't have to answer her.

"I was hoping for some progress," she ventures. She's not going to let me off easy.

"Everything is okay," I say lamely. "We're doing okay."

She gives me a wry smile. "Well, that was a ringing endorsement if I ever heard one. How has it been since Dr. Walters moved back in?"

"Fine." My voice has not one ounce of inflection. What is she fishing for, asking me that? Do they suspect I overheard them last night?

"Do you want to talk about the change?" she ventures.

"No."

The last thing I need is her rooting around in my home life. I especially don't need her tipping anyone off that I think my mother and Evan are plotting against me. I keep my mouth shut and just stare at the carpet.

She makes a low, humming sound and scribbles a few notes. "Alright, then. We'll leave that alone for now."

I give her a nod of thanks and roll the glass of lemonade between my hands. Time to throw out a probing question or two of my own.

"Actually," I say slowly. "I do have something I'd like to ask you about."

"Go ahead."

"Is it possible to dream about somebody you've never met? Over and over I mean?"

"Like a movie star?"

"No, just a regular person—actually more than one person." I set the lemonade down and rub my hands on my legs. "I keep seeing the same people in my dreams every night, but I don't know any of them. I mean they're nobody I've met."

"Yes, you've mentioned that."

"But it's possible I saw one of them in a picture. Is that weird?"

"Well," she says, steepling her fingers together, "there's actually a theory that we never dream about strangers. That all of the people populating our dreams are people our mind has seen somewhere on the street, in a shopping mall, or in the background of a TV show. So—no, there's nothing inherently weird about dreaming people who seem familiar even though you don't know them in real life. Does that answer your question?"

"Sort of." Her theory makes sense. It makes a *lot* of sense. The thought is comforting—somewhat. I'm putting Mateo Ruiz from a picture I pass every day into my dreams and that's normal. But the rest of it? There's nothing normal about the rest of it.

"I'll even go further and say there's nothing inherently weird about dreaming at all," she goes on. "That's the whole point of dreams. They can be odd and unsettling, joyful, scary, or even dull. They're dreams. They don't have to be logical or serve any purpose."

"But I'm being shot at or drowned or burned by acid. So are they and I can't help them when it happens. It's awful."

"It sounds like you're worried about them as much as yourself."

"Yes." The word comes out with a groan.

She touches her pen to her chin, tapping thoughtfully. "That shows a good amount of empathy, which is a very healthy thing to have in your coping arsenal. What concerns me is that you're feeling guilt over your inability to control the direction of the dream."

Control the direction of the dream. What exactly is she getting at? Are those words meant to trigger a response of some kind?

"So you're feeling guilty?" she presses. "Feeling like you should have saved them—saved your father."

I stare at Dr. Grady in stony silence.

She lets out a sigh. "I don't mean that to sound like there was something you could have done to prevent your father's death, so please don't think I meant it that way. But whenever someone of great meaning in our life dies suddenly, it's very natural to have survivor guilt regardless of whether you were actually there at the time, or not."

I swallow hard and shift my eyes away, blinking a few times to clear them.

"Or perhaps you're manifesting some lingering guilt because you're finding it difficult to connect with your mother when she very clearly is trying to connect with you?

"I'm going to stop you right there," I interrupt. "I have no guilt about my relationship with my mother. None. So don't waste your breath."

"Duly noted." She sighs, then clicks her pen and scribbles a few words down. "They're just dreams, J.J. They're not some magical prophecy-laden thing, just a subconscious expression that, in this case, clearly points to the stress you've been experiencing. As you continue adjusting to your new normal, you'll hopefully see less and less of them."

"Right."

My less-than-enthusiastic response has her tapping her chin with the pen again.

"I know just what might help you." She swivels her chair to access her laptop, her fingers making a string of sounds as she types and clicks her mouse. "The first is an article on lucid dreaming that was presented at a consortium I attended a few years ago in New York. Some people are able to train their mind to recognize and control certain aspects of their dreams. Perhaps you could learn to do the same."

"You're going to hypnotize me again?"

She looks puzzled, then she remembers. "You mean the relaxation and focus exercises? Yes, a bit like that. But self-directed."

She seems unaware that I'm digging for information about her possibly hijacking my brain. So maybe I am delusional, after all.

"I've just emailed some information over to you," she tells me. "And here—" she reaches into her right desk drawer and fishes out a USB drive. "This has some guided meditations on it, set to soothing music. The files are too large to email without getting kicked back from our server. Try using these at bedtime for the rest of the week and we'll see if it's made any difference at our next session."

I lean forward to take the drive from her, but she suddenly pulls it back.

"Oh wait," she says. "You need the access code. Encrypted drives are the only kind of file backup we're allowed to use on the island." She scribbles down the code for me before finally handing me the drive. I pocket it and try to keep my face suspicion-free, because my delusional meter just ramped back up to ten.

"So, in your professional opinion I'm not crazy?" I ask.

She gives a little chuckle. "No, J.J., you're not crazy. Work on the directed dreaming techniques. Maybe you can learn to point your dreams in a more comfortable direction. Wouldn't it be nice to be lying on a beach or winning the lottery instead of being attacked and shot?

"I can lay on a beach here," I remind her, "but the lottery would be nice." *I would leave this place forever.*

"And certainly more restful."

"Better than being in combat," I say, shoving my hair off my face. "Or dropped into a war zone with a group of soldiers every single night."

"Soldiers?" She jerks like someone poked her with a pin. "The people in your dreams are soldiers?" The alarm in her voice is unmistakable.

"Every scenario, the squad gets attacked," I tell her. "And the funny thing is we all know that it's not reality, but we all put up with it anyway—I mean, it's not like we have a choice."

"You're talking to—interacting with—soldiers in your dreams?" She's gone very still. "And you used the word *scenarios*—"

"Yeah, combat scenarios—all sorts, too. Guns, spears, arrows, lasers. All different time periods. It's like someone's trying to drive us crazy." I shake my head.

"These combat scenarios—" Her pen is poised, frozen in mid-air. "Have they been a part of your night terrors all along?"

"Just since I got to the island," I say, keeping my tone even. "I've probably been through dozens of encounters by now—that I can remember. The whole squad getting wounded and killed over and over."

Dr. Grady's hand shakes as she writes in her notebook.

"Well, that's—" She stops talking and writes a little more. "That's certainly—" A few more furious scribbles. "J.J., I'm going to need to do a little research before we talk again. I don't really know enough about night terrors and I'm—it's just that—"

She starts to write again, then sucks in a breath and slams the notebook shut.

"Listen, do you mind if we break early today?" She stands abruptly. "I just remembered that I bumped somebody else up to an earlier appointment and I'm meeting them on the other side of the facility." She gives me a thin smile.

"Sure." I get to my feet. "No problem."

"Thank you. I'm going to get more information for you. We're going to figure out how to help you. I promise. I just—I need to research." She nods her head rapidly a few times then points to the doorway as she comes around the desk and ushers me quickly to the door.

"See you next week?" She asks brightly. Too brightly.

I've spooked her badly. It wasn't intentional, but I feel sort of guilty about it. Maybe I was right and I'm borderline psychotic or something.

"Is everything okay?" I ask warily.

"Fine. All fine. And don't worry, J.J." She puts a hand to my shoulder as she pushes me toward the door. "I know your dreams are very frightening and confusing for you. But they're only dreams. That's all they are. Not reality."

"Right."

"Only dreams." She opens the door, then suddenly freezes.

Armando is leaning against the wall in the hallway, clearly waiting for her, and she turns white as a sheet. Her hand clutches the doorknob like she can't let it go.

Was Armando the appointment she just remembered? Not that he hasn't probably done stuff he'd likely need counseling for, but he doesn't seem like the type to have a therapist.

"*Buenas tardes*, doctor." He inclines his head.

"Now isn't a good time to talk." She forces a smile. "Can we touch base later?"

He pushes off the wall with the grace of a stalking jaguar and moves closer. Too close. His eyes slide to me and he tips his chin in acknowledgment.

"Good to see you again," he purrs. "How is it that you know our lovely Dr. Grady?"

Dr. Grady's eyes flare, and she seems to remember her hand on the door because she wrenches it away to move it to the middle of my back and give me a nudge.

"She was just leaving." She turns to me. "I'll see you next week."

Her tone carries a clear and almost frantic dismissal, and Armando looks amused at her obvious discomfort.

I give them both a nod and start walking. I sure as hell don't want to get in the middle of whatever this is.

I'm halfway down the hall when Armando says, "I thought I might walk you to the laboratory before our meeting with Dr. Walters and Dr. Ashford."

"That's very kind but I need to see to a few things first," Grady says in that overly-bright way. "Go ahead without me."

"Your errands can wait." Armando's voice doesn't sound so friendly now. "You and I will chat without Dr. Walters around to redirect the conversation."

I'm nearly at the door, but I slow when I hear that. He sounds like Evan irritates him as much as he does me. Surprise, surprise.

"I-I really don't have much more to add to our last briefing—"

"I am sure a walk in the fresh air will help you fill in all the details I seek," Armando says smoothly—with a bite of steel beneath it. "Shall we?"

I open the door and step outside, wondering if I can hide somewhere and follow them but I run into Armando's two shadows standing right outside the building. The thought of Dr. Grady going for a walk with Armando—and the creepy sidekicks lurking behind—makes my stomach tighten. What has Evan pulled her into? And what doesn't Evan want her discussing with Armando?

What the hell is going on?

12

I LIE IN BED AND try to remember everything I've read about lucid dreaming from the links Dr. Grady sent me. They came from reputable sites like the National Institute of Health and the Mayo Clinic, so I'm willing to give this a try.

It occurred to me after I left her office that this might be a way for her to secretly subvert Evan if he's trying to get her to control in my mind. Maybe she's actually helping me in some way. I'm not watching the videos she sent me, though. I'm second-guessing myself every time I think I know what's going on, so I'll play it safe for now.

First, I start by squeezing and releasing muscles in my body, from my toes to the top of my head. Tighten. Release.

Tighten. Release. Then a series of five long, slow breaths, with a slight hold on count five. I do ten sets of those.

Then I use my mnemonic devices—sentences that I'm supposed to repeat over and over that my brain will hopefully go back and rerun while I'm in my nightmare.

"I am in control," I whisper. "Challenges help me learn."

I say each phrase a minimum of ten times until I feel like I'm reading inspirational memes posted by middle-aged moms on Facebook.

Finally, I *envision my trajectory.* This involves picturing a dream I have visited before. I have no urge to be shot at or blasted by drones, so I try to remember the dream with my father. I think of the way his eyes crinkle at the corners when he smiles. That ends up morphing into a memory of one of our many picnics in Lincoln Park, so I go with it. I see the river and trees. The flower beds and grass. The sound of insects. The smell of green, growing things and dirt. My father laughing as he hands me a sandwich. Once I get the picture in my head, I go back to squeezing and releasing my muscles.

With a long, exhaled breath, I run the entire exercise again, and I keep doing it until my eyes grow heavy and the reaffirming words are barely a mumble across my lips.

And I've mostly done it.

There's no river, but there are trees—a lot more trees than I remember. It definitely smells green and growing. The ground is spongy, and the air is thick and so humid, I can taste it. My hair clings to my face. Not the park. Not Chicago. And I'm alone. My disappointment runs deep, leaving an empty, hollow spot where my dad's smiling face should be.

And that's when I notice my clothes—or lack of them. I'm wearing an animal skin—a sleeveless shift of hide covers my body with one diagonal strap over my shoulder keeping it from falling down. It barely reaches mid-thigh and I feel like I'm almost naked. My feet are also wrapped in skins in a very clumsy fashion, the strips of hide knotted on the tops of both feet. My toes poke out at the ends of each makeshift shoe and the glittery silver nail polish Rio put on them yesterday after school looks ridiculous.

A long strip of plaited vine around my neck weaves into a sling supporting a large gourd hanging halfway down my chest. It's been hollowed out inside, and the top only partially cut to leave it attached on one side, able to flip over like a lid.

Inside is a primitive med kit. I pull out a handful of leaves, giving them a cautious sniff. Mint. That's good for stomach problems. The other bunch of leaves have small flowers, and I struggle to remember the workshop I attended at the hospital once: *Medicinal Herbs from Your Garden*. I think these might be primrose, which can treat rashes and eczema. Aloe Vera would be better, but I don't see any of that. There's also a stub of bright orange root—I'm guessing turmeric for its anti-inflammatory use, and finally, a piece of bone sharpened into a needle.

Bird calls echo around me and I jump as an enormous insect buzzes by my ear. My hand flails, swatting it away, and then I turn in a circle to get a better look at my surroundings.

Where is everyone? I calm my breathing and listen.

There. Something cracks over to my left.

"Hello?"

Another crunch to my left, and another, and another. Whoever it is—they're definitely coming toward me, and quickly.

"Sarge?" I call out. "Rookie?"

Just as I pivot to turn, a blur of fur and tusks breaks through the trees with incredible speed. I leap to the side as it skids and turns to come back at me, letting out something between a squeal and a roar.

I'd say it was a boar, but I've never seen one up close and any pictures I've seen of them don't look like this. This thing is enormous, standing nearly as tall as me, with a hide that blends perfectly into the dirt and mud. It has a square head like a cow with lethal-looking tusks and a muscular, long-legged body like a horse. I have a split-second to live and the only way to do that is by going up.

Luckily, the closest tree has one branch that's low enough to reach. I jump for it just as the beast reaches me, and swing my legs up, wrapping them around and hauling myself out of its reach as I climb higher.

It's definitely not happy as it skids again and wheels around—this time charging the tree and slamming into the trunk with enough force to nearly shake me loose. Its hooves and tusks score the trunk as it tries to reach me. The thing tosses its head left and right, bleating at me, furious to be denied its prize. It slams into the trunk once more, rocking the entire tree, then again, and this time I hear a crack.

My frantic mind registers that there's nowhere to go. *I am in control I am in control I am in control*, I whisper frantically, over and over, hoping that's going to help me somehow. Like hell I am. The tree gives a shudder as the creature backs up and hits it again.

I need to get to another tree! I look all around me and let out a shriek as the tree rocks violently again. I don't have much time. I scramble up two branches above me and start walking along the limb, holding the branches above me for balance until it intersects a limb from a neighboring tree. My arms burn from the exertion, and my palms tear as the bark bites into them.

I've just found my new path when the limb beneath my feet breaks, sending me plunging to the ground with a scream of pure terror.

The animal turns and I grab the only weapon at my disposal—the broken branch. The section is only a few feet long and about as thick as my arm but at least it's something to put between those vicious tusks and me. The end of it hits the thing right in the face, and it snarls, clamping down with its jaws and trying to wrest the branch from me. I hold on to it for dear life, and we engage in a violent tug of war that I know I'm going to lose. It's just too strong and I can't hang on much longer.

The creature opens its mouth to get a better grip and I push to my knees, shoving the jagged, broken end of the branch as hard as I can into its open mouth and down the back of its throat. It rears back, so I push forward, shoving harder. Blood sprays out of the creature's mouth.

I ram my knee into the dirt, bracing the end of the branch against my shoulder and shove again, as hard as I can. This time, the other end of the branch bursts out of the back of the creature's neck. It falls to the side, trying to squeal, but it makes only a watery, strangled sound. Its legs scramble, then slow. Then it stops moving, sides rising and falling in shallow breaths until with a final shudder it lies still.

I give the branch one more shove, just to be safe. The beast doesn't stir, and its sightless eyes and gaping mouth do not move or twitch.

Dropping the branch, I fall to my backside in the dirt, gasping for air and shaking like a leaf.

"Well. I'm glad you got it," a voice says from behind me. "All I have is a bone knife. It would have never gotten the job done."

I turn my head and I'm grateful when her name leaps into my whirling mind.

"Shadow! Oh my God. Oh my God." My hands are trembling violently and it's all I can seem to say.

She strolls out from behind a tree and Gears walks up to join her.

"You okay?" He asks, reaching a hand down to help me up.

I'm shaking too hard to do more than stutter a reply. He wraps an arm around my shoulders and gives me a squeeze.

"Hey, it's all right," he says soothingly. "You got the sucker."

Shadow nudges the carcass with her foot. "Yes, she did."

"Oh my God, oh my God," I stammer again, rubbing my hands together and then gripping them fiercely as I try to make them stop shaking.

"You did well, Sparkles." Shadow pulls out a bone knife. "Who knew you were so fierce?" She gives me a nod of approval and moves around to the front of the animal.

I gape at her. Fierce? Me? I'm *terrified.* The thing is dead, and I am still terrified.

"He's too big to carry back." Gears says, rubbing his chin.

"We'll have to carve up what we can and leave the rest." Shadow takes a moment and glances around her. "We'd better be fast. He's not fully grown yet—there may be a mother nearby."

"He's not full-grown?" I squeak out. "Good God—how big do they get?"

"As tall as Beast." Gears replies.

Beast is well over six feet!

"There are also plenty of other predators out here that eat animals like him," Shadow adds. "They're going to smell the blood."

"What the hell is that thing?" I ask, giving a start as a bird squawks in a nearby tree.

"Is this a new scenario for you?" Shadow crouches down near the animal's head. "I thought we've been to this one before with you."

"I—I don't think so. Unless this is where I drowned in the river. But there were people on horses chasing us then."

"No one rides horses here," Gears says. "Not domesticated yet."

"This scenario—" Shadow digs her bone knife into the creature's neck and begins sawing her way down the hide. "This one is what we call Paleo Planet. You'll find lots of animals like this that can snap you in half with their jaws."

"Bugs that can suck the blood out of you while you sleep. Birds big enough to swoop down and carry off small children," Gears adds cheerfully.

"Tigers with tusks that make this thing look like a kitten." Shadow gestures to the creature's mouth. "Here, give me a hand."

"Wh-what do you need?" I ask, stumbling as I start forward.

"Are you injured?" She asks me sharply.

With all the adrenaline coursing through my system, I honestly don't know. I take a moment, shifting my weight from one leg to the other. Then I stretch my arms.

"My shoulder is sore, and I've got some bruises and cuts." I look at my palms, bloodied from the rough bark on the tree branch. "I don't think anything is broken. I fell on my butt." I wince a little. My backside is good and bruised.

Shadow wipes her hands on the animal's hide and then points to the long cut she made just over the creature's shoulder.

"Grab it." She says, "Right there. And then pull."

I look at her in dismay. "Grab the skin?"

"Yes. Grab the skin and pull. We need to get this hide off so we can cut into the meat."

I look over at Gears helplessly.

"He's keeping watch," she says sharply. "This is good meat and we need to eat. The others are back at camp, and they need to eat too."

"Are they close?" I ask.

"Grab the hide and let's get this done." Her tone brooks no argument.

I make a face as my fingers dig into the still warm and bloody flesh under the edge of the skin. We both tug, but it's hard to hold on to, slippery from blood and the layer of fat beneath it. Finally, after a lot of huffing and puffing and exertion on my already screaming muscles, we manage to get the hide folded down over the legs.

Shadow makes short work of cutting it away and laying it out on the ground, bloody side up. Then she begins carving at the meat inside, dumping chunk after bloody chunk of it on to the hide. She looks over her shoulder at me.

"Get some leaves and grass," she instructs. "Wipe it all down. Get as much of the blood off the meat and hide as you can. We don't want to leave a trail of drippings behind us as we walk."

I start ripping the large leaves off the trees and rubbing down the meat, squeezing it and patting it as dry as I can, feeling the nausea roil in my stomach and climb up to my throat as I do. Finally, Shadow uses her foot as leverage and snaps off the tusks. Then she sits back, wiping her hands and the bone knife in a patch of grass. Gears glances at my palms.

"You're going to need to wash those off and anywhere else you're cut. It's easy to die of infection out here."

He kneels and begins rolling the meat up in the hide, folding the ends in as if he's making a giant burrito. Then he hoists it up into his arms.

"Here." Shadow hands me a tusk. "You earned it."

Gears gives me a wink. "You're doing fine, Sparkles. Just keep those baby blues peeled, and if anything else comes at you—kill it."

"Kill it." I repeat, holding the tusk in a death grip. "Right."

He seems satisfied that I know what I'm doing. But I don't know what I'm doing. I almost died and from the look of this place, I'm probably going to die sometime very soon when something eats me. Unless I get a horrible infection instead, and then I'll die later after a lot of agony.

I'm not where I tried to dream myself to be, and when I did see a friendly face, it was only after I killed a face out of my nightmares.

So much for lucid dreaming.

Twenty minutes later we make it to the others. I look for the one face I really want to see, and there he is, strolling into camp, a makeshift bow over his shoulder and a few homemade arrows tucked in the hide belt that's holding up the hide kilt he wears, just like the other men. And like the other men, he's shirtless, his bronzed skin and defined muscles shining with sweat. I look away quickly when I realize I'm staring, and from the smirk Rookie gives me, he knew it, the jerk.

"Are you kidding me?" He lifts his arms in a gesture of defeat. "Am I the only one that didn't bag a meal?"

"They're keeping you on your toes, Rookie," Sarge says over his shoulder as he unwraps the meat that Gears lays at his feet. "I may need to replace you on hunting detail and leave you here plucking chickens." He motions to two large, dead birds lying on the grass.

"Why do we pluck them?" Shadow asks. "Their skin is thick enough. Just peel it off them."

"The skin is the best part," Beast protests.

"The *best* part," Chef echoes.

"You can't cook them without the skin," Gears says incredulously. "It'll dry them out."

"Suddenly you all have culinary training?" Shadow shakes her head. "I'm hungry. Besides, the skin is full of fat."

"Fat equals calories," Sarge reminds her. "In this environment, we're going to be covering a lot of terrain, and we don't know when we'll eat again. Calories are a good thing. Fat is our friend."

"If you don't want to wait for a bird, we've got steaks." Gears points over at me. "Courtesy of Sparkles."

The others turn to look at me in surprise.

"What, did she flush it out into your path?" Rookie asks.

"She killed it." Gears replies. "All by her damn self and without a weapon."

Beast leans forward and extends an enormous arm, with his hand held high. I return his high five.

"Go Sparkles!" He exclaims, with a full measure of admiration. "If this is what I think it is, you've got bigger balls than me."

"I can't believe you killed it," Rookie says, shaking his head.

"Stop being jealous," Gears says. "And somebody start the fire 'cause I'm roasting these slabs of ham."

"There's a stream over that way," Shadow tells me, pointing behind a line of trees. "Be careful, there's a slope going down. You can wash up there. Rookie, go with her."

"It's okay," I say. "It'll only take me a minute."

"A lot can go wrong in a minute," Chef warns me.

"There are things worse than this guy out there," Beast says, tapping a homemade stone knife against the pile of meat Gears is working on.

"You just had a taste of going it alone," Sarge reminds me. "I don't recommend it out here."

I nod. They're right, of course. Just because I got lucky and killed whatever the hell that was, doesn't mean I'll get lucky again. And even though Rookie looks like he'd rather fight one of those things to the death then spend five minutes with me, I'm glad to have him watch my back.

Looking at him closely as I crouch down next to the stream to wash my hands, I can see how I might have mistaken him for Mateo Ruiz. I dreamed of some generic dark-haired, good-looking guy and my mind filled in the blanks with the guy from the picture. It makes sense. Well, none of this makes sense, really, but I guess that does. His voice breaks through my thoughts.

"You're not still crushing on me are you, Sparkles?" He smirks as he looks down at me. "You're staring."

I open my mouth, close it, and open it again. "For the last time—I am *not* crushing on you."

"This climate is pretty warm, so you won't need to be snuggling up to me tonight. Unless you want to."

I don't dignify that with an answer.

"Although, next to me is the place to be," he goes on, with no small amount of cocky attitude. "A man with a bow can hit whatever is coming out of the night faster than anybody else."

"I got by without one."

"Yes, you did." His voice actually sounds admiring—not mocking. I feel my skin flush in response.

"So—this is Paleo Planet." I splash water on my face and neck, taking off the sweat, dust, blood, and hopefully this stupid blush.

"That's what we call it. Lots of prehistoric bullshit trying to kill you. Not all of it is armed."

"There are things that are armed?" I asked warily.

"Oh yeah." He keeps an arrow nocked, and his eyes are scanning the trees. "They haven't figured out bows yet. But they get the job done with spears and rocks—and teeth."

"People?"

"I guess you could call them that. They don't talk much. At least not in a way that we understand."

"Have you tried being nice to them? Maybe offer to share your food?"

"To them, we *are* food."

A shiver goes down my spine as I straighten to my feet.

"Let's get back." He motions with his bow and we make our way up the slope and through the trees. True to his word, Gears is roasting chunks of meat on a spit over the fire.

Sarge points at my palms. "Looks like you're still bleeding," he says.

I wave my hands in the air, trying to dry them. Scrubbing all the dirt off reopened the gouges and scrapes. I squat down near the fire, and not wanting to put my hand down in the dirt, I lean back and fall the remaining three inches, letting out a groan when the ground slams into my tender backside.

"Somebody's got a war wound." Beast says, reaching for a chunk of meat off the skewer.

Gears slaps Beast's hand with a stick. "Those are raw."

"I like my meat mooing," Beast insists.

"You like your crap full of worms, too?" Sarge asks snidely. "Wait a few minutes. The last thing we need in this place is a raging case of dysentery. Ask the medic, she'll tell you."

I raise my eyebrows. "I'm not much of a medic here—I don't even have a proper kit." I gesture at the gourd necklace.

"And I ain't got a grill," Grills says. "But I can still season and cook meat to perfection with a little ingenuity and a good sense of smell." He waves a bundle of leaves and bulbs under my nose.

I sniff and my eyes widen. "Is that wild garlic?"

"Yes ma'am. Only wish we found some potatoes to mash it into. But I'll settle for rubbing it into the meat."

"Can I have some of that?" I ask. "Wild garlic is antimicrobial. I can use it on my hands."

"See?" Sarge says as I break a bulb open and rub it into my wounds, tucking the rest into my gourd pouch. "That's what a medic is good for. They know the plants that can heal you."

"Unlike Chef, who knows the rocks that can kill you," Gears says.

I look at Chef and he waves one hand dismissively as he turns the spit with the meat. "I found a cave with feldspar—that contains potassium nitrate—in the walls when we were trying to complete our mission objective."

"What could be important here?" I ask, looking around at the primitive conditions.

"Cave paintings," Sarge answers. "The indigenous map their food and weapons caches on the cave walls. We just have to find the right cave, and this one wasn't it."

"Chef thought he could make homemade gunpowder from the potassium in the cave," Shadow says.

"If we could find a vein of sulphur, which isn't likely in an area with no volcanic activity," Chef says. "Add it to charcoal—but good quality charcoal."

"Nothing with meat drippings, I'm guessing," Gears says, still rubbing garlic into the meat.

"Can I eat the meat now since its antimicrobial?" Beast asks me hopefully.

"You really shouldn't." I give him an apologetic shrug. "We have no idea what kind of bacteria we're dealing with here. The longer the meat cooks, the less chance of something nasty or parasitic finding its way into our bodies." I look at Sarge. "You should probably boil the water, too."

Sarge gestures to a large hollowed-out gourd brimming with water, set carefully at the edge of the fire pit. "Already on it."

Beast gives a long-suffering sigh as he settles back against a rock and stretches out his legs to wait for his food.

It's growing dark around us now, and I can't help but flinch at every little hoot or croak or screech in the trees. Coming out of the pitch black, everything is amplified. I'm hungry, but I don't know if I'm this hungry. But I suppose Sarge is right—in this environment and without knowing how long I'm going to be here in this scenario, I should eat while we have the meat.

I try a piece of the roasted bird first. It's tough and stringy and the greasiest thing I've ever eaten in my life. No amount of wild garlic is going to make this taste good.

The creature I killed is slightly better. The meat is almost like ham, which makes sense if this thing is some prehistoric boar. It's a little more palatable, but my stomach still turns over as I remember the horrible sight and sound of it dying in front of me. I'm not a vegetarian or anything, but it definitely makes a difference when you're literally eating the flesh of your enemy.

"How much longer are we going to be here?" I ask.

"Who knows?" Chef shrugs.

I look around at all of them and ask the question that's been plaguing me since I started having these dreams: "How do you keep going? I don't know how any of you ever sleep."

"You don't sleep, you don't function properly," Shadow explains. "You get stupid and sloppy, and it only gets you wounded or killed faster."

Sarge hands me the gourd full of water. "We need rest in order to keep our reflexes and instincts sharp. If it's constant chaos, you get burned out and desensitized too quickly. That's why we get rewarded with rest periods when we complete a mission successfully."

"Just enough to get us to boredom," Gears says, "and then the action kicks in again."

I shake my head. "And you just keep going?"

Beast shrugs. "What other choice do we have?"

"Be like Boomer and just not wake up." Chef says.

"Or Scribe," Beast adds.

"Or Wizard." Shadow's face is grim.

"Boomer? Have I met him yet?" I look around at the others.

"He died before you came in, and so did the others." Sarge's voice is clipped. He clearly doesn't want to talk about this.

"So, they died," I say. "We've all died, right?"

Shadow tosses a stick into the fire. "Sometimes when you die—you stay dead."

"We were in a rest period," Chef explains. "Boomer went to bed and he did not get back up again."

"And he didn't reset?"

"Nope," Gears says, shoving a long blade of grass on his mouth to chew on. "Eventually we moved on to the next scenario, and he didn't. We never saw him again."

"Scribe got the shakes," Gears says. "He was the first."

"Wait—what are the shakes?"

"That's what happened to me in the Citadel," Chef says quietly. "We forget who we are. Why we're here."

"It starts with the shaking, and then periods of serious brain fog. Then the vertigo and paranoia set in," Beast continues. "They start feeling like everyone is trying to kill us."

"Everyone *is* trying to kill us." It seems pretty blatant to point out.

"Everyone," Beast repeats. "Including us."

"They turn on the squad," Sarge says tightly, throwing a bone into the fire. "Then they turn on themselves—with a gun, a knife, even their bare hands. If it happens too many times, they're removed."

"Removed?" My voice sounds entirely too high and thin. "By who? The scenario gods?"

Gears snorts at my question. "This ain't no religion I ever signed up for."

"Baptism by fire," Shadow growls.

"And Wizard?"

"Same thing, more or less," Sarge replies flatly, ending the conversation. "Beast, you've got first watch. Normal rotation after that. We'll work Sparkles in after Rookie."

I realize with a good deal of embarrassment that I really need to see to my needs and it's not like there's a porta-potty anywhere on Paleo Planet.

"Um—I need to go back to the stream," I tell Sarge.

"Not a good idea." He shakes his head. "You don't want to be near a water source in the dark."

"But I need—I mean I have to—" I stammer.

Shadow knows just where I'm headed with this. "Go behind that tree," she says, gesturing with her bird leg. "You don't want to be far from the fire."

"We won't listen," Rookie smirks. "Much."

I shoot him a dirty look and walk to the tree, grateful it's large enough to squat behind. Once I'm out of the bright circle of the fire, things start emerging from the dark. Shifting shadows. Rustling leaves. I'm aware of every little sound I make and every little sound in the foliage around me.

"Don't wipe with the big triangle leaves," Beast calls out. "They'll give you a rash."

Great. I look around, but all the leaves look triangular in the dim light bleeding off the fire. I'll just have to drip-dry. I make a face as I stand up. There is grass nearby—not a lot, but there's a decent-sized clump under the next tree. A handful of that is a better gamble than those rashy leaves.

I walk over and wrap my fingers around the grass, yanking hard since the stuff seems to be rooted somewhere down in the Earth's magnetic core. I let out a loud grunt as I yank again, and my face burns with embarrassment as Rookie's voice carries on the breeze.

"You're making a lot of sound back there," he snarks. "You don't want to attract predators."

Terrific. I pat myself dry as best as I can, and I re-adjust my hide dress.

This time more than a grunt comes out of my lips as my hair is gripped hard in a meaty fist and my head snaps back to get the full view of whoever—or should I say *whatever*—has grabbed me. I suppose he's a man, but the brow is heavy, the eyes deep-set. His teeth are large, not animal-like but much bigger than a normal human's. He's shorter than I am, but he's *strong.* His eyes are wide as he snarls in my face, something like words, but they're monosyllabic and come out more like a series of growls than a language. His breath makes me gag as his other arm comes around my waist and he starts dragging me backwards.

I can only make a strangled sound—his has a vice grip on my ribs, keeping me from drawing in a full breath. I claw at his hand and arm, kicking my legs and ramming my elbow into him again and again like Shadow showed me. He slams the blunt end of a crudely sharpened stone into my head, and I see stars.

I flail my arm behind me to slap at his face, and my hand explodes in pain. Suddenly, I'm jerked backwards. We both fall, landing with me on my back on top of him.

I try to scramble off, but I can't. My arm is stuck, and it takes a second for me to register the fact that he isn't moving. That's when I see the arrow. It's pierced right through the center of my palm and lodged firmly in his eye—so deep that I can't get free.

Rough hands grab me by the shoulders and lift me.

"Wait!" I try to stop him, but Beast practically throws me. Pain lances through my hand and shoots up my arm as I scream.

"Hold it! Hold it!" Sarge calls out. "She's hit."

"She's hit?" I hear Rookie voice as he comes up behind Sarge. "Shit! She must have just put her hand up."

I'm on my knees now, arm and hand twisted at an odd angle and still pinned to the primitive man's face, with his one sightless eye staring up at me.

"I can't—I can't—" I groan, feeling my stomach lurch.

"It's okay," Rookie says, holding my shoulders in his hands again as he squats in front of me. "Hey," he reaches up to cup my chin in his hand, his thumb stroking gently across my jaw. "Look at me."

I drag my eyes away from the horror in front of me and try to focus on Rookie's face. On that tiny scar right next to his mouth. Then I glance over at Sarge as he bends over my neolithic attacker.

"Look at me," Rookie says again, and a moment later I understand why as Sarge snaps off the end of the homemade arrow and rips it off my hand.

I scream again, and that quickly, Beast is wrapping my hand in leaves.

"Those aren't the triangle ones, are they?" I ask in a daze.

Everyone around me breaks into laughter, and Rookie falls back, sitting hard in the dirt. "Man! Oh man. I wasn't sure I was going to make that shot. I was so afraid I was going to hit you."

"You did hit me," I remind him. How can they laugh? The primitive man stares at me with his sightless eye, and I can't stop shaking. I've been murdered over and over here but this time the attack feels more personal, somehow.

"I wouldn't have let Rookie make the shot if I didn't think he could take this troglodyte down," Sarge says, gesturing at the primitive man. "You're alright?"

My head nods—a non-verbal lie. He looks around at the others.

"Come on, we've got to move. Now."

"Are there more of them?" I ask, clutching throbbing my hand to my chest.

"Most likely," Beast answers.

"We'll leave the rest of the meat," Sarge says. "We don't have time to smoke it and it'll keep them busy—hopefully too busy to come looking for us."

"Unless they're not here for meat," Shadow says flatly.

I look up at her for an explanation, but she just looks away. I'm still shaking violently, and an arm slides around my waist.

"Can you walk?" Rookie asks as he helps me to my feet.

"Yeah. Yeah, I'm fine," I answer, hoping I sound tougher than I feel right now. Then I blow it spectacularly as I lean over and vomit up every bit of my paleo dinner, shuddering and shaking all over.

A hand comes to the middle of my back and just stays there. Another holds my hair back until I finish. Yet another hand presses the gourd of water to my lips. I rinse my mouth and spit.

"I'm sorry," I say to all of them. "I'm sorry."

"It's okay," Shadow says. "We've got you."

"You've had a hell of a day," Sarge tells me. "Let's move."

Rookie falls into step next to me. "I grabbed some of that garlic," he says to me. "You should put it on your hand when we make camp again."

I whisper my thanks.

"I'm sorry you're hurt," he adds. "I didn't mean to hit you."

I turn my head to look at him. "You saved my life," I tell him. "I should be thanking *you*."

"He probably wouldn't have killed you right away," Rookie says quietly. "At least, not intentionally."

Things are finally starting to add up in my overloaded brain and I go cold all over as the color drains from my face.

Rookie bumps me with his shoulder. "Besides," he says, forcing a joking tone. "Beast was right behind that arrow. You wouldn't have gone more than another ten feet, tops."

I look over at Beast. "Thank you," I say. Then I raise my voice so all of them can hear me. "Thank you all."

"Part of the job," Gears says. "Looking out for each other."

"You fed us," Chef chimes in. "No Wahala."

No Wahala. My mind stretches, trying to place the familiar phrase, but I'm still not firing on all synapses yet. I'm too shaken.

When we finally make camp in a small cave, I settle in with Shadow lying next to me. Sarge and Beast take first watch, while Rookie, Gears and Chef curl up in front of us.

"Are you okay?" Shadow asks me softly. "Did he hurt you—anywhere we can't see?"

"No," I tell her quietly. "He didn't have time."

"Good," she says. "While we are here, don't go anywhere out of calling distance alone. Ever." She reaches out and squeezes my good hand. "Promise me."

"I learned my lesson," I tell her. "The boar was bad enough to handle by myself."

"If you hadn't gotten lucky, that boar would have killed you too," she says. "We don't have the weapons we need here."

"Speak for yourself," Rookie's voice carries in the darkness.

"Not all of us can be president of the archery club," I reply dryly.

"What's that supposed to mean?"

Well, I guess that didn't ring a bell for him.

"I just meant that you're really good with a bow and arrow."

"A target is a target," he says. "Gun, arrow, spear, rock—whatever works."

I look back to Shadow, and she's staring blankly off into nothing. Was it the shakes? Her hand felt like it was trembling when it squeezed mine, but she doesn't seem like she's going to turn violent. Then I think about her warning again. *Promise me.*

"Did what happened to me happen to Wizard?" I whisper. "Was Wizard a girl?"

"Yes," she says quietly. "Wizard previously had an episode or two of the shakes with memory loss and that day we were all trying to flush out and kill a flock of birds. None of us saw her wander off. They must have knocked her unconscious and gotten her away before we even knew she was gone. We heard her screaming a few hours later as we increased our search grid."

"She wasn't the same after that," Gears adds, having listened in.

"They did not kill her, but she wished that they had," Chef finishes grimly.

"I found her first," Shadow whispers. "I couldn't help her. They would have only turned on me if I showed myself and— and there were too many of them. I had to leave her and find the others, bring them back. She saw me." Her voice breaks. "She saw me. She knew I was there. And I had to turn around and run."

I reach over and find her hand with my good one, squeezing it. "But you brought the others. She knew what you were doing. She knew you'd get help."

Shadow drags in a breath. "Maybe later she did. But in that moment? I was all she had."

"Did she—" I almost hate myself for asking. "Did she die later? After everything?"

"The shakes set in harder on the next scenario. And the next. And the next," says Shadow. "Maybe the added trauma—God knows we have enough as it is—made them so much worse."

"She mowed us all down at the supply depot," Rookie says. "I managed to stay alive long enough to watch her slit her own throat when the gun ran out of bullets. We didn't see her anymore after that,"

"Enough talk," Sarge's voice cuts the darkness. "We don't need to be making unnecessary noise. Get some rest."

I have no idea how I'm going to fall asleep with my hand throbbing and my head whirling. Oh my God, what happened to them all . . . My logical mind knows none of this has really happened, but it's still a long time before my eyes drift closed.

When I open them again, I'm staring at the ceiling in my bedroom. My hand is unmarked, my sheets are soaked in sweat, and I turn my head, retching over the side of the bed.

13

R**IO PACES THE CLASSROOM** furiously, waving her hands as she fumes.

"The planet is burning up around us! Our seas are rising! Air is becoming unbreathable, polar ice caps are melting, entire species are being wiped off the globe, and no one can give forty-five minutes out of their week to address it?" She slams her tie-dye spiral notebook shut in disgust.

"They'll come around," I soothe. "Maybe we need posters?"

Her eyes light up. "Posters! Yes!"

"We could show a movie at a meeting," I suggest. "Like a disaster movie featuring climate change. Or would that be stupid?"

"Entertainment is good!" Rio scribbles some more. "It's not like there's a thriving nightlife in this place. Or a shopping mall. Or a movie theater. Or concerts."

"They show movies in the warehouse sometimes, at least that's what Dr. Grady tells me."

"It's all Disney movies and Rom-Coms." Rio says, with a look of disgust. "But we can do movies. We need to pick a good disaster flick. I'm thinking tidal wave or new ice age."

We both look up as the door opens. Akoni backs into the room with his janitorial cart, clearly not seeing us. Once the door closes, he crouches down and reaches under a stack of cleaning cloths on the lower shelf of his cart and digs out a notebook. He makes careful, concise notes on the page.

"So, are you writing a tell-all book about the secret lives of Codonexus employees, or something?" Rio asks him. "Or do you write poetry about cleaning windows and emptying waste baskets?"

Akoni jumps and turns to face us, clutching the notebook to his chest. "You two again!"

"We had to switch to Wednesdays for Climate Champions," Rio tells him. "What are *you* doing?"

"Nothing!" He closes the notebook and shoves it behind his back. "It is nothing. Sometimes I get ideas and I have to write them down before I forget them. Please do not tell anybody—I do not want to get in trouble."

"Custodial work gets your creative juices flowing?" Rio asks.

"We won't tell anyone," I assure him. "I would imagine it's a boring job. Anything you do to pass the time is no big deal. We'll keep your secret if you won't tell Mr. Silva we ate half the bag of beef jerky in his drawer." I give him a smile.

"No wahala," Akoni tells me, smiling back.

My eyes widen. "Say that again."

"No wahala?" Akoni repeats. "It is just something we say in my country."

"I know. You told me before. But I know someone else who says it too. He looks—" I swallow hard as the realization sinks in. "He kind of looks like you."

Akoni goes still. *"What?"*

"I mean—" I fumble, trying to find a way to phrase this. "I recently met someone who talks like you, and he even looks a little like you and—" I give a laugh, realizing how ridiculous this sounds. "But maybe it's just the accent that makes me think of him when I talk to you."

"What is his name?" Akoni tries to play like he's just making conversation, but his body is tense, and his eyes are practically drilling into mine.

I shift nervously. "Um—I don't know his real name. Everybody just calls him Chef."

Akoni's shoulders sag.

"Are you—are you looking for someone?" I ask.

Rio's eyes widen. "That's why you're always snooping around, right? Or is there another reason?"

His eyes widen. "I am not a corporate spy." He holds up a hand. "I swear it."

Rio looks pointedly at the notebook in his other hand. "So, what's that for, then?"

"I need to go," he says hastily. He moves to shove the notebook back under the paper towels on his cart, but I hop off the desk and walk over to put my hand on his arm to stop him.

"Who is he—the one you thought I was talking about?" I ask. "It's kind of obvious you're not here to just be a janitor."

"You can totally tell us," Rio reassures him. "We're not going to turn you in or something. We don't even like most of the people in charge here."

"That's an understatement." I lean back against the desk.

"Maybe we can help you," Rio offers. "My dad works in security, and her mom is banging the president of the company.

"Will you stop that?" I snap.

"Just saying." She shrugs. "We've got resources."

Akoni glances around as if there are other people hiding under the desks or peering in the window. Finally, he takes a deep breath, and I can see in his eyes the desperation that pushes him to take a chance on us.

"I am looking for my brother," he says quietly. "His name is Kalu. He's twenty-one years old, and he was hired here under an internship program with Codonexus. He disappeared eight months ago. The company told us he resigned and left the island, but no one has heard from him."

"Maybe he just had a really bad time here or something," Rio says. "Did they fire him? Maybe he's embarrassed and doesn't want you to know."

"He would have never gone this long without talking to his family. Without talking to me," he clarifies. "My brother is my best friend. There are only three years between us, and he would email or text me nearly every day."

"They did institute communications screening a while back," Rio says. "They have a big fear of corporate espionage here. Maybe he told you too much, so they blocked him."

"No, it was nothing like that," Akoni says. "Not with Kalu. And his texts before his disappearance—they worried me. He said the internship was not what it appeared to be. He told me he regretted his decision to come here."

"What was he studying?" I asked.

"Neurochemistry. My brother is a very talented chemist, but our father was in an accident and suffered a brain injury shortly after Kalu started university. He wanted to put his studies to use healing people's brains instead of working on fuel or plastics. It was a field he was passionate about."

"Chemistry." I stare at Akoni, and I have to remember how to breathe. "Could he use his knowledge of chemistry to make explosives? Or poisons?"

He gives me an odd look. "Yes, I suppose he could, but Kalu would not do that."

"Do you think they were trying to use him to make weapons of mass destruction?" Rio asks in a tone dripping with awe.

I rub my hands over my face. "Okay. Okay. What I'm going to tell you is going to sound crazy." I practically fall into Mr. Silva's chair. "I mean completely, *completely* crazy."

They both stare at me, and the only sound is Rio smacking her gum while they wait.

I forge ahead. "Ever since I got to the island, I've been having really bad night terrors. In my dreams, I'm with the same group of soldiers fighting battles over and over again."

"You told me all this," Rio says.

I look at Akoni. "This guy Chef is one of them, and they call him Chef because he's good with chemicals and compounds to make explosives or weapons. And he looks—he looks just like you. He uses that same phrase: *no wahala.*"

Akoni's eyebrows are raised so high they're practically a part of his hairline.

"He's making weapons—in the dreams?" He asks. "Like he is a soldier?"

I nod. "We're all soldiers in my dreams. Each scenario, we're in a different time and place but always in a battle or being hunted by an enemy. Sometimes we accomplish our objective, but most of the time we just end up getting killed. Then it all starts over."

"And you think you're dreaming about his missing brother?" Rio asks.

"I don't know. Maybe." I shake my head. "I know that sounds crazy."

"I have pictures," Akoni says, pulling out his phone. He scrolls through, then turns the phone to face me. There they are, Akoni and Chef, side-by-side with their arms around each other's shoulders.

I don't need to say a word. My face tells the story as Akoni swipes through picture after picture. That's him. That's Chef. I am sure of it.

"You saw him," Akoni's body tenses with the knowledge. "Kalu."

Locking eyes with him, I nod.

"Trippy," Rio breathes.

I rub my suddenly sweaty palms on my knees. "It gets crazier. That day when Rio showed me the trophy case, I recognized someone else from the group of soldiers."

Rio's eyes widen. "That's why you got all weird about the archery team photo?"

"Mateo, the team captain," I say nodding. "He's Rookie. But he doesn't recognize his own name. None of them remember who they are."

"Daaaamn," Rio says, exhaling loudly.

"And you've never met Mateo before this?" Akoni asks. "Or my brother?"

"I only got here a few months ago," I tell him. "I've never met your brother, and Rio said that Mateo left for college before I arrived."

"That was kind of strange," Rio says slowly, remembering. "I mean, it wasn't even the end of the semester. All of a sudden one day he just wasn't here, and the teacher said he had enough credits to graduate early, and he had to leave or risk losing some major scholarship or something."

"When was that, exactly?" Akoni wants to know.

Rio's eyes look up as she tries to remember. "Maybe four months ago? A couple of months before J.J. got here."

"All of this is very strange," Akoni says evenly. "But I believe you. This place, this company, is nothing but layers of secrets upon secrets. Something is going on here and being covered up. I think Kalu knew it, too."

"So how am I dreaming about him—if it is him?" I ask warily.

"Maybe you're a prophet," Rio says, her eyes lighting up. "Maybe your night terrors are *paranormal*," she finishes in a hushed tone.

I want to roll my eyes, because this all sounds ridiculous. But there's a knot in my gut that tells me we're onto something, here.

"What do you know about the company?" I ask Akoni. "Is it really in trouble? There are rumors they're having difficulty finalizing some big contract. I have a feeling that's why they— they might want my father's money. Or whatever else he had that has value."

"They *are* in trouble." Akoni glances at the closed door before he pulls his notebook back out and flips through it. "I have made extensive notes. The company's primary research area is neurology—specifically the study of neurotransmitters and brain chemistry in the therapeutic areas of trauma and cognitive decline—all in the emerging field of nanotechnology."

"That's like microscopic robots, right?" Rio says, jumping down off the desk. "They're building killer microscopic robots! Like in that show you made me watch. Starpath."

"Not very much like *Stargate*," I tell her. "They're not building full-sized self-replicating people. My dad used to work on that development team when he was with the company. Microscopic is right—all the research is done in a Petri dish."

"They were exploring nanotechnology for the treatment of mental health-related issues." Akoni fishes out papers tucked between his notebook pages—articles printed off the internet—and spreads them across the desk. "They had contracts from a few universities and pharmaceutical companies for developmental work. Then two years ago they landed a contract with the United States Department of Defense."

"The government?" I ask. "They're working for the government?"

"In conjunction with the military, yes," Akoni says. "They received a large amount of grant money and solicited volunteers for a program that studies methods for treating the effect of battle-related PTSD on brain chemistry. Kalu was excited about the possibilities, to be able to help soldiers and others who have experienced trauma. Not long after he arrived, he stopped being so excited. He knew his correspondence was being monitored so his words became guarded. Then one day—nothing."

"We need more information," I say. "If your brother is being held somewhere, if they're using him—and others—to test this nanite therapy or something like it, where are they being kept? And how am I able to interact with them?"

"Maybe you're being targeted next," Rio says. "Do you think your mom slipped something into your food? Like she fed you a nano-burger or put it in your coffee or something?"

"No." I make a face that tells her just how ridiculous that idea is. "That's not how the science works. The nanites have to enter the bloodstream to—"

My brain suddenly flips back through time and I freeze.

No. No, it's impossible.

Not impossible, my thoughts tell me. *Highly improbable. But not impossible.* My mind fixes on a memory of a broken coffee cup, a Petri dish, and my bloody finger.

"I'm betting it was Dr. Walters," Rio goes on. "You know I think he's secretly a serial killer."

"Not Dr. Walters," I struggle to say the words. "My father. He worked on the prototypes for the nanites they use in their research."

Akoni's brow creases. "And you think he tested them on you? Deliberately infected you with them?"

"Not deliberately." I begin to shake as the scope of it all—of what I've actually been witnessing these last months—seeps in. "I used to visit my father's lab with him sometimes. Once, I touched a Petri dish—one containing the prototype nanites—and I had a cut on my finger. I never told him. I could have infected myself. But they were only prototypes."

"Duuuude," Rio breathes.

"And you never had these sorts of dreams before you came to the island? Even though you were near his lab?" Akoni presses. "The project Kalu was on involved using nanites to access parts of trauma memories, but they put the subject's consciousness in a safe environment where the subject could examine and address the after-effects of the trauma."

"We lived miles away on the other side of Chicago from the lab, and they were still in the early phases of development then—nothing like whatever this is. I've always had night terrors, but never like now."

"Duuuude," Rio says again.

I have nanites in my body. In my *brain*. I swear, I can feel them. I have an insane urge to scratch my head. Tiny, microscopic robots in my body. I shudder.

"Okay," I protest, waving my hands. "This is getting into the realm of batshit crazy." I know I'm trying to talk myself out of this. Out of what I already know.

"Will you dream again tonight?" Akoni asks. "Can you take this man—Chef—a message? If he is Kalu, maybe your nanites are able to access a part of the program he developed for the project. There may be a clue there to where he physically can be found."

"Or maybe he's dead and trying to get a message to us through your nanites," Rio says, nodding her head eagerly.

I shove an elbow into her side. "Rio!"

"Sorry," she says, giving Akoni a sheepish look. "I probably shouldn't have said that."

"No apology is needed," Akoni says grimly. "It is a thought I have had myself, many times."

"Okay," I say slowly, "just on the odd chance that I am theoretically, possibly, somehow communicating through my dreams with your brother—" Part of me is hoping Akoni will tell me how completely nuts this sounds but he just looks at me steadily.

"Just in case," I say again. "How can I be sure? He won't remember his own name. They've all had their memories wiped."

"Perhaps hearing his name will help him remember," Akoni theorizes.

"I tried that with Rookie—Mateo," I say. "No luck."

"If that does not work, there is another way," he tells me. "When we were children, I stole a bag of sweets from Kalu. He chased me through the house. I tried to shut the door to keep him from following me into the bedroom, and I shut it on his hand hard enough to cut him. He needed stitches, and I had to do all of his chores for the next month. My mother made me buy him two bags of sweets to repay him."

Akoni smiles at the memory. "Kalu has a scar that crosses the knuckles of his left hand from here to here." He touches my hand, showing me where to look. "If you see that, you will know it is Kalu."

"We also need to find out more about the project your brother was working on," says Rio. "How do you know so much already?"

"I was planning to study cybersecurity journalism at university," he says. "I know some things—have made some connections that aren't entirely reputable. Some of the information on Codonexus is publicly available if you search for it. Then I moved to the nearest port on the mainland and asked around, then bribed enough people to get hired onto the island. With my custodial badge, I can get into all the buildings—but not all the offices and laboratories. In the research facility, an entire wing is security coded. I cannot get Into that area. The answers may be there."

"I could see if I can find the entry code," Rio offers. "On the days I work with my dad, I mostly do data entry of the overnight security logs and email the daily security reports. But I'm sitting right there, and I have access to the system."

I shake my head in a vehement *no*. "I don't want you doing anything that's going to get you in trouble," I tell her. "Or get your dad fired."

"I'm not going to change anything," she protests. "Just look it over. I'll write everything down in my notebook and as soon as we get the information, we'll burn those pages. Under a full moon."

I take a breath and my stomach clenches. "I can look through the files in Evan's office."

Rio's mouth forms a little 'o'. "Duuuude," she breathes.

"Dr. Walters would kick you off the island if he caught you going through his files," Akoni protests. "He may even have you arrested."

"He's welcome to send me packing," I say emphatically. "Nothing would make me happier. But he won't do that."

"Not if he wants to keep banging your mother," Rio adds.

"Let's meet back here in a week," I suggest. "Akoni keeps trying to dig up information, and I'll try to talk to people in my dreams and also find a way to get into Evan's office." I shake my head, realizing how completely and utterly crazy all of that sounds.

"We need a super-secret project name," Rio says excitedly.

I give her a look. "Rio."

"Oh, come on. It might keep us focused. We can be a squad, too." She raises her chin defiantly.

"Why don't you draw up a list of potential project names," I tell her with a sigh. "We'll vote on them next week."

"Oh, this is going to be *so* cool," she squeals.

My eyes meet Akoni's, and despite Rio's enthusiasm, both of us know we're in over our heads.

14

MOM AND EVAN MAKE small talk as they prepare dinner together, and I hesitate in my bedroom doorway. It's now or never. My hands ball into fists, then I realize how counterproductive it would be if I walk out there looking like I'm ready to punch them both.

I really would like to punch them both.

If Rookie and Chef really are Mateo and Kalu—and Evan is behind this somehow—I'll need more proof than just my freaky dreams. If there's more going on here, Evan would know about it. And if he knows, that means my mother probably knows, too.

A wave of acid churns in my stomach. I may not be close to my mother—hell, she's practically a stranger. But she's still my mother. I want to believe she's not capable of putting people through something like this.

Then there's the matter of my nanite infected brain. What the hell has that done to me? What are the long-term ramifications? I swear, I was up most of the night imagining them burrowing into my gray matter—even though I know I've had them for years and that's not how the science works. I have enough to deal with without throwing brain-altering nano-robots onto my mental load.

After one more deep breath, I force my face into a pleasant expression and step out of my room, making a show of sniffing the air.

"Mmmm! Smells good," I exclaim. "What's for dinner?"

They both look at me with surprise and it's possible I'm laying it on a little thick.

"Just hungry." I add a shrug.

Mom gives me a genuine smile. "Linguine with clam sauce," she says. "You probably smell the garlic bread."

"She's definitely not smelling the salad," Evan says with that stupid, grating laugh of his. I force myself to turn my head and smile at him in acknowledgement as I take my seat.

"So," Mom begins as she passes me the pasta. "How did your club meeting go yesterday?"

"Not much to report," I answer. "So far it's only me and Rio."

"Maybe it'll pick up as time goes on," she offers.

"What sort of club?" Evan asks. He's chewing his salad and for some reason—probably because I hate him—it sounds ridiculously loud.

"We call it Climate Champions," I reply, helping myself to garlic bread. "We're both really passionate about climate change."

"It's a good cause," he says approvingly. "And a burgeoning field. Lots of money to be made there."

I reply with a non-committal noise even though I want to grind my teeth. Of course, Evan only sees the money-making opportunity. Of course, he does. But I have the perfect opening and I should use it. Here goes.

"The club was Dr. Grady's idea," I tell them. "It's one of the things she suggested to help me acclimate to my new life."

"And—does it help?" Mom asks hesitantly.

"A little." I make my shoulders droop as my voice grows quiet. "It's just hard."

Something flashes in her eyes that might be sympathy but more than anything she just looks uncomfortable and so does Evan. Good.

"Dr. Grady thought maybe if I had something else to keep me busy it would help," I tell them. "Like a hobby or—or a job."

"I thought she canceled today," Mom says.

"She did. But we've talked about it before. A lot."

"Do you have any hobbies?" My mother asks. "You haven't shown any interest in that sort of thing."

I fight the urge to roll my eyes because dad would have known everything about all my hobbies. "I was thinking about a job."

"A job? Where?" Mom asks. "It's not as though there's a mall nearby."

"I have less than six months to graduation," I remind her. "And I'm starting to narrow down my college choices. I've even applied for early admission decisions at a few. I was thinking it would look a lot better on my college applications if I had an internship on my record."

Evan frowns. "Most of our work is very highly classified, J.J. I'm sure you understand."

"I totally get it," I reply. "And I'm not asking to be let into the labs or anything. It doesn't even have to be anything medical. Just working for Codonexus in any capacity would look impressive on a college application."

That remark puffs out Evan's chest exactly as I thought it would. He can't keep the smug, self-important smile off his face.

"Yes, I would imagine having your name associated with a company of our quality would get your application to the top of the stack."

"So, I was thinking—" I pause a moment to twirl some pasta on my fork. "Maybe I could work for you." I give Evan a hopeful smile. "Just in your office. Maybe proofreading letters or working spreadsheets, answering phones—you know, like a personal assistant.

"I don't know, J.J.," Mom starts in. "Maybe we can find a way for you to work with me, instead."

"I think I'd lose some credibility if I'm interning for my mother." I turn back to Evan. "Honestly, someone at your level within the company really should have his own assistant, anyway, don't you think?"

That remark falls right into a sore place for him. As CEO of the company, he definitely feels like he should be treated more importantly, and I know it bugs him. I've overheard enough conversations in these last few weeks to know that—and to know he doesn't already have a personal assistant. Still, he doesn't jump on the suggestion.

"It's just that—" I turn wide, imploring eyes to Evan, "Maybe if I can spend a little more time with you, get to know you, things will get easier between us." I suck in a breath and make it sound like a shudder. "At least, that's what Dr. Grady thinks. And I'm willing to give it a try."

Mom bites her lip and she and Evan share a glance. He nods his head and leans back in his chair.

"Well," he says, considering. "Yes. Yes, I think we can make this work. There would be some guidelines. Certain phone calls or meetings you can't be in the office for."

"I'm sure there are times when you'll need me to track someone down or maybe deliver something," I offer helpfully. "Or I can even get you coffee or food. Just send me on an errand when you need me out of the office."

Another well-placed strike. I can see that he loves the idea of having a personal assistant to fetch his coffee. He rubs his chin, looking satisfied.

"You know, J.J., this is a stellar idea," he gushes. "A really stellar idea." Mom is smiling at me now that Evan is on board.

"You can come by tomorrow, right after school," Evan goes on. "We'll outline the job parameters, write up some objectives for the internship, maybe discuss a small salary."

"It's not like I've got a lot of other competing offers," I joke.

"Who could compete, right?" Evan says, raising his glass. He sounds like a used car salesman again.

"Seriously." I raise my glass and clink it to his in a show of faux solidarity.

Evan glances down at his watch. "I need to get over to the lab," he says. "I've got to meet with Armando—then check on a project." His eyes dart to meet my mother's, and she nods slightly.

"We'll circle back after," she tells him.

We both watch the door close, and an awkward silence descends between us.

"Well, this is nice, just the two of us," mom says, offering me more pasta. I hold up a hand to refuse, but I do help myself to more garlic bread.

"J.J.," she says tentatively. "I know this has been hard for you, moving here. And—" she takes a deep breath. "Losing your dad. What you and he had was special, and I could never—" She pauses. "What I'm trying to say is—I appreciate you giving me a chance. I think it's fair to say that from your point of view, I might not deserve one."

"I didn't say that." It comes out muffled around a mouthful of garlic bread.

"You didn't have to," she says. "Neither of us was expecting this, and it's never easy rearranging your life to accommodate other people. But I want you to know that despite all of that, I'm glad to have you here. I really am. I only wish it had happened under different circumstances."

"It wouldn't have happened under different circumstances." The words come out before I can stop them, and they're sharp and ugly.

She swallows hard, and I see her eyes fill up, but her mouth tightens, and the tears don't spill over. Guilt twinges, and I'm not entirely comfortable with it.

"You're right," she says quietly. "I wouldn't have tried to make you live with me. What kind of a life would that be? I've been working sixty-hour weeks for years, moving all over the world—and I would never have tried to take you from your father. But I should have tried to see you more. I wish I had. I'm so proud of who you've become."

"Thanks. That means a lot." It surprises me that it's kind of the truth. Maybe she's just saying it to ease her guilty conscience, but it's nice to hear, all the same. She did rearrange her life to include me. She also got me help for my grief and my night terrors with a therapist. I can't forgive the past, maybe never will, but if she's trying, maybe I could too. Slowly. Part of me still rebels at the idea but another, smaller part of me wants a family again. Needs a family again, even if it's fractured. Maybe if we get closer, I can convince her to drop Evan and leave this lousy company. There's one long-term goal I've set. Dr. Grady would be proud.

"And now you'll be working with us," she says brightly. "I'm glad to see you're finally finding your place here."

"I think it's becoming clearer now," I tell her. "Maybe this is the first step to having it all fall into place."

"Maybe it is." She smiles at me again as she stands to clear the table. I smile back but the question is burning in my mind—in my heart—and I wish I knew the answer.

How much does she know?

15

BULLETS STRIKE THE GROUND entirely too close to me as I desperately try to get my bearings. In the dream scenarios I've picked up enough by now to know that the safest thing to do is drop low and run for cover, so I do that as quickly as possible. A familiar clocktower stands at the end of the street and something catches my vision on the periphery.

Chef leans around the corner of a half caved-in building, then pulls back as a shot zings off the wall next to his head. His hand reappears down low and motions me over.

"Sparkles! Finally!" He exclaims as I race across to him. "Hurry. Gears is down."

"What do you mean down?" I say breathlessly, clutching my med bag.

"He went backwards over a wall trying to get away from the soldiers who ambushed us. We got rid of them and tried to press forward, but of course, there is a sniper—"

"And you can't get past him," I finish. The sniper is kind enough to punctuate my sentence with a volley of bullets that hit a wall just a few feet away. I try to look at Chef's hand for scars, but it's too hard to do while dodging gunfire.

He pulls me further into the alley. "Stay out of his line of sight," he admonishes. Then he leads me in a zigzag pattern between buildings and down alleys, over piles of rubble.

"Are the rest of the enemy soldiers all gone?" I ask.

"For the moment. We have to get past the sniper—once Rookie takes him out—then follow them to their next encampment and steal the latest battle briefs."

"If anybody can get the sniper, Rookie can," I say. Chef gives a nod of affirmation and leads me through the doorway of a mostly intact building. He taps quietly on the door before he gives an odd little whistle like a birdcall, then heads back to the end of the alley.

The door cracks open and Shadow's face appears in the opening before she steps back to let me in.

"Where have you been?" she asks. "We've got wounded."

"Sorry," I say. "I only just got here."

I follow her to the back of what looks like an abandoned tavern. Beast is lounging on a chair, eating some bread he scrounged from somewhere. A bottle of amber liquid sits on the table in front of him. He raises a hand in greeting as I walk by. Sarge is in the back of the room, and much of his body is covered in blood. I start to reach for his shirt to examine him, but Shadow stops my hand.

"That blood isn't from him," she says. "Gears has an injury to the back of his head." Gears is propped against the wall.

"Gears?" I squat down in front of him. "Hey, can you see me okay?"

He looks up at the sound of my voice, squinting his eyes as though he's having trouble seeing my face.

"Kind of seeing two of you," he mumbles, squinting. "Why is it so bright?"

Grimacing, I open up my medical bag. There's a small flashlight inside and I shine it into his eyes. His pupils are uneven in size.

"I'd like to just take a snooze," he says, "but I'm guessin' that's not a good idea."

I move around behind him, blowing on his hair to get the dust out of it before I gently prod his scalp with my fingers.

"Ouch! Dammit!"

"Sorry. You know you've got a concussion, right?"

"I figured."

I turn and look at Shadow and Sarge. "Keep him awake for a while, then he can sleep, but only for short periods. We'll have to wake him every hour, ask him some questions."

"Make sure his brains aren't scrambled," Sarge says. "Any more than usual, I mean."

I grasp one of Gears's hands. "No shaking?"

"No, but I might be drooling a lil' bit." He forces a grin.

"You've still got your sense of humor," I tell him. "That's a good sign. I can give you some aspirin for the pain. I think I saw aspirin powder in here." I fish around in my med bag. "Is there any water?"

Shadow moves off to go and fetch some, but Gears calls after her.

"Find beer if you can!"

I scowl at him. "No alcohol. Or food—you might throw up."

"I know," he sighs. "Not my first concussion."

She returns and I open the packet of aspirin powder, dissolving it in the cup and stirring it with my finger before I hand it over. Gears makes a face as he drinks it down.

Sarge motions me to the other end of the room.

"I've been meaning to have a chat when we got a free minute," he says. "But we got interrupted by all that nonsense on Paleo Planet."

"Yeah, not a great time to chat."

"I suppose not. You okay?" he asks. His eyes are warm and full of sympathy. "How are you holding up?"

"How is anybody holding up under these circumstances?" I shake my head as I repack my med bag. "Please don't tell me I need a therapist."

He huffs a laugh. "I'd wager we could all use one, but you're new, but you're not always where we can watch over you. I guess I'm worried about you when you're away."

I arch a brow. "You're worried about me?"

"Maybe in another life, I've got a daughter your age," he says, bumping my shoulder with his. It's a gesture Dad used on me often, and my throat tightens in response. "And after what's happened to the others, with the shakes and all—"

His voice trails off and the silence hangs there a moment, settling on me, dragging my shoulders down. I really need a hug, but it sounds like he needs one more, so I give him one. He stiffens in surprise, but doesn't pull away. He just ruffles my hair when we let go.

"What's the word on the sniper?" he asks loudly, changing the subject. "I'm still hearing gunfire."

"Rookie is on it," Shadow tells him. "Chef is doing recon to be sure the rest of their battalion is staying put."

"Do you need me out there?" I ask.

Shadow gives me a look. "The way you fire a gun?"

She's right, of course, but it rankles.

"Check on Beast, Sparkles," Sarge jerks a thumb towards the doorway.

"He's hurt? He didn't say anything."

"He doesn't enjoy the spotlight like I do," Gears says with a groan. He reaches up and squeezes my hand as I walk by. "Thanks."

"Yeah," Sarge says. "Thanks."

"I didn't do much."

Sarge puts a hand to my shoulder. "You look after us. I couldn't ask for more from one of my squad."

I find myself clinging to his words. I'm part of the squad. My eyes fill up at the thought—the thought of belonging somewhere—even if it's this hellish place.

"I've got your six—just like you've got mine," I tell him around the lump in my throat. "And I think I might be close to figuring out who you all really are and why you're here."

He gives me a surprised look, so I lean in and lower my voice. "I'm trying to piece things together and I hope to have some information for you soon." I glance to the doorway. "I don't want to get anyone's hopes up. Just know I'm working on things—behind the scenes."

"Behind the scenes," he repeats, but his eyes are thoughtful and he's only half-listening.

"Let me check on the others and we can all talk." I make sure Gears is as comfortable as he can be under the circumstances. Sarge's eyes follow me as I move to the front of the room where Beast has one leg propped up on a chair.

"Where are you hurt?" I ask, opening my bag.

He raises one thick eyebrow. "Got winged by a bullet on the top of my thigh near the inside," he says.

"Why are they always shooting near your crotch?"

Beast cracks a wicked grin. "They aim for the largest target. And it barely even bled." He waves me off.

My cheeks redden, and I bite my lip, determined to be professional about this.

"I need to make sure it doesn't get infected," I tell him.

"It's not infected."

"You can't know that. Not without looking at it closely."

"All you're going to do is clean it out, right?"

"Unless it needs stitches."

"If it needed stitches, it would still be bleeding," he reasons. "And I can clean it out."

He reaches in front of him for the bottle on the table and then he stands up, tips it over and jams it down the front of his pants, pouring it liberally all over the wound. He flips the bottle back up and takes a drink.

"Disinfected inside and out," he says, giving me a salute.

I blink twice, shake my head, and turn to look at Shadow. "You're okay?"

She nods, but Beast disagrees.

"She got confused out there," he says somberly.

My head snaps to look at her as she protests.

"I'm fine." She inhales, tucking her hands behind her. "I just got a bit dizzy dodging gunfire."

Shadow is the most agile person I've ever met. I eye her suspiciously.

"Put your hands out."

"I'm *fine.*" She's emphatic. Too emphatic.

"Shadow—"

"It's just a little tremor." She's still not pulling her hands out from behind her back. "I've barely eaten today—"

A birdcall sounds and Chef steps through the door again.

"He got him!" Chef declares. "Rookie took the sniper down. And when I was doing recon, I found one of their radios." He holds it up. "The courier with the battle plans will be arriving just after sundown." He holds the radio out to Sarge, who shoves it in his shirt pocket.

"Great job, everybody," Sarge says. "This ought to get us at least a week of rest time if we can nab that courier."

"You get a week for every successful mission?" I ask incredulously.

"Sometimes," Shadow replies. "Sometimes more if it's a more complicated scenario."

I shudder. "Like the Citadel?"

"We haven't beaten the Citadel—yet," Sarge says. "But that's the big one. The grand prize."

"The grand prize?" I ask. "Like a month in Tahiti with no one shooting at us?"

"Like our ticket out of here," Beast says.

"That's the theory," Sarge interjects. "All these other scenarios just sharpen our skills and teach us to work as a team more efficiently. We're rewarded with rest when they're successful—"

"But the Citadel is a whole 'nother level," Gears adds from his place in the corner.

"Which means there's probably a reason for that," I theorize. Sarge acknowledges with a nod. We both jump at the sound of breaking glass. Shadow stands over the shattered remains of a waterglass.

"I didn't injure myself. I'm fine," she says yet again. "Just clumsy."

"You should sit down," I tell her. She stiffens at the worry in my voice—and in everyone else's eyes—but she sits, gripping the edge of the table hard.

Sarge's eyes narrow skeptically, and from the look of everyone else nobody believes a word she's said. Shadow is always in control and never clumsy.

Chef drops into the chair next to Beast, who slides the bottle toward him. I try to look at Chef's left hand without being obvious, but it's down at his side. Finally, I just reach out and grab it.

"Speaking of injuries, I need to see yours," I tell him firmly. "It looks like you've cut your hand."

He doesn't object as I peer down at it, and sure enough, there's a thin white scar on the back of his hand, right across the knuckles.

"That is an old scar," he says, pulling his hand away. "Not fresh."

"Any idea how you did it?"

"I do not remember." He shrugs, and I take a breath, not sure exactly how to tell him what I need to tell him.

The door suddenly flies open, with no warning birdcall. Beast has his rifle up and Shadow is kneeling with hers trained on the entry before I can even reach for my gun. Rookie clears the doorway, shuts the door behind him and leans his gun against it.

"Is that alcohol?" He points at the bottle on the table.

"Bourbon," Beast replies. "Aren't you a little young?"

Rookie only walks over and takes a long, gulping swig from the bottle before he sets it back down. Something about the look on his face keeps anyone from stopping him. He moves back toward the door, grabbing his gun along the way.

"Wait," Shadow says, stopping him. "Take Sparkles with you if it's clear. She needs more shooting practice, and we can't make a move before dark."

I can't argue with that, but Rookie really doesn't look like he wants company right now.

"Someone needs to stay with Gears," I say. "And you." And now that I'm certain Chef is Kalu, I need to speak with him—and then Rookie—about what I know.

"I've got her," Beast says, and Shadow strangely does not object.

"I will look after Gears," Chef promises. "Stay close and we will find you when we need you."

Rookie just keeps walking out the door. Okay, then. Rookie first. With a worried glance at Shadow, I pick up my gun and hurry out the door after him.

"We're safe?" I ask. "I know you got the sniper but—"

"Safe enough for now," he says tersely. "The enemy is at their encampment, and with the extra gun fire from the two of us, they're probably going to think the sniper is still keeping us busy."

"Okay." I pause and he rolls his eyes, annoyed. "It's just—I need to talk to you."

"Talk after you shoot," he grumbles. "Shadow's second in command, and this was an order."

I nod my agreement. Maybe it'll be better to ease into it anyway instead of just hitting him with *hey, our brains have been invaded by nanites and I think you've been trapped here by an evil corporation.*

Rookie spends a few minutes refreshing me on the parts of this particular rifle. Then he points at a crumbling section of wall a good twenty yards away. It stands like a pillar in the middle of a pile of rubble.

"Hit that," he says.

I bring the rifle up to my shoulder and line up my shot.

"You're closing one eye," he growls.

"Of course, I'm closing one eye. How else am I supposed to sight a target?"

"That's taking the easy way out."

"Since I'm new to this," I remind him sharply, "I would imagine the easy way is the best way."

"You imagine wrong." His voice is cold. Why is he so angry? "When the enemy is firing at you," he says, "your heart rate is going through the roof. Your breathing is three times as fast, and your pupils dilate. You'll be in full fight or flight mode, and you're not going to think for one minute about closing one eye." He touches the barrel of the rifle, shifting it left just a fraction.

"Your body is going to be telling you to gather as much information about the coming threat as it can," he continues.

"If you practice firing with only one eye your brain is going to get a lot more confused than it needs to be at a critical moment. You need to develop your muscle memory and train your brain to assess with both eyes open."

"Okay," I grumble. "Okay."

I squeeze the trigger gently and shoot nowhere near the target. I don't even know where that bullet went. I shake my head to clear my ringing ears. Gunfire is so loud. It's nothing like the movies.

"Try again," he says. "You were too high."

I lower the rifle slightly, and as he leans down, his cheek brushes mine. His hand comes over to the barrel, pushing it down a little more, and then nudging it slightly to the left.

"You keep drifting right. Try now."

I get off another shot, hitting an abandoned vehicle behind and to the right of the pillar.

This time, he comes around behind me, wrapping one arm around my right arm and the other around my left, his hands coming over mine on the rifle. He sets his chin down on my shoulder, and the warmth of his cheek is again next to mine.

"Easy," he murmurs, "take a breath before you fire."

Right. For some reason it's not easy to take a breath. I force myself to focus, and I pull the trigger.

This time I hit the pillar—all the way on the outer edge— but I hit it.

"I did it!" I turn my head as I exclaim. Rookie still hasn't moved and we're suddenly nose-to-nose.

"Now do it five more times," he commands.

I back up with a nervous little laugh. "I don't think my shoulder can take five more times," I roll my arm around. The gun really has a solid kick, and my shoulder is already sore.

"You'll get used to it."

"And then I'll be the one who takes down the snipers. Good job, by the way."

His face changes to an expression that can only be described as fury, and his body goes utterly still.

"We're done here," he snaps, turning on his heel to go.

What did I say? He moves quickly over the rubble, and I don't want to be left out here alone. More than anything though, I don't want him to be as upset as he clearly is.

"Look, I'm sorry." I run up next to him. "I know I'm not doing very well but I'm taking this seriously. I really am."

"It's fine." He rams a hand through his hair. "It's not you."

It's not me?

"Wait." I grab him by the arm and turn him to face me. "What's wrong? What happened?"

"Nothing. I killed the sniper." He looks almost like he's going to be ill, but the anger is still there, simmering. The hand not holding his rifle is clenched into a fist, and his neck is corded and tight.

"Did—did he hurt you? The sniper?" I feel bad for not thinking to ask sooner if he was injured. I review him top to bottom, but he only shakes his head. Then he drops down, sitting on what's left of a low crumbling wall, and sets his rifle down next to him.

He pulls in a long, shuddering breath. "It wasn't a *he.*"

"The sniper? He was a—she was a girl?" Wow. I didn't see that coming. "Has it always been a girl in this scenario?"

"I don't know," he says. "This is the first time I've seen the sniper up close. Usually I shoot him—shoot *her*—out of the clocktower and the body falls somewhere into the rubble. I've never gone looking for it. Once or twice, the sniper has moved to another building, and I watch them fall from a distance and not get up. She wears a hat, so I never knew."

"And today?"

"She was closer than I thought. She somehow sneaked around to a building behind me and got a bead on me from a nearby roof. She almost took me out like she has a dozen times before. But I got lucky and heard her when some rubble shifted underneath her. I turned and fired. She fell and landed right in front of me."

I don't know what to say to him. As hard as it is for me to watch my squad members die, I hadn't realized how lucky I am. I haven't yet pulled a trigger and ended a person's life up close and personal—yet.

"She was young," he says, and his voice is low, guttural. He rubs a hand over his face. "Really young. Eleven, maybe twelve, at the most."

"Oh God—she was just a kid!"

"Yeah. Just a kid."

Tears sting my eyes at the obvious pain on his face. The agony is written in every line of his body. I sit down next to him and slide my hand over his.

"I'm sorry," I say, wishing I had more to give. More comfort I could offer. "I'm so sorry."

He shifts his hand, clasping mine. Then suddenly he tugs me into him. He wraps his arms around me and clings tight, burying his face in my neck and taking deep, shuddering breaths. What can I even say to him? There are no words that will ease this or make it better. He shot a child, killed her, saw her dead body. I squeeze him fiercely, wishing I could take every bit of this memory from him.

Finally, he releases me, rubbing quickly at his eyes.

"Sorry," he mumbles.

"Don't be."

"I guess sometimes you just—I just need—"

I push his hair gently off his forehead. "You just need to be held. I know." My eyes fill with tears because I know it well. I've needed it badly since my father died. Having Rookie's arms around me made me realize just how much I needed it.

"The rest of the squad, they've all got their own stuff to deal with," he tells me. "I know you do too, but you're different. Part of the squad, but different. I guess that's why it's easier for me to—"

"You can talk to me anytime," I say, meaning it. "Whatever you need, I'm here." *You should tell him. You need to tell him.* The words circle in my mind, but he's dealing with enough at the moment.

He sucks in a cleansing breath, and then another one. "Do you mind too much if we don't use the rifles right now? I'm kind of done with shooting a gun until I absolutely have to."

"It's fine. I totally understand."

He hops off the wall and pulls me with him. "You're still going to do target practice. We'll just use a different weapon."

I look at him curiously and he reaches down, selecting several chunks of rock and concrete. Then he lines them up on the wall behind me.

"See that bucket over there?" He points down the street. "We're going to go for that."

"If I can't hit a target with a gun, what makes you think I'm going to hit it with a rock?"

"You will with practice," Rookie promises. "A target is a target, and in some of these scenarios, a rock might be your closest or only weapon. Learn to use what you've got."

"Okay," I reluctantly pick up a rock. "Here goes nothing."

He stands behind me and puts his arms around me again, holding my wrist and showing me the proper practice swing.

"Line it up," he says. "Don't second-guess. Take the shot."

I let the rock fly and come up short.

"Not bad," he says.

I give him a dubious look.

"No, really—not bad," he reassures me. "This time you need to feel your wrist snap at the end of the arc. Think of your wrist being on a rubber band. You want that whip of tension at the end before you release."

He hands me another rock. "Line it up. Don't second-guess. Take the shot."

"Line it up. Don't second-guess. Take the shot," I repeat.

This time, the rock sails past the bucket. He already has a third rock ready for me.

"It's not going to get better until after it's been worse for a while," he tells me.

"Is that a target practice pointer, or a life philosophy?"

"Maybe a little bit of both. I guess we'll just have to live through this nightmare and see."

"Guess so."

I take the shot.

16

I'M DOING MY BEST not to zone out as I sit in Evan's office. And by 'my best,' I mean I'm staring off into space and have lost my train of thought so many times I think it's permanently derailed.

I can't stop thinking about my squad. About the hell they're going through. How many times have they died, have they killed, over these nights? I can see their faces, and their pain, both physical and emotional weighs me down until I feel like I'm made of sand. Like I'll spill out if someone slices me open. And I think about Rookie. I still can't seem to call him Mateo. I think about the way his arms felt around me, warm and strong despite the vulnerability he was showing.

I should have told him. I really should have told him.

I didn't get the chance before a shell slammed into the tavern last night, collapsing the ceiling and taking us all out.

I glance down at my computer screen. I've been stuck in my Rookie mind loop again so long that the screen on my laptop has gone black. Evan has me typing up proposal requests to send to various product vendors—everything from automobiles to medical equipment to food service vendors. The letter specifically mentions an expansion of the company compound here on the island. I get the feeling Evan is spending the money from that big contract the second the ink dries on it—and maybe even before.

Luckily for me, he isn't watching me, judging by the curse words that keep bursting through his lips in between the furious clicking of his mouse and the typing of his fingers. I don't dare ask him what's going on because he's obviously not going to tell me.

"Evan?" I say it quietly, but his head jerks up like I screamed at him.

"What?" He snaps.

"Sorry," I say apologetically. "Would you like me to get you some more coffee?" I point to his empty cup.

He shoves fingers into his perfectly coiffed blond hair so hard that they snag in his hair gel.

"Might as well. I'm going to be here for a while."

I push out of my chair and reach for his mug.

His hand covers the mug. "You remember how I take it right?"

"Four sugars, splash of cream, stir it twice."

He slides his hand away and lets me take the mug.

"Glad to see you're paying attention," he says. "Wish I could say the same for everyone around here."

I give him a fake smile and step out in the hallway, closing the door behind me before I walk down to the break room.

As I make Evan's coffee, my mind plays over the conversations Rio and I had at lunch with Rookie's—I mean Mateo's—friends yesterday. I tried to sound casual as I inquired about the guy in the trophy case picture, and it turns out he still has fans.

He has a wicked sense of humor. I knew that.

He's an excellent archer. I knew that. There was even talk about him trying out for the Olympic Archery team.

He broke his rib surfing on the south side of the island. I didn't know that.

He had a dog named Goliath. And it's a Chihuahua.

He once ate four burritos from the food stand near the turtle beach and barfed on the elementary school teacher. I'll have to tease him about that, if he ever remembers who he is.

And finally, some girl named Milena told me he was a very good kisser. Not that I cared to know that.

I stare down at my hand, which has stirred Evan's coffee so long I've practically turned it into a whipped drink. It settles down quickly and I'm willing to bet money he'll never know how many times I stirred it.

Walking back down the hall, careful not to spill, I force my mind to stay on the task at hand instead of on the memory of Rookie's arms around me, of his shoulders shaking as he held me. As I near the door, it becomes clear that Evan is not alone.

My mother's voice is easy for me to pick out. With a quick glance up and down the hall to make sure no one will witness me eavesdropping, I stop before the doorway to listen.

"So, what—they're talking about backing out?" She says angrily. "You told me they were on board and willing to wait while we worked out the bugs."

"I think I've got them talked around but they're not going to hold out forever." Evan fumes. "They're being scrutinized, just like we are."

My mother's voice lowers. "Interpol?"

"Not to mention the other interested factions," Evan says with an exasperated noise. "Maybe we should let them all tear into each other and we make a play for whoever is left."

"Keep your voice down," my mother admonishes. "We can't let Armando or one of his goons think we don't have this under control."

"I don't know how much longer I can stall them. And Grady isn't coming through—she says she can only spin the reports for so long."

"We can't let this get into a situation where mouths are running and money is passing through too many hands," she says. "We're getting too much notice as it is."

I hear Evan slam his laptop shut. "It's all so damn infuriating," he snarls.

A loud sigh. Then my mother's voice again. "We'll figure it out. The pieces are going to come together. I stopped by to let you know I thought of something."

"What?" The tone in Evans voice sounds like a drowning man who just got thrown a rope.

A pause. "Where is J.J.?" she asks.

Before she can open the door and look for me, I beat her to it.

"Did I hear my name?" I enter, the picture of unconcerned innocence.

"That took a while," Evan chides, looking at me through narrowed eyes.

"The coffee machine was in the middle of making a new pot," I tell him. "I had to wait."

He takes the cup from me, but he doesn't drink. He just sets it down.

"What did you need me for?" I ask my mother.

Her face goes blank for a moment and then she recovers quickly. "I was going to ask if you would go out and pick up dinner. Evan and I need to work late on a project, and I was craving empanadas from that place in the village."

"Great idea," Evan says. He digs some money out of his pocket. "Empanadas for everyone. And take your time. Ask for the fresh ones."

"I can finish what I was working on first," I offer. "It's still early for dinner."

"Then you'll definitely get them fresh," my mother says. "Oh, and ask them for a bottle of that papaya soda they carry."

"Make it two," Evan chimes in, "and get whatever you want."

"Why don't you invite Rio along?" My mother suggests. "She can help you carry."

Wow, they *really* want me out of here. But I'm not looking a dinner horse in the mouth. They're not likely to keep talking about whatever they were talking about while I'm hanging around anyway. I take the money from Evan.

"On it." I close out of my computer and grab my bag. "Be back soon."

I shut the door behind me and walk away before tiptoeing back quietly and leaning toward the door again. They're talking too softly now for me to make out the words, and I can hear someone rounding the corner at the end of the hallway, so I quickly step back—but not before I'm seen.

Armando and his two men are walking straight toward me. I make a show of patting my pockets.

"Did you see my security badge in the hallway?" I ask. "I think I might have dropped it."

Armando studies me for a long moment, the scar at his lip twitching.

"That's a serious security issue," he says. "Dr. Walters—he is very protective of his secrets. It wouldn't be good to have someone careless jeopardizing his great work."

"I—I think I just left it in the kitchen," I stammer. "I'd better go."

"What's your name, *chica?*" He smiles, but it doesn't look friendly. I'm saved from answering him when my mother opens the door. She freezes when she sees us both.

"J.J." She speaks to me, but her eyes are on Armando. "You need to go."

"Stay safe, J.J." Armando's voice follows me down the hall, and my mind is whirling, lending speed to my steps.

Things are obviously not good—Interpol is investigating? How does my father—and whatever he left me—figure into this? How does my squad figure into this?

A cold fist clenches my gut. What has my mother been doing all these years? What has she been pulled into? How far into this are my friends and I going to be pulled? And Dr. Grady is involved? I may not like having to see a therapist, but I thought she was mostly okay.

Suddenly, the thought of a free dinner only makes me nauseous. I have a feeling that as complicated and chaotic as my life is on the overnight, my daytime reality is on its way to being just as bad.

I'm glad they told me to bring Rio along. Maybe Akoni can meet us in the village, and we can do a little more planning. Akoni will be thrilled that I positively ID'd his brother but not so much when I tell him I haven't been able to speak to Chef about it yet.

We need to get moving on this, before Evan—and my mother—get hauled away by the police or murdered by a terrorist faction. God only knows what else the company is mixed up in.

I'm still not entirely convinced that I'm not delusional, but I am a hundred percent sure that my mother and Evan are neck-deep in something I should stay far away from.

Just like the members of my squad, I'm as trapped as they are now.

17

"**Can I pick your** brain for a minute?" I ask Sarge.

This scenario they call *Kings and Castles*, and the mission is to intercept or steal the king's personal adviser's diaries. Shadow just scaled a castle wall while the rest of us laid false trails to confuse the king's hounds. Sarge and I sit in an abandoned mill while we wait for the others to join us.

"Not much there to pick." Sarge pats a spot on the ground next to him, and I settle down, my back against the wall. "What are we chatting about?"

"The scenarios," I begin. "Who exactly decides these missions? You always mention 'getting' the orders."

Sarge nods. "That's right." He picks up a few moldering stalks of wheat from the floor and rips them into pieces as he talks. "They're given to me at the start of each scenario. No person hands them to me if that's what you're asking. They just appear."

"That's crazy."

"It takes some getting used to," he agrees.

"There has to be someone overseeing the game." My finger taps on my knee with agitation. "Someone with answers." *I'm afraid to know who.*

Sarge eyes me shrewdly. "What's this all about, Sparkles?"

"I've just been thinking a lot—in my off time."

"Your *off* time," he repeats, looking at me as though I'm speaking pig Latin.

"It's just—you've all been dragged into these nightmare scenarios, getting slaughtered over and over—don't you want to know why? Or how to get out of here?"

"Of course, we do," Rookie says as he comes in through the door. The others are right on his heels, bearing bows, swords, and daggers. Beast's sword is nearly as big as he is. Gears has an arm about Chef's shoulders, but before I can ask if he's injured, Chef pulls away hard, then sinks to the ground, holding his head in violently shaking hands.

"Make it stop," Chef pants, and I can hear the pain and fear in his voice. I start to rise to my feet, but Sarge puts a protective hand on my arm to hold me back.

Beast sets a large hand in the middle of Chef's back, and it seems to calm him. He takes several long, shuddering breaths until finally, the tremors stop.

"You okay?" Beast asks. "That's twice this scenario."

Chef gives a shaky nod as Beast helps him to his feet. "I will be all right. I just need to get out of this scenario."

"We'll all get out," Rookie assures him.

"If our brains aren't mincemeat," Beast adds with an unsettling air of resignation.

"What if—" I wet my lips nervously before I put this out there. "What if I know who some of you are? Who you *really* are?"

Gears turns from where he was keeping watch by the door. "Come again?"

"Where are you going with this?" Sarge looks at me warily, but he motions to me to continue.

I pull in a breath. "I know who Chef really is. And Rookie."

Rookie freezes. "*What?*"

"You know who we are?" Chef moves over to crouch in front of me.

"I think so. I told you I can leave here—wake up and go back to the real world."

"The *real* world," Sarge echoes.

I nod. "I live on an island. I go to high school. Rookie went there, too. He was captain of the archery team, and his name is Mateo Ruiz."

Rookie looks at me blankly, as though I told him he was Abraham Lincoln. Or just plain John Smith. He takes no meaning from this information.

"And me?" Chef asks hopefully.

"Your name is Kalu," I tell him. "You have a brother on the island and he's looking for you. His name is Akoni."

Chef shakes his head. "This is not familiar to me."

"Why only them?" Beast asks. "Why can't you tell us anything about the rest of us?"

"If I hadn't seen Rookie's picture and run into Chef's brother, I wouldn't know any of you," I explain.

"This is all very interesting," Sarge says, slowly pushing to his feet. "But who's to say you're not just blinking out to some other scenario? What makes your 'other life' any more real than this one?"

"Why would I lie about this?" I spread my hands wide. "I wake up from this—these dreams—every night. And the rest of the time, I'm a normal kid. I go to school. I hang out with friends."

"A friend who's an undercover spy and your school is on an island," Sarge fills in.

"Yeah. It's partially owned by Codonexus." I wait to see if that has any effect—but there's no recognition there, either.

"What's a Codonexus?" Gears asks.

"It's a bio-tech company," I reply. "With secrets."

"The company runs a school?" Chef looks as confused as the others.

"What secrets?" Beast asks at the same time.

"I'd like to know—" Sarge is interrupted by Shadow, as she sweeps through the door.

"Sorry to interrupt a fascinating conversation," she says. "But we need to move." She closes the door and leans against it, panting. "I walked into an ambush. I barely got away."

"The intel?" Sarge demands.

Shadow shakes her head as the others begin gathering their things. I scramble to my feet, pulling out my dagger, but Sarge's voice stops us all cold.

"Hold up a minute."

Clearly, something is wrong. I can hear it in his voice, see it in the tense way he's holding himself, the tight line of his mouth and the way his eyes are boring into me as if he can see through my skin.

Before I can ask what's going on, Sarge twists the dagger from my hand. In two quick steps I'm against the wall and he has the blade at my throat.

"Wh-what? Wait!" I stammer. The rest of the squad are behind Sarge, looking at me as though I've grown a second head.

"I don't understand." I look frantically from Sarge to Rookie. He's staring at Sarge in confusion.

"Whatever it is you think she's done—" He begins.

"Command has been monitoring an increased need for threat resistance," Sarge tells them in a tone as cold as ice. "Her inclusion in our squad was not sanctioned by any orders I've seen, so I've been keeping an eye on her. And tonight, she got here just in time to set up an ambush for Shadow—right after she mysteriously appeared from wherever it is she goes all the time."

"But she's a medic," Rookie says, still defending me. "She's treated our wounds, fought with us!"

Sarge has a pained expression on his face. "When you've been a soldier as long as I have you learn the best double-agents are the ones you call friend."

"Sarge—" I start to protest, but he digs the edge of the knife in a little deeper, sending a trickle of blood down a path over my suddenly icy skin.

"But it doesn't make sense," Rookie shakes his head.

"It makes perfect sense," Sarge goes on, every word snapping like a whip. "What better way to infiltrate our group than to send someone to heal you and befriend you personally? She's been privy to all of our plans, to all of our mission directives. Who knows how much damage she's done when she blinks out of our sight—a trick none of the rest of us can do, I'll remind you."

"I'm not a threat!" I turn pleading eyes to Shadow, to Rookie—to all of them. "You know that's not true! Doesn't it bother any of you that you're fighting blind?" I ask frantically. "No one knows what's going on!"

"No problem," Shadow says in a growl. "We'll have all sorts of new information in a few minutes." She brings her own dagger up, twirling it in her fingers.

"We need to know every word of what she knows," Beast says, stepping closer to Sarge.

"There's no time for that now," Sarge says. "Interrogating her will only slow us down, and we have a mission to accomplish."

"Wait!"

Rookie's voice rings out, but it's too late. I see the flash of the knife in the corner of my eye and the rage on Sarge's face. There's a burning slash of pain and my knees give way as I crumple slowly to the ground. Blood gushes out from between my fingers as I frantically attempt to cover the ragged hole in my throat, choking and gasping, writhing as I fight for my life.

And I see the hard, cold look in Sarge's eyes as the rest of my squad's shocked and angry faces fade to black.

18

ON MONDAY NIGHT, I tried to reason with them as we all stood near the banks of a rushing river. I didn't get ten words out before Gears slammed the handle of his musket into my skull. I tumbled down, down, down into the water, where once again, I drowned.

On Tuesday night, Shadow caught me hiding behind the kennels at the castle. She simply shouted for the guards, who couldn't be troubled with an unarmed young trespasser. They loosed the hounds on me instead. It took a long time to die. I missed school the next day, spending the whole day in bed. When Rio stopped by, I pretended to be asleep. I couldn't talk. I just couldn't.

On Wednesday night, it was the Citadel, and the feel of Chef's trembling hand on my back as he shoved me hard, sending me stumbling into the Fibonacci tiles. I didn't even have time to gasp before I was blown to bits.

On Thursday night, they pulled me backwards from my hiding place in a thicket. I clawed at the dirt but it was no use. They dragged me by my hair into the center of a clearing and shot me. It was Sarge that time, and the look of cold determination in his eyes as he pulled the trigger sat in my stomach like a ball of ice for a solid day afterward.

On Friday night, it was Beast's turn. I'm not sure where we were, because just about everywhere has rocks, and the one he swung at my head did the job on the first blow.

On Saturday night, Shadow finished me quickly with the tusk of a large animal. I like it better when they kill me fast.

And on Sunday night, I took an arrow through my heart. You'd think that would have killed me instantly, but it took a few minutes. Long enough for me to see him move closer, and crouch down beside me. Long enough to watch him judge whether or not I needed a second arrow. Long enough for me to remember his expressionless face and the coldness in his eyes before he stood and walked away.

I managed to go to school the next day, but I still felt that arrow in my heart.

19

EVAN HAS LOVED HAVING me at his beck and call this last week. I fetch his coffee, his dinner when he works late—he even gave me the keys to his car so I could take it to the motor pool and get it washed.

Earlier this week he had me type a few business emails. I was hoping he'd give me proxy into his email account so I could send them, but he's too paranoid for that. He scrawled out some thoughts on a couple of post-it notes and had me type it up on my own email account and send it to him instead so he could copy and paste. Still, I've had a few opportunities to gather information. I keep his calendar, so I know his schedule now.

I know he has a daily meeting at ten a.m. with all of his department managers. I know he meets with Finance on Wednesdays at eight-thirty a.m. He visits the lab complex every Tuesday, Thursday, and Friday at four p.m. I leave early on those days, or he sends me out to run errands. He even has a standing appointment with Dr. Grady every Monday afternoon at her office. I'm sure he wants to know how many employees are having anxiety attacks or hate his guts, along with the other covert stuff she's apparently privy to.

I've met a few of the managers, most of whom seem nervous all the time. They're apprehensive in a way I can't put my finger on. One or two of them seem cordial with him, but I wouldn't say he's respected or liked by many of them. And then there's Armando and his shadows redefining *creepy menace* on a daily basis. Maybe that's just me projecting, but those are my impressions.

Evan spends a lot of time on the phone or reviewing spreadsheets full of data. I happened to glance over his shoulder once when I was delivering coffee and saw one with the heading Clinical Data Preliminary Conclusions and then the words *Evening Time* or something like that.

Every single day he saves whatever he's working on onto two different USB drives, which he locks in his desk. He backs nothing up to a network drive. The USB drives are encrypted, just like the one Dr. Grady gave me. There's no chance they both use the same access code, so I have to figure out a way to get my hands on it.

Today is Tuesday, and Rio, Akoni, and I will be enacting our plan. Evan told me I'll be taking his car to the motor pool for a wash and wax at four o'clock, while he visits the lab. Then I am to drive over to the lab complex and drop the car by five.

One hour.

I have one hour—less if you count the commute time—to get whatever I can off those USB drives.

I try my best not to look nervous as Evan sits down at his computer after lunch. Smiling sheepishly, I walk around behind him, holding up the watering can.

"Can I get the plants on the windowsill?" I ask. "Or will that bother you?"

"Go ahead," he says, casually waving one hand over his shoulder without looking at me—which is a very good thing, because if he turned to look at me now, he'd see me holding my phone behind his shoulder, taking video of his keyboard as he inserts the USB drive and types in his access code. I pocket the phone quickly and turn back to water his plants— thank God he practically has a jungle back here, so this can take a few minutes.

Two hours later, and it's time for his afternoon coffee, which I leave to fetch from the kitchen. I duck into the bathroom on the way. My shaking fingers are barely able to latch the door on the stall before I sink down onto the toilet, taking deep breaths to calm my racing heart.

The hard part is over, I tell myself.

I watch the video over and over until I'm sure I have the code correct—including capital letters, numbers, and special characters. At least, I hope it's correct. I scrawl it on a sticky note and cram it into my bra, like I expect him to pat me down or something. Totally paranoid.

In the hallway I stop again to take a few more deep breaths, otherwise I'm going to spill coffee all over myself from my hands shaking.

It's stupid to be this afraid. What's he going to do? Yell at me? Fire me? I couldn't care less.

Just please don't let him hurt my friends. I hate that I think it.

A few minutes before four o'clock, Evan removes the USB drive and dutifully locks it in his desk drawer. Then he calls my name and after I look up from my computer, he tosses me his key ring—the key ring that has his car key, our house key and the keys to his desk, among other keys. I keep my face cool and polite as I pocket them.

"You ready to go?" He asks, holding the door.

I pin a pained expression on my face. "I'm sorry," I say. "I'm just finishing up the projections spreadsheet for the lab supplies. I know you need it for tomorrow morning's finance meeting." I wince apologetically. "I only need like, ten more minutes."

He gives me a curt nod. "Make sure you lock the door before you leave."

I offer him a jaunty salute. "Will do, boss. I'll see you in an hour—if I don't run off with your gorgeous car."

His chest puffs up and he gives me that stupid car salesman grin. "Take good care of my baby," he says.

"Nothing but the best for you," I reassure him as I look back down at my keyboard. I type a bunch of random numbers and letters until he closes the door behind him.

I give him five minutes, then ten, just to make sure he doesn't backtrack because he forgot something.

I move to the windows and close the blinds, then text Akoni, who is at the other end of the building, sweeping floors.

A few minutes later a quiet knock sounds.

I let him in quickly, a little out of breath with mounting panic. This is crazy. I've worked myself up into an extreme state of nerves and I am completely second-guessing every step of this stupid plan.

"Do you have the keys?"

"Hold on." I walk over and open the bottom drawer before tossing him the key ring.

"Take the car somewhere no one will see it," I remind him. "It's barely dirty. If you and Rio hose it down and then buff it up with some rags, he'll never know the difference."

"I will have it back in twenty minutes," he tells me.

"Make sure nobody sees you," I say again.

"We will be very careful."

"And don't let Rio use any glittery soap or essential oils. Just water and a rub down."

"Got it," he says, and he slips out the door.

I run my suddenly sweaty palms against the fabric of my jeans before I reach for the unlocked drawer. Outside in the hall a door slams and I startle, slipping in the chair. I count to ten and nothing else happens. Probably just someone leaving for the evening.

Reaching in the drawer, my fists closes around the two USB drives. I move back to my desk and pull my personal laptop out of the big tote bag I brought into work with me. The laptop boots up and my fingertips drum the desk with impatience. My eyes are on the clock, as it all seems to take forever.

Finally, I'm able to login and I disable the wi-fi before I access the Climate Champions sub-folder of the "Homework" folder I put on my desktop. Hopefully, this looks bland enough to fool Evan or my mother if they should ever come snooping.

I take a deep breath and insert the USB drive, smoothing out the crumpled sticky note and rereading the combination of numbers, letters, and symbols one more time as the drive boots up. It flashes a box on the screen asking for the encryption code.

Here goes.

Oh God—what if it's wrong? My fingers slide back from the keys. What if I type it wrong? Will it set off some sort of alarm? Will Evan be able to tell?

Do it now, I scold myself. If there is some way to show when files were accessed, I'm still close enough in time that Evan might just think the record is of him. The longer I take to do this, the less plausible that will be.

I flex my fingers and type with one hand while the index finger of the other carefully points at each character on the sticky note.

With a silent prayer, and a giant knot of tension in my stomach that also seems to be gripping the back of my neck, I press *Enter.*

"Yes!" The exclamation slips past my lips a little too loudly. I look at the door, terrified, but nothing happens and no one comes in. I copy the folders over. They transfer quickly, but not quickly enough. I feel every second as it stretches into a mini eternity, finally snatching the drive out the moment it finishes copying and then the second drive goes in. I repeat the process with the log on, working myself into another fine state of anticipatory terror at the thought of them each possibly requiring a separate encryption code, but I get lucky.

I suppose the encryption codes are unique to the person. It would be a good way to track who's accessing what data.

The second drive has fewer files. The clock shows nineteen minutes gone. I take a moment to spray some glass cleaner onto a paper towel and I carefully use it to wipe down each drive before I place them back in his desk drawer. Then I wipe the drawer handle like I expect them to dust for prints.

Dammit! Which direction were they facing in the drawer? Were they side-by-side or end-to-end? I think they were side-by-side. One might have been a little crooked.

My logical mind reminds me that Evan just tossed them in the drawer without looking but I'm still paranoid about it. I look up at the clock again.

Nearly twenty-five minutes gone.

I shut down my laptop and shove it back down in the bag.

Where is Akoni? Did someone see him? Did Rio make too much noise? She was probably singing while she worked. I love the girl, but she's not exactly good at being subtle. I look out the window and gnaw my lip. When the knock comes at the door it makes me jump.

"Who is it? I ask quietly, throwing my bag over my shoulder.

"It's me," says Rio, in what has to be the loudest whisper I have ever heard in my life. Her head peeks around the corner of the door, but before I see the face, I see the poofy purple pom-poms on each ponytail.

"All set!" she says. "The car's out back. Akoni wanted me to remind you that we're meeting in the maintenance shed behind the motor pool at six-thirty."

"Got it." I nearly bowl her over rushing to get out the door. Her hand—complete with neon orange fingernails—stops me as I'm about to close the locked door behind me.

"Dude, don't you need these?" She dangles Evan's key ring in front of me.

"I would have asked you for them before I got in the car." I roll my eyes at her.

She lowers her voice. "For the drawer."

I nearly forgot to lock the drawer again! I take back every impatient thought I ever had about her. Rio is brilliant.

I lean forward and kiss her forehead loudly. "Thanks for having my six," I tell her gratefully.

"I don't want you getting locked away in Dr. Walters' secret island dungeon or something," she says with a shrug.

I quickly lock the drawer, double-checking it, with a jiggle to the handle that probably upset the carefully placed USB drives inside. I use my Windex-soaked paper towel to wipe down the handle of the drawer again, and then I toss it in the garbage and follow Rio out into the hall, checking the door to make sure it locked behind me.

"Is this phase one of the *Operation Chimu Trio Masterforce* plan a success?" she asks.

"That's what we're calling our squad?"

"That's what I've decided on today," she says as we walk down the hall. "I reserve the right to revise. And wow, Dr. Walters has got a sweeeet ride."

"I know." I grumble.

"The cup holder lights up."

"I know."

"And the sun visor makes the cutest whirring sound when it drops into place."

"I know." I give her a side eye. "Please tell me you weren't playing with all the gadgets and devices. He has everything set a certain way—he'll know."

"I only touched what I had to wipe down," she swears to me. "He totally has to be an evil genius with a car like that."

I don't know about the genius part, but something in my stomach warns me I might not like uncovering the evil.

20

I WORRY MY MOTHER suspects something as I rush through dinner. Luckily for me, she also knows next to nothing about me, so even though she might think I'm hiding something, I doubt she suspects that I'm trying to take her company down from the inside. *Seriously* inside.

After dinner, I tell her I have to meet Rio so that we can do our next homework assignment together for biology. Even though it feels like I'm leaving a limb behind, I put my phone under the pillow on my bed. The last thing I need is her tracking my location. I take my time walking toward the general housing area and then circle back the long way on the service road just to be sure no one's following me. I reach the maintenance shed without any issues and breathe a sigh of relief when Rio opens the door for my triple knock.

"Dude," she says. "That wasn't the right knock."

"Then why did you open the door?" Akoni asks from behind her.

"I mean, it was close," she tells me. "It's not one-two-three, it's more like one-two-pause-three. There's a rhythm." She nods her head for emphasis.

"Does it matter now?" I unsling the bag from my shoulder and remove the laptop. "Let's get to work."

"When it boots up," Akoni says, "you should disable the internet access."

"Already on it," I tell him. "I shut off the Wi-Fi before I ever copied the files."

"But it's not a network computer," Rio points out.

"I'm not taking any chances with using their internet access. This is serious cloak-and-dagger stuff, here. I don't think we can be too cautious."

"We're not going to get caught in here?" Rio asks nervously.

"No one is in here after five," Akoni tells us.

"Great," I say, dropping into one of the chairs at a metal work table set against one wall. "Here we go."

I access the files we copied over, clicking in and out of various folders, many of which just contain spreadsheets full of numbers and other sorts of data and research proposals. I find a few PowerPoint decks with what look like pitch presentations for the company, and then one of the folders catches my eye.

"That's interesting." I lean forward, scanning the screen.

"What?" Akoni leans in on the other side of me from Rio, who's driving me crazy with her right ponytail in my face.

"I think I found something." I point to a folder. "What's *Project Eventide?*"

Akoni chews his lip. "The name is similar to something I've read about—there was a project called *Evenglow.* It was the research that started the company—and it was the project Kalu was recruited for."

"They might have renamed it or something," Rio says. "If the first name wasn't catchy enough."

"Project Evenglow was developed as a therapy tool for post-traumatic stress disorder," Akoni explains. "They programmed nanites to access the hippocampus, where memory is stored. The test subjects would then review their trauma in a virtual setting that would not put them in physical jeopardy. They could deconstruct the things that trigger them and work through them in a safe, controlled environment."

"My dad helped develop the nanite interfaces early on," I add, remembering.

"That's messed up," Rio says. "Who wants to re-live their worst memories?"

"The idea was that the soldiers would be in control through the process," Akoni says. "This is what Kalu told me. The soldiers would know it was a simulation, and be able to pull themselves out, or maneuver themselves within the simulation—under direct psychiatric care. Alternately, the nanites were also a delivery mechanism to switch on parts of the brain that release dopamine and serotonin when needed."

"The Eventide files were the ones Evan was looking at today, I think." I open the Eventide folder and click into the *Program Parameters* file.

"Project Eventide," I read from the summary. "A direct corollary to project Evenglow, was developed as a virtual training alternative for military special forces, leveraging the scenario-building capabilities of Evenglow and incorporating advanced combat and covert operations practices to ensure real-world experience in a no-risk environment."

"They've militarized it," Akoni says, in a voice as cold as ice. "Next, they weaponize it. They trap people in it, perhaps to extract information, possibly even for torture."

"That's not what my father was working on." My stomach turns at the thought. "This isn't what he planned."

"Didn't you say he left the company?" Rio asks. "Now you know why."

I'd always assumed my father left because of my mother's affair with Evan. Could there have been more to it? I force myself to focus on the files, and among all the many sub-folders full of spreadsheets, charts and data, I find one titled *Test Subjects—Specialist Squad.*

"Seriously?" Rio asks. "That's the best name they could come up with?"

"Can we move forward, please?" Akoni asks impatiently. "I am supposed to be on my dinner break."

I scroll through the documents and click open the file marked *Roster*—then gasp as the file comes up.

My eyes scan the pictures—the faces just as I remember them, alongside a brief bio for each. "This is my squad," I say, though the first bio is for someone I have never met.

"Erik Andersson," I read aloud. "Squad designation: 'Boomer.' Age: twenty-eight. Two years as an investigator with INTERPOL. Norwegian Special Operation Forces, OED certified, specialized training in bio-weapons and electronic trigger mechanisms. Declared deceased day sixty-three. Initial health status categorized as 'optimal,' updated due to previously undiagnosed aortic aneurism. Languages: English, Norwegian, German. Intelligence scores above average.

So that's what happened to Boomer. I keep reading.

"Kalu Bolaji. Squad designation: 'Chef.' Age twenty-one."

"Kalu!" Akoni exclaims.

"College internship program, Georgetown University," I continue. "Seeking dual degrees in chemistry and neuroscience. Health status optimal. Intelligence scores well above average. Languages: English, French and Igbo."

"Smart guy," Rio interjects.

"He is." The pride and affection in Akoni's voice is evident.

"William Capaldi," I continue. "Squad designation: Scribe. Age: thirty. Aeronautica Militare (Italy). Specializations in linguistics, cryptology and interrogation techniques. Languages: English, Spanish, Italian. Health status optimal. Intelligence scores above average. Declared neurologically compromised on program day 158. Black protocol enabled.

"Travis Hawkins. Squad designation: 'Gears.' Age: twenty-two. College internship program, University of Alabama. Seeking advanced degrees in engineering and robotics. Languages: English. Health status optimal. Intelligence scores above average.

"John Maiava. Squad designation: 'Beast.' Age: thirty-six. Former US Navy SEAL, three tours of duty in classified combat situations. Languages: English, Samoan. Health status optimal. Intelligence scores above average.

"Marianne Lao. Squad designation: 'Shadow.' Age thirty-two. Skilled mercenary specializing in stealth operations and intelligence. Advanced skills in hand-to-hand combat, nine years with MI6. Languages: English, Chinese, Russian,

German, French, Italian, Spanish, some Arabic. Health status optimal. Intelligence scores well above average."

"Wow," says Rio. "Just—wow."

"They're all impressive," I tell her. "But they're not all soldiers."

"Kalu said they wanted a mix of subjects for the project, civilian and military," Akoni explains. "My brother is in good company."

"The best." I keep reading.

"Prisha Sharma. Squad designation: 'Wizard.' Age: twenty-one. College internship program, Penn State University. Seeking degree in software systems architecture with an emphasis on cybersecurity and threat assessment. Languages: English, Hindi, some Bengali. Intelligence scores above average. Health status optimal at initiation. Declared neurologically compromised on program day 224. Black protocol enabled."

"This man," Akoni points at Boomer's summary. "It appears he had a heart problem?"

"An aortic aneurysm," I read.

"That mean all of this was too much for his heart?"

"It looks like it," I answer grimly. "I mean, if he had an undiagnosed heart condition and they kept putting him under stress—even if it's psychological—it's still going to have a physical effect on his body, wherever that is."

"He died in his dreams, and it killed him in real life," Rio's voice is hushed, her eyes wide.

"It was murder," Akoni says harshly. "They may not have meant to kill him, but they put him in an environment that certainly did."

My cursor moves back down to the entry for Scribe, then Wizard. *Deceased on program day 158. Black Protocol enabled.* I read it again, and my finger freezes over the words *Black Protocol.*

"What does this mean?" I minimize the data folder and search the remaining folders until I find the list of protocols.

Green Protocol: Serotonin and/or dopamine levels elevated to reward group participation and objective focus.

Yellow Protocol: Altering of scenario to focus action primarily on one participant for research or instructional purposes.

Red Protocol: Participants behaving outside of structured norms, immediate corrective synaptic direction taken.

White Protocol: Triggers program transparency.

Black Protocol: Termination.

Termination.

I lurch to my feet, feeling like I'm going to puke.

"They deliberately killed them," I whisper, my horror growing as I realize what I've just read. "Scribe was the first to get the shakes, and—"

"The shakes?" Rio interrupts.

My eyes shift to Akoni, then I quickly look away. "It's a condition—they shake all over and lose control, sometimes by blanking out, sometimes by trying to kill the squad or themselves."

"That is not a good thing," Akoni says, "And this also happened to the girl? Miss Sharma?"

"Wizard was traumatized in one of the scenarios—I mean, more than just the usual bullets and arrows and getting blown apart—"

Both Rio and Akoni look at me with their eyebrows raised.

"I know, I know." I wave a hand. "You get used to it, sort of. Well, not really used to it. But resigned to it. It wears you down and you just accept that death is probably going to happen, and you'll wake up in the next scenario—except sometimes you don't."

I feel a chill skitter down my spine at the memory of those hands grabbing me, the strength of the primitive man as he dragged me back. How quickly he moved before I even knew he was there.

"It's not an exaggeration to say that Wizard underwent an extreme amount of torture," I explain. "I can only imagine what that did to her psychologically. She was already showing signs of the shakes, and this sent her over the edge."

"So, they decided that her mind was broken. She was no longer of use to them," Akoni says in a hard voice.

We're all silent for a moment as we stare at the file picture of the lovely young woman with the flawless copper skin, raven hair, and bright smile. And at the curly-headed Scribe, with his wide grin and the creases around his eyes that tell me he used to laugh a lot. At Boomer's bright blue eyes, so full of life. Gone, all of them. And for what? My mind once again asks the question I ask every night in my dreams as I die and die again. *Why?*

I turn suddenly from where I've been pacing. "Wait—where's the file summary for Sarge and Rookie?"

"Maybe they weren't originally meant to be there," Rio observes. "Like you."

"Rookie is a recent addition to the squad?" Akoni asks.

"He came in after the others—I can't say by how much exactly since time is all over the place there," I explain. "Rio says Matteo Ruiz been gone a few months."

"Ruiz—as in Dr. Manuel Ruiz?" Akoni looks alarmed.

Rio nods. "That's his dad."

"Dr. Manuel Ruiz is the world's foremost authority on nanorobotics," Akoni says.

The name clicks suddenly. "He worked with my parents," I say. "I never met him, but my dad talked about him. I didn't make the connection before."

A thought swirls in my head and slides down to my stomach, making me nauseous. Did his dad send him into this? Did my mother?

"So where did they get Sarge?" Rio asks. "You said he's been there the longest."

"We think so," I reply. "But no one's really sure how much time separates all their arrivals."

"He may very well have been the first subject," Akoni says, scanning the file. "The program called for direct psychiatric observation and intervention during the scenarios. If he's a psychologist or therapist, he wouldn't be there as part of the squad—more like an embedded resource to help facilitate scenarios."

I can believe that. Sarge just naturally makes you want to trust him. When he's not intent on murdering you, anyway. It's possible, he doesn't have much choice in that if the program somehow perceives me as a threat and he's been put there to intervene. We've got to fix this so I can get my Sarge back. The squad needs him.

"So Mateo *is* in there," says Rio.

"You thought I was making it up?" I turn to look at her.

"You've been under a lot of stress," she says. "Mateo was a hot guy, and you seeing his picture and then dreaming about him later isn't really that much of a stretch. This?" She gestures at the screen. "This is crazy. Why would they take Mateo Ruiz? Why would his father allow it?"

"I do not believe he did," Akoni says. "A few months ago, he went into seclusion. Talk around the island is that Dr. Ruiz has a drinking problem, so they are keeping him out of the public eye. That seemed odd—from what I have found in my research, Dr. Ruiz is known to be very conservative, an honest family man. Since his wife's death from breast cancer four years ago, he dotes upon his only child."

"Dude, you know all that?" Rio is impressed.

"I have files on everyone important in this place and a lot of people that are not as important." Akoni answers. "I even have files on the schoolteachers—that is why you caught me going through the drawers of the classroom that day. As I said, this company is layers of secrets upon secrets. All the little pieces show the bigger picture."

"And that is?" I ask.

"I'm not entirely sure yet." Akoni shakes his head. "But Dr. Evan Walters is known for being driven in his pursuit of monetizing nanotechnology for maximum investment potential. Militarizing that technology would definitely open up the investor pool."

He pulls the laptop over and does a quick search through the file and pulls up another document, motioning us to look with him. It's the Evenglow file again.

"See this? This is what they were supposed to be working on—what Dr. Ruiz intended the technology to be used for. A therapeutic tool to help soldiers."

"That's not what's happening," I tell him. "There is no therapy. There's no talking things out. There's no transparency. No one remembers who they really are. They're not even facing realistic, modern-day scenarios. None of them have lived through cavemen or knights with swords or laser-blasting drones. There's no end for them—just fighting and dying again and again."

"And you say Kalu had no memory of his own name?" Akoni presses. "Or of me?"

The pain in his eyes squeezes my stomach. I sit beside him, touching his arm. "I tried to get through to him—to all of them. It just got me killed when they turned on me."

"Why did it take them so long to murder you?" Rio kicks back and puts her feet—in mismatched neon flip-flops—up on the table. "I mean, why not off you on day one or something?"

"I have no idea," I reply. "It was like they suddenly decided out of nowhere I was a threat. Sarge made it sound like command—whoever they are—had been watching me."

"You said you were asking questions," Akoni points out.

Rio points a finger at the screen. "You must have triggered Red Protocol: Remember?" She takes the computer mouse from Akoni and clicks through to the *Protocols* folder.

"Participants behaving outside of structured norms, immediate corrective synaptic direction taken," she reads.

"The program targeted you as a threat and weaponized them against you," Akoni says.

The blood drains from my face and my mouth goes dry. "They know I'm in there? Evan—and my mom?" *And they tried to kill me.*

Akoni shakes his head as he resumes perusing the files. "We don't know that. It is odd—there is almost not data. No details of what happens in each scenario, or what was said. I don't think they see anything but physical responses to the scenario and whether or not protocols were triggered." He scrolls through another document. "If the squad has some of their memories—in order for them to retain their skills—it stands to reason that they might occasionally trigger a deep-seated memory tied to something. The program would take corrective action through these protocols, erasing or redirecting that line of thought."

"Great."

Akoni sets his hand on my shoulder. "I'm sure it is frightening for you, but it also makes you the one person who can act independently of those protocols. You may be the only one who can get them out—perhaps from the inside. We only need to figure out how."

"And we need to figure out how to keep me alive long enough to get them to trust me again." Because I'm the enemy now.

These people were never meant to be trapped in there, any more than I was. They have lives and families who miss them, worry about them, are probably looking for them, just like Akoni. They're my squad, and I care about every single one of them.

Despite everything I've been going through on a nightly basis for the last two months, I've almost been—the thought is ludicrous—but lately I've almost been okay with falling asleep at night. Just seeing my squad again. Listening to them all roar with laughter at something funny that Gears says, watching Shadow and Beast spar with each other, mocking each other good-naturedly as they try to take each other down. Sarge's fatherly advice colored with a good deal of sarcasm. Chef and his innate kindness. And Rookie, teaching me to throw, his arms around me.

I can get him out. I can get them all out.

I *will* get them all out.

21

THE TREES TOWER BEHIND me. This, of course, tells me nothing. I've been in several scenarios with trees. I stay very still, listening. From somewhere far off, there comes the dull roar of engines. Wheels rolling. Cars, or maybe something louder, like a tank. Small scurrying sounds come from the forest around me.

If I'm hearing motor vehicles, at least I know I'm not on Paleo planet. It also means I'm probably not facing the king's soldiers or anybody with a musket in their hands. It's daylight and I can clearly see the tall peaks of the mountains before me, and the sheer rock face where the trees end. It's possible this is where my parachute landed in a previous scenario. I'm on the edge of a large clearing, but it's warm now. The trees are full and green, and the clearing is high with grass. My uniform and med bag are green and brown camouflage, the better to blend in.

I can't stand here all day. I don't know how long it will take for the enemy—or my squad—to decide I'm fair game and open fire on me. Moving as quietly as possible, I back into the cover of the trees.

There.

Off to my left—a sound. It repeats. Not a scurry, not a sound of wind or branches rustling. This was a crack, as if a stick was breaking under the weight of something or someone. Then—a shuffle. I move behind the nearest tree that's big enough to cover me, slowly leaning my head out to get a closer look in the direction the sound came from, and then I leap back as a blur explodes from the trees. Shadow is on me before I can react. Her high kick to my chest sends me staggering backwards into another tree—a good thing because I would have hit the ground otherwise. As it is, the breath is knocked out of me in a whoosh.

I leap back just in time to avoid her next sweeping kick, meant to knock my legs out from under me. My training is now so ingrained that my hands come up instantly to block Shadow's blows, angling my body to the side to minimize access to vulnerable areas. I've sparred with her for weeks now—which feel like months in these scenarios.

Blocking and dodging so swiftly I can barely register it, I move on pure muscle memory. I even get in a couple of solid hits, but this is Shadow—I can't keep this up for long. Another kick—this time to the stomach—sends me staggering but I recover enough to use the momentum to pivot and run. I'm not good enough to beat her, but I am the fastest out of all of them. Three years of sprints and relays in high school track have equipped me to literally run for my life.

I take off, gasping raggedly as I try to fuel my body with the oxygen needed to run. I don't risk looking behind me, not when there are so many trees I can collide with, so many rocks and sticks and patches of rough ground to trip me up. She's close, judging by the sound of her footfalls behind me.

I race like a deer through the trees, leaping when I need to leap, shifting when I need to shift. Part of me wonders why she's not firing her gun but I'm not going to take the time to question it. I just need to get far enough ahead of her that I can lose her and hide somewhere.

Another movement catches my eye off to the right. Beast! His long legs are eating up the distance between us on a path that is sure to intersect my own. And now to my left I see Chef closing in. I'm being herded, and there's nowhere to go but forward—right into Sarge, Gears and Rookie.

They step out from behind the trees, armed and definitely not looking friendly.

My legs slow, stumble, stop. I bend at the waist, putting my hands on my knees and breathing deeply.

"You—" I gasp. "Have to. Wait. Listen to me." I put up a hand. "Please."

Sarge steps forward and relief floods me as he puts his hand on the barrel of Rookie's rifle and lowers it.

"Use a knife," he says coldly. "We don't want anyone hearing gunfire."

"Sarge, listen to me." My breath is still coming in short, ragged pants and my heart is thundering in my chest. "You've been in this program longer than anyone else. But you had a life before." I look at the team imploringly as they circle me. "You all had lives before you came here. Don't you want to go back to them?"

"You know they do." Sarge's mouth flattens into a thin, grim line.

"She's trying to play with our minds," Shadow says, and she pulls her own knife.

Gears looks over his shoulder as the sound of engines gets closer. "We need to get this done," he says.

Shadow takes a step toward me, but I push out a hand, begging them to stop and *listen.*

"Chef! Akoni loves you very much," I tell him. "We're working together to help you. Rookie! Six months ago, you were in high school just like me. We have a mutual friend." I look at Shadow. "Marianne. That's your real name."

None of them looks back at me with any kind of recognition.

"Finish her," Sarge orders, in a resigned voice, tinged with exhaustion. He turns to go.

Shadow moves in for the kill, knife raised. In a desperate move, I throw out the only thing I can think of.

"You're all part of the Eventide program!" I shout, backing away, preparing myself for another run. "They're keeping you prisoner in here!"

Shadow stops the knife in mid-air, freezing in place. I stare at her in confused shock for a moment before I realize the rest of them are motionless, too. Finally, Sarge turns slowly and looks at me.

"What did you say?"

Shadow lowers her knife, taking a step back. She shakes her head as if to clear it.

"Wait." Gears moves to step around her. *"Eventide?"*

"Who the hell are you?" Beast asks, rounding on me. "I remember Eventide, but I don't remember you. Not before any of this." He gestures all around him.

"You remember?" My eyes search their faces—their shocked and confused faces.

"Eventide is a trigger word," Sarge says. "For White Protocol."

White Protocol. My adrenaline-soaked mind strains to remember. *Triggers program transparency.*

"Akoni!" Chef pushes his way between Sarge and Shadow to take me by the shoulders. "My brother. You know him?"

"I do," I tell him. "He's on the island, and he's been working to find you."

"He's here!" He exclaims. "So, we will go now? The scenarios are finished?"

I stare at him, at all of them, uncertain of what to say.

"She doesn't know how to free us." Shadow's voice is soft, flat. "She would have done it already, if she knew how."

"No, I don't," I admit. "Not yet. We just got our hands on all the confidential files for the program. Akoni is going through them now. We're going to find where they're holding you and get you out. I promise."

"You have access to the data?" Sarge's eyes are sharp. I can practically see the thoughts swirling in his head now that the fog has lifted.

"You're not where we are?" Chef asks, confused.

"It's a long story, but not exactly," I tell him. "But I think we're close."

Sarge suddenly looks around at the sound of gunfire coming closer. "We need to get out of here," he says.

"How long has it been?" Shadow grips my arm, her eyes showing a touch of fear for the first time since I've known her. They all look at me, and my heart twists in my chest. I wish I had better news.

"Eight months, for most of you. More for Sarge, I think. Only a few months for Rookie."

No one says a word as the shock of my statement sinks in. The weight of every one of those days, weeks and months away from their families and lives hangs heavy in the air and is carved in every devastated line on their faces.

"All right." Sarge rubs neck. "All right. Look. We all have a million questions. Let's find somewhere safe to hunker down and get them answered."

"There's that cave," Gears suggests. "The one on the east side of the mountain. You have to push through a narrow opening to get in—we've laid low there before."

"Worth a try," Sarge says. "Let's move."

Everyone starts off through the trees after Sarge. Everyone but Rookie. He hasn't said a word. He's just standing there looking at me.

"Rookie—Mateo." I say his name softly, and in two long strides, he reaches for me, pulling me into him, lifting me off the ground. I hold him tight as we sway, until finally, he sets me down but doesn't let go.

"I'm sorry. I'm so sorry I hurt you," he says over and over into my hair, my neck.

"It's all right. We're all right," I keep saying, until I pull back to look at him.

"You know who I am—the real me," he breathes.

"I'm J.J."

"You're Sparkles," he says. "And we didn't need real names to know each other."

We stare at each other, frozen for a moment. Then he pulls me in and kisses me, hard. With a lightning flash of heat, I'm kissing him back fiercely, afraid I'm going to wake up because this is what I've wanted—needed. Him. Real and warm against me, his mouth hot and nearly frantic on mine. We break apart, both of us panting, and I give a relieved little laugh.

"I thought you were never going to do that," I whisper.

"I've been wanting to for a while," he confesses. "I did it fast because I thought you might punch me, after the way we've all treated you. The way *I've* treated you."

"It's all right now."

"I almost feel like I should introduce myself," he says.

"I know who you are," I remind him. "And you just kissed me. I think we can bypass the formal introduction."

He grins. "You said we have a mutual friend?"

"Yeah." I smile. "Rio Nakamura."

He looks up a moment, sorting through memories. "Quirky girl? Wears a lot of glitter?"

I hold up my free hand, waving my glittery silver-tipped fingers at him. "The nail polish was her idea."

"It's going to be weird, not calling you Sparkles."

"It's fine. It's kind of grown on me. Makes me feel like part of the team."

"You *are* part of the team," he reminds me, "I don't think anybody here questions that—not anymore. You really think you can get us out of here?"

I touch his face, smoothing back his hair. "I'm not going to stop trying," I promise him.

Something in his eyes softens, and then he pulls me in again, slowly enough for me to say no this time, but I don't want to. His mouth comes down on mine, his lips gentle, warm, and lingering, sending a spreading heat through every part of my body .

"Nobody's getting out of here if they mow you down while you're smooching!" Beast's voice calls out from ahead in the trees.

We pull apart and I blush furiously as Rookie laughs. "Come on," he says, taking my hand. "We've all got a lot of catching up to do."

The cave is damp and a little small but relatively well-hidden behind thick underbrush. We can still hear the sound of an army mobilizing in the distance but so far, nothing has come after us.

Sarge passes out some provisions while I debrief the team, catching them up on everything that brought me to them, and everything I've discovered since—including Boomer's cause of death, and Scribe and Wizard's probable murders. Sarge sits on my left, not saying much, like he's having a hard time digesting it all. Rookie is on my right, his shoulder leaning into mine, lending me his quiet strength. The others take it all in, their faces cycling through stunned disbelief to confusion, and then varying levels of anger.

"This was intended to be a short exercise," Sarge says. "Ten days. That was the original plan."

"Is that what they told all of you?" I ask.

"Yes," Shadow says. "They recruited me for a special study. To help soldiers."

"To help people deal with trauma," Gears amends.

"And if White Protocol was engaged, the scenario would end immediately," Beast adds. "If something went south, we'd be pulled out."

"Something went south," I tell them.

"That is an understatement," Chef scoffs. "I am an intern. I attend university."

"So do I," replies Gears. "I remember you. I saw you on orientation day. You and Wizard."

Her name hangs in the air a moment. Shadow tosses her knife into the dirt, point down.

"Someone will pay for what they did to her," she vows.

"Damn straight," Beast growls. "What went wrong with the program? And how the hell do we get out of here?"

"I'm not entirely sure yet," I tell them. "Akoni—that's Chef's brother, has been keeping files on everyone on the island. He works in maintenance and janitorial, so he has badge access to just about everywhere. The only place he doesn't is the east wing of the lab complex. Our guess is they have you in there."

"That's where they took us when we started," Shadow says.

"That's right," Gears nods.

"I understand the soldiers being used in the study," I tell them, "but why use interns?"

"It was part of the research," Chef explains. "PTSD does not only happen to soldiers. Many people experience trauma that can linger. In my case, it was the death of a friend at university. He was a suicide—I found his body." He grimaces at the recollection. "They asked for intern volunteers to see if there was a marked difference between the way soldiers and non-military personnel react to traumatic circumstances."

"And now you're all trapped, no matter what your background is," I say grimly. "I recently got my hands on two

USB drives full of program data and this is all stuff with the security level of Dr. Evan Walters—"

"Walters!" Beast exclaims. "Is he the slimy guy with the shit-eating grin?"

I choke on my laughter. "That is exactly how I see him," I reply. "But he'll have the highest level of security in the company so everything I've got on these files—and we're talking a large amount of information—would have to be the inside scoop."

"And where's that information now?" Sarge asks.

"On my laptop, but I made two copies—one to give to Akoni, and one for Rio to hide. Akoni's working tonight, but he's off tomorrow so he's scouring the data to see what else he can discover. In the meantime, Rio helps her dad by posting security logs—she may be able to find out more about the cameras and access points at the lab complex."

"I never realized I was engineering my own downfall." Gears says, shaking his head in disgust. "I worked on the design systems for the pods."

"Pods?" I look at him blankly.

"I remember them from the orientation," Beast says. "They were wondering if they had a pod big enough to fit me."

"The pods keep you in a semi-catatonic state and enable the neurological interface between the nanites and the program," Chef remarks.

"Along with the neural interface," Gears explains, "there are electrical stim probes and contact points—not just to monitor your vital functions, but to keep muscles from atrophy during the process. There are food and waste tubes attached to the subject as well."

"That sounds . . . uncomfortable," I say. "There's got to be some way to let you out."

"There is," Chef tells me. "But the scenario program has to be disengaged first, or you risk severe neural damage to the test subject."

"Once the program has been disengaged," Gears goes on, "there's a red EVAC button at the back of each pod, as well as one on the control panel that will trigger the pods all at once and shut off the neurological interface."

"They were originally programmed to open upon completion of the exercise," Chef says. "For whatever reason, they extended these scenarios."

"They're looking for us to complete the circuit," Sarge interjects. "I still hold to it that we need to make a successful run of all the scenarios to end this."

I shake my head. "Not necessarily. We need to figure out how to disable the program, and then trigger the failsafe on the pods."

"That should do it," Chef says, and Gears nods affirmatively.

"Once we get enough information from the files, we should be able to at least alert someone, the police or the media. Then we can get you out of here," I promise.

"Are our families are looking for us?" Gears asks. "Other than Chef's brother, I mean?"

"The company seems to have come up with an excuse for your disappearances," I answer. "They told Akoni that Chef left the program and took a boat to the mainland. It's possible they said the same to all the other families and they're out searching the world for missing persons. I overheard Evan talking about Interpol, so maybe they're investigating."

"My father works for the company," Rookie says, spearing a hand through his hair. "He's got to be going crazy looking for me."

"It's possible he knows you're in here," I say grimly. "And Codonexus is using you as leverage to keep him working on the program."

"Bastards." Beast spits the epithet.

"They had a cover story for you, too," I tell Rookie. "Something about you graduating early and leaving the island to start college. And no one has seen your father since you disappeared, and he's not showing his face, either."

His eyes grow wide. "What did they do to him? He's not in here with us."

"I guess that's another question for my list," I answer. "But I found info on all of you. I'll find him, too." I squeeze Rookie's hand, hating the look of dread on his face.

"About my brother," Chef leans over to hand me a canteen so I can wash down my food. "You tell Akoni I will not trade my life for his. Tell him I said he must look after you and the other girl, too." He leans across Rookie to set a gentle hand on my shoulder. "You have been a good friend to all of us. You must be careful."

"He's right," Shadow says. "These people cannot be trusted. If they've killed three of us already, that makes them very dangerous."

"I don't like this," Gears shakes his head. "Too much can go wrong. We can't have a bunch of kids in danger. You should find a safe way to get a message to someone in authority."

"I'm with Gears," Beast says. "You and your friends step back and let the adults deal with all of this."

"We need to be sure you can trust whoever you give this information to," Sarge cautions.

Shadow makes a sound of disgust. "Dr. Evan Walters is a powerful man, a rich man. I did my research on him before I took this job—I very nearly backed out and now I wish I had listened to my gut. You don't know who he's bribed or who he's in business with."

"Watch your six," Sarge warns.

"Yeah," say Beast. "We can all stay in here a while longer if it means you and your friends stay safe."

The group echoes him in their agreement, but like hell I'm leaving them in here one minute longer than I have to.

"I'll be careful," I assure them. "I might be able to get a message out to your families—if they'll believe a teenage girl who claims to see you in her dreams."

Shadow shakes her head. "Too dangerous. If you're intercepted, we're all in jeopardy."

Sarge chews his lip. "Yeah, hold off on that. Eight months is a long time to be gone. If something else should go sideways here, I don't want to get anybody's hopes up only to have it all ripped away from them again."

The looks on their faces range from sad to furious, but they all nod their agreement.

"I promise all of you, this is going to be over soon." My voice cracks with emotion. "I'm going to—"

A thundering boom splits the air, and dirt and rock rain down all around us. I'm thrown violently to the side as another boom follows the first.

"They're shelling us!" Sarge yells. "Take cover! Take—"

But there is nowhere to take cover, nowhere to hide as the mountain crumbles around us, crushing us beneath it.

22

All that I've learned in these last few days loops in my mind as I drop my backpack in my room and head to the shower. I'm sweaty and sandy because class was held on the beach today. We were talking about changing acidity levels in the ocean and the effect on ecosystems.

My mother is home early for some reason, and I can hear her starting dinner as I step from the bathroom into my bedroom. I brush my wet hair out and reach for my locket to put it back around my neck.

Only it's not there.

I could have sworn I laid it down on my dresser before I left. That's where I always put it. It's solid silver so I don't take it near the water and the salt spray.

Padding back into the bathroom I check the counter there, wondering if I took it off while I was changing my clothes earlier. Not there either.

I check the floor of my bedroom, under the bed, then I tip out the contents of my beach bag. Did I forget and leave it on? We were in the water for a time—it could have been ripped off while I was pulling my wet hair out of my eyes.

In a panic, I text Rio. Did she remember me wearing my locket? Did she remember seeing it around my neck?

She isn't sure.

I throw on a sundress, slide into my sandals, and rush for the front door.

"Wait J.J.!" My mother calls out. "Where are you going? It's almost dinner."

"I have to go back to the beach," I tell her. My hand goes reflexively to my neck to feel the emptiness there. "I lost my locket—I think while I was there today. I'm going to retrace my steps. Maybe I dropped it on the beach or on the way home while we walked."

She stares at me for a moment and then she gives a funny little laugh.

"Oh," she says, laughing again. "Your locket! I found it. I was going to tell you when you got out of the shower."

She gives me a bright smile as she stirs something bubbling in a saucepan. "You must have forgotten that you took it off out here in the living room. I put it in my bedroom for safekeeping." She gestures for me to come over. "Stir this for me and I'll go and get it."

I turn instantly and run for her bedroom door as she calls out again.

"Wait!"

"Where?" I say over my shoulder.

She laughs again—a forced laugh. Why is she nervous about this? And why would she bring it in here—why not just leave it in my room? And I know I took it off there.

She pushes past me, and then opens her dresser drawer. The locket is there, sitting open on top of a bunch of silky lingerie I wish I could scrub from my mind.

"Why were you looking inside it?" I asked.

"I wondered what sort of picture you had in there. You almost never take it off, and I didn't know how to ask you."

I give her a wary look. "You just ask. You don't go pawing through my things."

Snatching the locket out of the drawer, I loop it around my neck and try to close it up, but it won't shut tightly. It's bent.

"It's broken." I say to her accusingly. "What did you do?"

"I found it on the floor," she says. "I accidentally vacuumed over it. I put it in my drawer because—well, I was hoping to get it repaired before you noticed it was gone."

"You didn't think I would notice that the only piece of jewelry I wear was gone?"

"I feel just terrible about this J.J.," she says with a frown. "I'd be happy to replace the locket. Get you something nicer."

I look at her incredulously. "Dad gave me this. I don't want another locket."

She holds out her hand. "Then at least let me get this one repaired. I looked around to find the picture you had in it, but I couldn't find anything."

"There was no picture," I say flatly. "Don't bother repairing it—it's good enough."

The locket does close, it just doesn't snap tight. I stroke my fingers across the Pegasus wings etched on the front.

She makes a face. "I really am sorry. I wish you'd let me take care of it."

"It's fine. I have college essays to work on." I turn and walk back to my bedroom.

"But I've got dinner—"

The door slams on her before she can finish her sentence. I'm turning eighteen tomorrow, and my dad's not here. He won't be making cheesy jokes when I blow out my candles. He won't be singing bad pop songs and embarrassing me in front of my friends. And we won't be adding a memory to my locket.

It was a special thing just between the two of us, starting on my twelfth birthday—the first birthday after my mother left. He took me to Disneyworld. We spent all day at the park, indulging every one of my childish impulses. I had ice cream for breakfast. We rode every ride I wanted to ride, and he bought me four sets of mouse ears and six tee shirts. At the end of the day, I sat on the grass watching fireworks with my father's arms warm around me .

He gave me the locket right there and asked me if I wanted to put a picture in it. I told him I wanted to put the memory of the whole day in it instead because it had been perfect. From that day on, anytime we shared a perfect day together, we had a ceremonial opening of the locket to capture it, and then I'd snap it tight again, swearing to hold the memory in there forever. The perfect picnic at Chain-o-Lakes Park, the trip we took to London where we had tea on a boat cruise on the Thames. The night we sat up watching a meteor shower from our campsite in the mountains. The trip we took to Utah and the beautiful view from atop a canyon in Moab. All memories shut tight in my locket. All pieces of a life I once had.

The tears run unchecked down my face as I lay on my bed stroking the locket. I want to be home. This place is not home, and it never will be. It's just as well that the locket doesn't shut now. I don't have beautiful days to put inside it anymore. My hand remains around the locket as I cry myself to sleep.

23

THE PYRAMID LOOMS IN the distance, the walls of the maze stand before us, and the triple moons shine down.

"It's that time again, folks," Gears says dryly.

"Lovely." Chef sighs.

Beast just lets out a string of curse words that's practically a work of art for its complexity.

Sarge rolls his shoulders. "You know the drill—get into that pyramid—push through to the inner chamber, find the coded intel and call it a day."

"Call it a nightmare," grumbles Shadow. "No offense."

I wave her off. My nightmares are their reality and none of us want to be here.

"I'd be happy just to make it to the damn pyramid," Gears says with a good deal of disgust.

"No splitting up this time," Sarge shouts. "Let's try taking it together. Sparkles—stay sharp and take the wall. Shadow, you're on point with Chef."

I give him a shaky nod, wrapping my fingers around my rifle.

"Gears, Beast, you take right and left drones," Sarge rattles off. "Rookie and I have your six. Let's move!"

The words are barely out of his mouth before the drones are upon us, and I swear to God, they appear to be targeting me. Blasts and drone parts rain down all around as I run with that cumbersome medical bag slung across my chest, trying to zigzag as best I can in the middle of a group of people who are firing guns and trying to zigzag as well.

Chef's voice rings out through the cacophony of shots and exploding pieces of wall.

"Slime!" He shouts.

That fast, we all lose our footing, going down awkwardly, some of us landing on each other. Sarge, Beast and Rookie see it coming and hold at the edge, giving us cover fire as we roll to get out of it. Once we're on the other side and begin firing, they make a dive for it, rolling through the slime to join us. We wipe off as best we can, but it's slippery going.

Chef moves down the next corridor and we follow as quickly as possible. A laser blast singes the edge of my med bag, but doesn't cut through the material. We're almost at the end of the corridor when Gears dodges drone fire and stumbles into a wall that shoots flame. My eyes take in with sickening fury the body burned beyond recognition as it falls.

A sudden stinging impact to my cheek explodes into pain that tears through me as a shot hits the wall in front of me, sending chunks of marble right into my face. I recoil as the blood rushes down from my temple to my neck. The pain in my right eye is searing, and a strong hand—I'm not sure whose—wraps around my upper arm and supports me.

"Is it bad?" Shadow's voice says in my ear.

I want to scream, *Yes! Yes, it's bad! It's agony!* But I think about Gears, and I know I have to keep going.

"I can't see very well," I grit out. "It got my eye."

"I'll be your eyes." She pulls me harder as we pick up the pace.

Another shout as someone else is hit. I struggle to make my good eye focus through the haze of splintered rock and ricocheting bullets.

Beast is before us trailing blood, and parts of his arm are literally sliced into pieces.

"Razor wire!" Shadow calls back.

Sarge and Chef work quickly, using the barrels of their guns to wrap around the nearly invisible, needle-thin strips of wire. They break apart when enough force is exerted by something it can't cut through, but we're losing valuable time. With us all in one place the drones don't have to split up to find us.

Before all the wire is down, we lose Chef. I hear his scream and turn instinctively to it, but Rookie is there, stepping in front of me as he fires on a drone, taking it out.

"Don't," he says, herding me forward. "Just don't look."

But it's too late. I saw the headless corpse. How many times can you witness murder? How many times can you witness a truly horrible death—and still retain your sanity?

I'm shaking, but don't have time to answer existential questions. The Fibonacci tiles are next, and Shadow gets me through them in short order. Rookie is the last to go, and a falling drone nearly becomes his downfall as the entire section erupts, blowing him into the wall. He staggers to his feet, limping and bleeding.

There are five of us now, and the drones seem to be slowing finally, thankfully—until the next section reduces us to four. We were nearly reduced to three, as I am close behind Beast when the darts hit him. Two of them ricochet harmlessly off my med bag, the metallic mesh too tight for them to penetrate. I guess it was good for something after all. But it's no help to Beast, who was dead before he hit the ground.

"Keep moving!" Shadow screams as she takes point. Sarge is now guiding me, pulling me with one hand and firing his rifle with the other.

"Shit!" Shadow shouts. "Spinner!"

"We're finished," Sarge says in a hard voice.

"No, we're not," Rookie snarls. "She can run faster than anyone here. She can do this."

I step forward as the remaining three surround me, firing on the last of the advancing drones. Before me is a perfect circular platform set in the floor, spinning, and spinning. It is surrounded by the high walls of the maze, also a circle in this section, and each wall—other than the exit passage on the opposite side—is covered bottom to top in deadly, pointed, spikes. Stepping onto this would mean instant death as it flings you into the walls.

I turn back to look at Rookie.

"I can't," I tell him. "I can't do this. No one can."

"You can run across it. Beast almost did it once," he tells me.

"Head left of center and stay on your toes," Sarge says firing a rapid sequence of shots an approaching drone. "Go! Fast!"

"But what about the rest of—"

"Go!" He shouts again.

"Get through," Shadow calls out as she lets loose with a round of gunfire.

"You can do this!" Rookie screams, dodging a drone blast.

I take a deep breath, rocking back on my heels and trying not to focus on the outer edges of this spinning circle of death. With one more breath I'm off and sprinting for it.

My best shot is to leap high and hard. The fewer times I touch the platform, the less chance of me being thrown. I dig my foot in on the last step, launching myself into the air, extending my legs as far as I can.

I land hard and start to twist as I push off, but I manage to do it. I'm airborne again in an instant. I lean and adjust my legs in the air, throwing myself forward and I clear the edge of the spinning platform, landing in a heap on the left side of the passage opening. I'm thrown partly into the spikes, and they tear into my clothing, grazing the flesh of my side and leg, but I'm not seriously wounded. I push myself shakily to my feet and turn back to the others.

Two. There are only two of them now. A cold fist grips my chest when I only see Sarge and Shadow. Rookie! Where is he?

"Keep going!" Sarge shouts.

Sobbing, I turn and run, partially blind and bleeding all over as I hurtle down the passageway, dashing the tears from my good eye. *This is crazy. This is suicide. I don't even know what I'm looking for. I don't even know what to watch out for. I don't even—*

I put my hand out as I stumble, grabbing at the wall for support. White light sears the vision of my good eye as thousands of volts of electricity pass through my body, stopping my heart in an instant.

24

 Grady has been canceled again for today. My mother sent me a text at lunchtime to say the therapist was "under the weather." Of course, that could just be code for *she got beaten up and/or murdered by a Venezuelan hit squad.*

In any case, I'm relieved. Now that I know what's going on I don't want to discuss anything with her. I'm not going crazy. I'm not experiencing subconscious psychotic behavior. I'm not in danger of losing my mind in real life. And more than ever, I'm determined to get to the bottom of all of this. That means I have to be careful. I can't be sure who's reporting what back to Evan, but the last thing I need is for him or my mother to figure out that I'm infiltrating their experiment on a nightly basis.

There's another upside to my canceled session with Dr. Grady—it means that Rio and I can meet with Akoni since he's on an early shift and finishes at three. The maintenance shed isn't an option at this time of day, but Rio and I found an awesome cave near the beach. I text mom and tell her we went swimming, then I pick up some shells and stones as we wait on the beach for Akoni. Rio's empty water bottle is my target, sitting on a nearby rock ledge.

Line it up, don't second-guess, take the shot, I repeat again and again, hearing Rookie's voice in my head.

Twenty-five tries and twenty-one of them I manage to knock the bottle off. Not bad, if I do say so myself. I only wish Rookie could see it.

"You're really good," Rio observes as I take my last few shots.

"I learned from the best," I tell her, smiling as I remember Rookie's hand on my shoulder, his chin on my neck as he showed me how to flick my wrist. And then I remember his lips on mine and the way he held me.

"Earth to J.J.," Rio calls out in a sing-song voice. "You're drifting off on the memory of his kiss or something."

My cheeks redden. "It's that obvious?"

"I totally would be, too."

"But it wasn't real. Who knows if he'll even remember it when he ever wakes up?" *If he ever wakes up*, a treacherous voice whispers in my mind.

Rio makes a heart with both hands and bounces it on her chest. "The captain of the archery team took a shot and won your heart," she says dramatically. "It's as real as you want it to be."

"That reminds me, is there anywhere in the village where I can buy a bow?"

"The school had to get them from somewhere," she shrugs. "Maybe you could re-start the archery team."

"I'm nowhere near ready for that."

"Just as well," says Rio. "When the company falls apart, I guess we'll all be leaving the island."

I hadn't really thought about it that way. If what we know goes public, it's quite likely the company won't survive It. All of these people will have to find new jobs—including Rio's parents, Rookie's father, and my mother.

"I'm starting to have second thoughts. Not about letting them out of there," I hastily assure Rio. "I mean, they've got to get out of there. But destroying a company? That's going to hurt more than just Evan."

"You mean your mom?" she says. "Are you worried she's going to end up back in America, living in a trailer? Working at a McDonald's or something?"

I shake my head. "My mom has a Ph.D. in neurobiology and twenty years of research experience. I imagine she'll be all right after the fall out."

As long as she's not in prison.

"So, you're worried about people like Dr. Grady and my parents," Rio says.

"Aren't you?"

"I guess. Seriously, we can't think too much about it," she says. "It's not like we have a choice or something. We have to do what's right—for Akoni, and for everyone in there."

As if she summoned him, Akoni rounds the bend on the beach and makes his way over.

"Are we ready?" he asks. "Where is this cave?"

Rio leads the way, speaking to him over her shoulder.

"It's nice and dry. I put a blanket down. If anybody finds us, they'll probably think we're in here looking at porn or something."

"You be sure and tell them that," I suggest.

Once inside the cave, Akoni pulls out his laptop as Rio flops down cross-legged next to the two of us. "What've you found?" she asks Akoni.

"Quite a bit, actually." His eyes shift to me. "Fair warning: I found a lot of information relating to your father, J.J."

"My father?" *Oh God. Oh please.* "Is this something about his death?" I make myself say.

"No, no," Akoni waves his hand. "Here is what I have been able to reconstruct." He boots up the laptop and points at the first document on the screen.

"It appears that J.J.'s father was still monitoring the company just before his death through public records and through contacts within the company itself. I believe these were friends and former colleagues. All of the people identified in the investigation no longer work for the company. That led in part to the decision by Dr. Walters to consolidate the company's global offices and move here."

"Where he could better control all the communication in and out of the company." Rio adds.

Akoni nods. "It appears the intense communication surveillance went into effect when a new computer virus was detected in the network. A virus specifically targeted to the Eventide program."

"What?" I'm having a hard time believing what I'm hearing. "You—they—think my father hacked into their system to plant a virus?"

Akoni traces the lines of text on the screen, so that I can see he's only reading off their conclusions.

"The virus created a series of protected sub-folders within the program that keep Eventide from running successfully. The protected folders have the majority of the information gleaned by the nanites within the program. They also prevent it from building upon what has already been developed."

I'm going to be suddenly, violently ill.

"My dad trapped them in there?"

"No."

Akoni's firm reply allows me to breathe again.

"From what I read in the files he worked within a gamification framework to create real-life therapeutic scenarios delivered through the nanite programming. But there was a definite global military market for this program from a training perspective," Akoni explains. "In some of the correspondence I've found, it appears Dr. Walters may have been in contact with certain foreign government factions, particularly after the US military pulled out after they discovered the program didn't work."

I shudder at the memory of Armando and his shadows with Dr. Grady, their dark clothes, and darker expressions. Their guns.

"That's scary," I say. "Really scary."

"But profitable," Akoni replies. "These factions have deep pockets—especially for technology that produces soldiers who are battle-trained with little to no physical risk."

"They would be battle-hardened the second they leave the pod," Rio says. "It's like learning to fly on a simulator or something."

"And they'd be traumatized and brainwashed to stick to the mission objectives," I add with dawning horror. I lean forward, wrapping my arms around my knees as the pieces fall together.

"There was an attempt made by Dr. Walters and an external specialist to disable the virus and modify the code," Akoni says. "It appears to have made things worse, creating a series of cascading errors in the code and locking the program into the alternatively developed but not previously utilized military scenarios."

"Sarge thinks they need to solve all the scenarios in order, and the program unlocks," I tell them. "They haven't had much luck with that."

Rio snorts. "Obviously."

"Every scenario has an objective, from hunting for cave art, to stealing battle plans from the king's messenger, to taking down a supply hub. Every scenario, we have our orders," I explain.

"But not every scenario is built to root out the invasive program," Akoni says, searching through folders again, his finger tapping on the laptop mouse pad. "Most scenarios were merely training exercises, more of the indoctrination. There is only one program scenario directly linked to the invasive virus. If that scenario ends successfully, all the protected folders should be unlocked, and White Protocol can be fully enacted. The program will end."

"Wait—didn't J.J. engage White Protocol? Why aren't they out of their pods and walking around or something?" Rio asks.

"The virus originally was intended to simply block the transmission of program data. The militarized modifications to the interface that were bungled by Dr. Walters in his battle against the virus now prevents the program termination without the successful completion of the key scenario," Akoni says. "Without that, the program will continue. And the program—the business—is not worth any money unless they can successfully release the participants and re-create for a new group of test subjects." "In other words, Armando and his henchmen won't buy in if their soldiers will be trapped inside the program," I say.

"So that means one of those scenarios is the big one." Rio spreads her hands out in front of her like she's envisioning a movie screen. "The mega scenario. The supreme ultra-mega scenario."

"Yes." Akoni nods. "The only one they have not been able to complete. That scenario has the same name as the virus your father designed, J.J."

I know what he's going to say, and my voice joins his as we say it together.

"The Citadel."

25

"The Citadel." Gears repeats, shaking his head. "You've got to be shitting me."

We're all sitting around a fire here on Paleo planet. No sign of giant boars or knuckle draggers with unibrows, thank God. I've been debriefing my squad on what we learned about the program—all except for my dad's part in their entrapment. He may not have intended that to happen—it's Evan's fault, really—but I'm not sure they'll see it that way. We really need to work together, and I'd rather not go back to being a target.

"Think about it," I say. "It's the only scenario we haven't beaten."

"It is true," Chef says. "Everywhere else, we have fulfilled the mission a few times at the very least."

"Lots of times on some of them," Beast injects. "Gimme that." He gestures toward the food on the fire.

Tonight's dinner consists of fish caught from the nearby stream bare-handed by Beast, of course. It has next to no flavor, and you have to bash it with a rock to get through the skin, but it'll do. With a couple of hollowed-out gourds for bowls that we can boil water in, and a few handfuls of small, tart berries, we've got ourselves a Paleolithic feast.

Sarge scratches his head. "Even if we get through the maze, we still have to fight through whatever we find on the inside of the pyramid."

"And we can't get through that maze," Rookie reminds us glumly. "No matter how hard we try."

"Maybe that's because we need more than us to solve it," Sarge gestures at me.

I look at him with surprise. "I don't know what's coming any more than you do."

"Yeah, but you're an unknown variable," he tells me. "If we can get you into that pyramid, you might just be the unexpected thing that gets us out of here."

"I've done at least a dozen runs at that maze with you—maybe more before I started remembering," I say, offering

Beast the rest of my tough, tasteless fish. "The thing is just impossible."

"Going on the assumption that she is our wild card," Gears muses. "What does she have that we don't have?"

"She can leave the scenarios and live in the real world?" Beast offers.

"And she's always known who—" Rookie's head suddenly whips to the side as Chef pitches forward, gripping his head in violently shaking hands. His lips peel back from his teeth and a howl of pure, violent rage rips from his throat.

"Chef!" We all shout his name together. Shadow puts herself between Chef and me while Gears gets an arm around him, rubbing his back. Beast yanks his gun away from where Chef laid it down.

"Give him a minute," Sarge says. We all watch as Chef breathes and breathes and shakes.

"This is two scenarios in a row," Shadow says grimly.

"Chef?" Sarge keeps his voice calm. "Talk to me, buddy."

Chef sucks in a long, shuddering breath and waves us off. "I am all right. I am all right now."

Gears lets out a breath of his own and we all join him.

"That didn't stop even after White Protocol?" I ask.

Chef shakes his head. "The disorientation is getting worse. This is something we occasionally saw in early trials for the Eventide program. Dr. Ruiz counter-acted the neuro reaction with a combination of drugs, and we thought it had been successful."

"Maybe it was temporary solution," Shadow says. "No one was meant to be in here this long."

"Did your research on the other side mention the shakes?" Beast asks me.

"Nothing beyond mentioning Scribe and Wizard being neurologically compromised," I reply. "We're still sifting through files."

"We need to know how to block it," Gears says, tossing a stick into the fire. "And how to shield ourselves from it if we're ever getting through the Citadel."

Shield ourselves. *Shield ourselves.*

"My med bag," I say suddenly, thinking of those poisoned darts bouncing off it. "It's something none of you have." I point down at my primitive gourd of a med bag. "Every single scenario, I have a medical bag, or whatever passes for it within the time period."

"That's right," Sarge says, realization dawning on his face. "You don't go anywhere without it."

"Maybe my nanites tapped into my desire to go into the medical field as a profession," I say.

Rookie nods. "We all have nicknames and functions that all play to our strengths. Sarge is a leader, Gears is an engineer, Chef is a master chemist, Shadow knows all about espionage, and Beast is . . . well, he's Beast."

"And you're a crack shot," I remind him. "Captain of the archery team."

"But the newbie until you came along—and not intended to be part of the original crew, so he's Rookie," Sarge says.

"I don't always have a bow or a rifle," Rookie says. "Sometimes I have to find materials and make my weapon."

"I don't always have things to work with either," says Gears. "And it probably took us half a dozen scenarios to figure out Chef can't grill to save his life."

Chef answers that with a rude gesture.

"But Sparkles always has a medical bag." Sarge is rubbing his chin thoughtfully. "You have it in the Citadel, right?"

"I do, but it's a pain in the butt," I say begrudgingly. "It gets in the way and snags on things. It weighs me down. When we get into the slime, I have to work hard to roll over it. But it does repel the poisonous darts."

"What? Now you tell us?" Chef exclaims.

"I just now remembered it. Anytime I get near the darts, they bounce right off of the bag. It's that metallic mesh—it's a natural shield."

"Do we know what's in the bag?" Gears asks. "Devices? Equipment?"

"Chemicals?" Chef asks.

"Knives? Torches?" Shadow chimes in.

"Torches?" Beast gives her a comical look. "Most medics aren't looking to flambé somebody in the field."

"I thought for lighting Bunsen burners," she says, rolling her eyes.

"That's research, not field medicine," I tell her.

"I can give you a rough idea of a field medic's bag—at least I think I can," Beast says. "Sarge might be able to fill in some gaps."

At our questioning looks, Beast says, "What? I'm the guy they always pick to hold the injured guy down while somebody works on him."

I guess that makes sense.

"Okay," I say. "I can probably figure out some of the stuff. I used to work as a volunteer at the hospital and one of the things we did was pack and refill first aid kits for all the local government offices. We also helped restock the ambulances. There are probably some similar items. Gauze, bandages, alcohol, peroxide." I remember when I used my kit on Beast and Sarge before. "Iodine, aspirin powder, sutures—and there were scissors and a scalpel."

"I wish I had paper to write this down," says Chef.

"Wouldn't matter. You wouldn't be able to take it into the next scenario," Sarge reminds him. "Might as well write it in the dirt."

"That's not a bad idea," Gears says, grabbing a stick.

"I know in the med kits I've seen there were tourniquets, and heavy painkillers like Morphine and Vicodin," Beast offers.

"Splints," Shadow adds.

"There's probably more," I say. "Maybe even some futuristic stuff since it's the Citadel." Why did I never think to look in the bag? Probably because I was too busy fighting for my life.

"I see a few things here that can be of use to us already, if they are in that bag," Chef qualifies.

"You give me a scalpel and I'll open one of those drones up and rewire it to call me Daddy," Gears promises.

"Okay, so let's finish the list," Sarge says, rubbing his hands together.

"We know what we likely have," I say. "We've seen most of the booby traps this thing has to throw at us. What can we use and where? And what do we have that might be helpful against something we haven't seen yet?"

Gears, Chef and Shadow start talking all at once, and Beast is reaching over them to point at things on the list and offer his suggestions. Rookie and I manage to throw in a few ideas until eventually, we've got a rough strategy mapped out.

As they run through the details once more, I excuse myself to go and refill our water gourds. Rookie grabs his bow so that he can stand guard.

"It feels good to have a plan." He watches me as I kneel at the edge of the stream. "I just wish I could offer more." He holds up his bow. "This is pretty much the only thing I can give insight on."

"You might be able to make a slingshot out of a tourniquet." I let out a laugh. "But I guess you're not going to take the time to make a slingshot when you're holding a rifle."

"Now you're thinking like a soldier," he says. "Guess we've both learned to look for the most convenient weapon."

"And to run like hell."

"And to run like hell." He leans back against a tree. "So—what is your real name, anyway?"

"I told you—everybody just calls me J.J."

"J.J.," he repeats.

It feels weird to hear my name on his lips.

He cocks his head to one side. "Does it bother you if I call you by your real name?"

"No," I answer quickly. "It just sounds weird. Do you want me to call you Mateo?"

He thinks it over for a moment. "Not in here. Why don't we save the real names for the real world?"

"Deal."

"What does J.J. stand for, anyway?" He moves closer.

I shake my head. "It's stupid."

"Oh, come on it can't be *that* bad. Jedidiah Jupiter?"

"No!" I laugh.

"Julia Jif? Were you named after peanut butter?"

I give him a look.

"Jelly Bean?"

"That would be J.B., not J.J." I roll my eyes, giving in. "I'm actually named for my grandmothers."

"Josephine?" he asks. "Old-fashioned, but not terribly embarrassing."

"Jennifer." I tell him. "They were both named Jennifer."

"Your name is *Jennifer Jennifer?*"

"I know—it's goofy." I shake my head ruefully. "It was my dad's idea. "I think he did it so I could always be part of one of his best Dad jokes."

"And that is?" Rookie looks at me expectantly.

"Jenny Jenny," I sing. *"Who can I turn tooo."*

He throws back his head and sings, *"Eight-six-seven-five-three-oh-ni-i-iine!"*

"Stop!" I laugh. "I heard the chorus every other week for the entirety of my life. At least until my father—until he died."

"I'm sorry," he says squeezing my hand. "I know what it's like to lose a parent. It never goes back to normal, but it gets easier after a while."

"That's how I ended up on the island," I tell him, swallowing hard. "I was sent to live with my mother, and then all of this started."

He twines his fingers with mine. "Would you hate me if I said I'm glad you're here? I don't mean here, exactly, but—with us. With me."

"I get it," I say, loving the feel of his hand in mine. He leans his bow against a tree, and I almost forget to breathe as his hands move to settle on my waist.

The warmth of his mouth on mine sends my fingers sliding into his hair, and his tongue traces the seam of my lips, parting them as the kiss deepens. He tastes like berries. This may not be reality, but he feels solid and real as his body settles on mine, pushing my back into the tree. The bow slides to the ground and I'm sinking into the feel of him against me. His mouth meanders along my jaw and down the column of my throat, making my breath hitch and my fingers dig into his shoulders.

Until Sarge calls our names from back at the campsite, breaking the spell.

"We should be getting back," I say breathlessly.

He gives my neck one last, lingering nuzzle, murmuring the word *later* against my skin.

Please, let there be a later someplace real.

26

THE EVENING IS WARM, the moonlight is shining on the water, and the beach is beautiful. The restaurant is lit with tiki torches, and the smell of grilling meat, exotic fruit, and simmering spices wafts gently on the breeze. As far as location goes, I have to admit the ocean view patio at the village restaurant is really nice. But it's still not enough to fill the aching empty place in the middle of my chest.

My first birthday without my father.

Rio told me that the first year is the hardest. Every single occasion is marked by the absence of the person you used to celebrate it with. I know this will get easier over time, but right now, it's hard. It's even harder because this is a milestone birthday, and my dad was big on celebrating milestones—any kind of milestone. My mother wants to have a nice dinner, give me a token piece of jewelry, and then pat me on the head and send me off to bed like she did when I was ten years old.

Despite that fact, I was actually looking forward to this dinner just because it's the nicest place on the island and I knew having Rio along would make it fun. But there is no Rio. Apparently, my mother—at the last minute—asked her to stay home tonight so we could dine "just the three of us."

"I know you're unhappy we asked Rio to bow out," my mother says as if reading my mind. "And to make it up to you, Evan and I have chartered a glass bottom boat tour for the two of you tomorrow. It's part of our birthday present to you." She gives me a smile that's supposed to placate me. It doesn't.

"What's going on?" The two of them share a look with each other and a sense of foreboding creeps up my spine.

"We asked Rio to stay home tonight," Evan finally says, "because we have something we need to talk to you about. Adult to adult," he adds with a wink that curdles something in my stomach.

"You can't talk to me at home?" I ask. "You've got to unload on me on my birthday?" *Unbelievable.*

"We're not angry at you sweetheart," my mother says, and the word *sweetheart* sounds like something foreign crossing her lips. She's never called me that. Not that I can ever remember, anyway.

"We actually want to discuss the other half of our birthday present with you," she goes on. "And it's a bit of a sensitive subject."

"So you want to do it in a restaurant?" I look at her like she's unhinged because she is.

"We know you can be a little—" Evan searches for the word. "*Prickly*—where talk of your father is concerned. We thought if we wined and dined you a little—"

"And had this conversation somewhere that you can't just leave and hide behind your bedroom door," my mother adds.

"We thought it might give you more of a chance to listen openly to what we'd like to discuss." Evan smiles, like this is just a friendly dinner conversation and not an ambush.

The server steps over to take our order and my mind is swirling so badly I don't even know what to say to him. I finally point to something on the menu—it doesn't matter what. I don't think I'm going to be able to choke it down.

I'm doing my best not to let my fingers fidget, or to wipe my sweaty palms against the tablecloth. Taking a sip of water, I breathe slowly through my nose, trying to calm my nerves.

What in the world could they have to talk to me about? Is it related to what I now know? Did they find out I'm spying on Evan? I'm doing my best to keep my face blank, but I don't think it's working as my mother and Evan share another long, charged look.

The server steps away, and Evan leans forward.

"I understand you've been working on college essays this week," he tells me.

"Yes. What has that got to do with my father?" My voice is cold and my mother gives me a look of reproach.

"He's just trying to make conversation," she says quietly.

"Can we cut the small talk?" I snap. "You've already ruined my birthday dinner so let's just get it over with."

My mother lets out a sigh and sinks back in her chair, nodding at Evan to continue.

"A woman who knows her own mind and appreciates candor," he says, giving one of his skin-crawling smiles. "All right, then. I was asking about your college essays because I am going to pull some strings and get you into the university of your choice. Your mother says you've narrowed it down to your final three, and whichever one you choose—no matter the price—I've got your admittance, tuition, room and board, and all of your related costs covered."

"I can get admitted on my own," I say, offended.

Evan takes a sip of his wine. "Confidence. I like it. But it's not realistic. You're a smart girl, J.J., you've got good grades—despite your recent rough patch—and your internship here is going to look impressive to any university. But they've got thousands of applicants, quotas to fill, and people on the inside pulling strings. You might have a good chance but that's not a sure thing. I'm a sure thing."

My eyes narrow. "Because you know the people who pull the strings?"

"Exactly." He offers me a silent toast with his wineglass. "And wouldn't it be nice to take all the money your father left you and set it aside for your first home someday? Maybe a wedding fund? Or possibly take a gap year after college and travel the world? If your father's money runs out in the process it'll only take a phone call from me to get you where you want to go."

The waiter arrives with our food, and mine sits untouched as Evan goes on and on, sawing into his sea bass and describing this dream of a life he wants to give me. I'm not buying it.

"What's the catch?" I ask. "You're not giving me all of this out of the goodness of your heart."

"J.J.!" my mother admonishes. "This isn't all coming from Evan, you know. I'm still your mother and I care about you. Evan and I have decided together," she reaches out and takes his hand, "that we've got a lot to make up to you. This is where we want to start."

I'm not even going to try to play nice after that fake-ass proclamation.

"So, you walk out of my life and now you want to buy your way back in?"

My mother makes a gasping sound and Evan squeezes her hand. The smile fades from his face and his lips compress into a flat line before he addresses me.

"We understand that you're in a difficult place, J.J. That's why we set you up with Dr. Grady. That's why we want to do something nice for you and your friend. We're not going to stop trying to make things easier for you because we understand just how much you have overcome."

Right. Sure he does.

Evan takes another long drink of his wine, then a bite of his food. He chews thoughtfully, swallows, and continues.

"It's perfectly reasonable that you blame your mother and me for some of that. But you're an adult now. Part of being an adult is weighing your options and making good choices. We're offering you a good, debt-free beginning to your future on a silver platter. Don't let your anger or your hurt take over. Don't walk away from this."

"Think about it, J.J.," my mother urges.

They're right. It's a great offer. And I do believe my mother wants to help me—even if it's just to ease her guilty conscience. Logic says take the money and run.

I can tell Evan wants to say more, but my mother is shooting him a warning look. A silent signal to be cautious.

And the more I look at Evan, the more I feel like something still isn't right.

"You said we needed to talk about my father," I remind them, "but you've hardly mentioned him. So what is it you really want to say? You're talking to me about weighing my options, but I get the feeling there's more going on here."

Evan looks over at my mother again before he looks at me. "She's clever," he says to her, shaking a finger in my direction. "I told you we need to be straight with her. She's a smart girl and she doesn't like to feel that her time is being wasted. I can appreciate that."

He cuts into his food again, gesturing with his fork before he puts it in his mouth. "So let's tell her. All of it."

My mother reaches across the table to take my hand, but I move it away. I don't miss the flash of hurt in her eyes.

"When your father died, he was working on some very special research," she begins. "We have reason to believe this was research that originally began with Codonexus. He was doing this on his own time—not at his new company, so we can't subpoena them for the information. We can't subpoena him either, now that he's gone."

"Subpoena?" I can't hide my shock or the trickle of fear snaking down my spine. "Like, have him arrested?"

"When your father worked for Codonexus, any research he did legally belonged to the company," Evan points out. "We had a pretty good idea that he might have made off with some important files, but we had no real way to prove it. Since the jobs he took after he left Codonexus weren't in direct competition, and our technology never surfaced in another company, we assumed he'd given up on the line of research."

"So, if he made off with your research but didn't sell it to anybody, you've got nothing on him," I reiterate. "And I certainly don't know anything about it, so if you're trying to get me to testify about something—"

"No, no of course not," my mother interrupts. "No one is accusing you of anything, J.J. We don't even want to accuse your father. The last thing we want to do is put any kind of black mark on his name."

"And that's where you come in," Evan says. "We've discovered that your father has a safety deposit box at a bank in Chicago. It's possible he may have left copies of the research in that box. We're not after this just because we're concerned about copyrights and trademarks. This research is literally going to save people's lives. It's going to ease the anguish of hundreds of thousands of people on a yearly basis. It's going to open up doorways to new treatments that can give people an entirely new lease on life. Your father's research will be critical in helping us achieve the next level on this thing."

"You mean the next level that's going to land you that big contract you want?" I ask pointedly.

My mother's shock is obvious, and Evan sets his fork carefully down on the table.

"I'm sure there's talk around the island." I can tell how much he wants to growl that instead of speak it. "I won't lie. The company needs this contract to stay in business. We want to stay in business because people need our help. We are almost there, and your father—your brilliant father and his meticulous research—can get us the rest of the way."

"I don't understand," I say. "If his research is years old, and that's what you were working with originally—how is that even relevant now?"

"Research isn't a straight path," my mother explains. "There can be different branches to the stream, various directions we take, building off what we've learned in our mistakes, and what we've gained from our advances. Sometimes you can follow the stream a long way and then it goes over a waterfall, and you realize you have to backtrack to the source and branch out in a different direction."

"We need to go back to the very early days of your father's research," Evan says. "Research that we should have but we don't because your father deleted our copies and took it with him. Now, I can open up a subpoena to get into the contents of that safety deposit box. If they find a laptop or a storage device, I can have all of the data reviewed in the presence of the Court, who can make the decision as to whether or not our intellectual property was violated. If it was, all of the information will be turned over to us, and your father's name will be tarnished forever. Any research he's published, any therapeutic areas he's been a critical assist for, all of it will come under scrutiny. His name will be splashed across websites and news articles, and everyone in the technology and scientific community will be shocked and disappointed."

I clench the edge of the table so hard, I'm surprised it doesn't crack.

"You would do that?" I look at my mother. "You would let him do that?"

She answers without a moment of hesitation. "Yes J.J., I would let him do that. I wouldn't want to, but this is bigger than one man's good name."

"And the beautiful part about all of this," Evan says, and now he's smiling again, "is that it can be easily avoided."

"How? I told you I don't know anything."

My mother leans in. "Did your father give you a key? To the safety deposit box?"

"No." I don't have to fake my surprise. "I didn't even know he had a safety deposit box until now."

"Do you have an idea of where he might have put the key?" Evan presses.

If they searched my storage unit, that would have had all of his personal effects—the ones I kept, anyway. And I can't think of any secret hiding places.

"No. Did you ask his lawyer?"

"Yes," my mother sighs, then she quickly amends: "On your behalf, of course."

At my questioning look, Evan explains.

"You're eighteen now. You are also your father's only next of kin. By terms of his estate, you legally assume ownership of the safety deposit box, with the key, by submitting his death certificate and a copy of his will, both of which are on file with his lawyer. One phone call from you, one signature on some paperwork, and all of the legal mess is avoided."

"Honestly," my mother says. "It's very simple and it's not the big deal that you probably think it is—or at least it doesn't have to be. We're not even sure what's in the box—the bank can't tell us. This may all be for nothing. He may only have another copy of his will in the box and some old jewelry left by your grandmother."

"All we're asking here is that you fill out the paperwork and let us get a look at it." Evan says.

"We can all fly to Chicago together," my mother suggests. "Then if there are any electronic devices inside, you give us first crack at them. Everything is returned to you once we get what we need."

"Think about it J.J.," Evan says, smiling like he wants to sell me a Lamborghini. "Your father can rest in peace, with his reputation intact. You can go to the college of your choice. No student loans, no dipping into your father's money. You'll graduate with a degree in your hand and I'm sure I can pull strings to get you the job of your dreams. That's how badly we need this data. That's how badly our potential patients need this data."

Did they think I kept the key in my locket? Is that why my mother had it? If I open that safety deposit box, I may find even more damning information that could sink this company. But I also might find information that can help my squad.

"I'll think about it," I say, trying to sound like I need time. My dinner is cold, but I force myself to start shoveling it into my mouth, if only to keep from talking anymore.

My mother reaches out like she wants to smooth my hair, then pulls her hand back. "Take tonight," she says to me. "Sleep on it. You'll feel better."

Sleep on it.

As usual, she doesn't really know me at all.

27

"**PEANUT BUTTER AND LETTUCE?** Really?" I make a face as I hand the jar of peanut butter to Rio.

"Try it! Maybe you'll like it," she says. "If you really want to make it interesting, it needs a touch—" She reaches into the back of her refrigerator. "Of Japanese mayonnaise."

"If you put that near my mouth, I will throw it across the room," I threaten. "You know I can."

"You can probably take someone's eye out with it," Rio smirks. Akoni looks puzzled, so she explains. "J.J. can throw rocks like a ninja throws stars."

"It's a skill I picked up from the squad," I explain. "I'm only kind-of good."

She holds up the sandwich again. "Maybe you'd be better if your body had the proper nutrients."

I push the sandwich away. "Pass."

Akoni looks over from his spot on her other side, "I will not have that, thank you."

She swivels to look at Akoni, tilting her head adorably and giving him big, puppy dog eyes.

"Perhaps one bite," he reluctantly agrees.

"One little bite," I qualify.

We're saved by the bell as my phone rings. I pick it up and freeze as I recognize the number. Rio mouths *who?* as I answer the call.

"Hello?"

"J.J.? It's Dr. Grady. How are you?"

"I'm okay." I keep my voice steady even though my heart is thumping loudly. "Did I forget an appointment?"

"No, no, of course not," she answers. "I feel bad that we haven't been able to meet recently. I know it's not our usual day, but I'm wide open this afternoon, if that works for you."

The odds are she'll rat me out to my mother if I don't go. And maybe I can get something more out of this and probe a little deeper.

"Sure, when?"

"How about now?"

I look over at Rio, who just bullied Akoni into a bite. His face says all I need to know about peanut butter, lettuce, and mayo. "Yeah, I can meet now."

"Great!" Dr. Grady answers brightly. "Let's not go to the office—why don't we get out for a little while? Do you know the shop at the beach near the nature preserve? The one that sells ice cream?"

"You want to go for ice cream?"

"My treat," she says. "I insist."

"I want ice cream!" Rio interjects in a loud whisper.

I wave her off with my hand. "I can be there in about twenty minutes."

"That'll be fine. I'll see you there."

I end the call and Rio looks at me questioningly.

"You're meeting Dr. Grady for ice cream?" she asks. "Did you win patient of the month or something?"

"She feels bad that we haven't been able to meet lately. She's missed my last two sessions."

"You are seeing the psychiatrist?" Akoni asks.

"She gets slaughtered every night in her sleep," Rio reminds him. "Her mother thought she was losing her marbles."

"*I* thought I was losing my marbles," I add.

Akoni shakes his head. "Your marbles are being used to play a bigger game."

"Exactly. This is perfect timing," I tell them as I drum my fingers on the counter.

Akoni's eyes widen. "Because the doctor is helping to oversee the project."

"Someone has to be reviewing and validating that data," I say. "Someone with professional certification. I'll try to get her to talk about her job. She knows something. At our last meeting, I let her know I'm dreaming of soldiers and she got good and spooked."

Akoni's reaches out, grabbing me by the shoulder. "That was foolish! What if they are aware you are in the program?"

"They would have said something by now," I say, shaking my head. "Or done something. Evan is still dumb as a box of rocks coated in hair gel."

"And you think Dr. Grady just going to tell you anything?" Rio asks, waving her sandwich around. "Not likely."

"I might be able to dig a little bit, if I'm careful."

"Be *very* careful," Akoni cautions.

"You think she can tell us much?" Rio asks.

"I don't know," I answer. "But like Akoni says, all information is helpful no matter how small it is. Plus, I'm getting free ice cream."

"So not fair," Rio whines.

"If you want ice cream, I will take you to it," Akoni promises her.

"Really?" Her face lights up and he smiles at her in response. I stare at both of them because I know Rio's face is lighting up for more than just ice cream.

"I don't like the idea of J.J. meeting her alone," he says. But he's still looking at Rio.

I hide my grin. "I'd better get going."

"Maybe we'll have another sandwich first," Rio suggests.

Akoni's eyes widen in horror behind her, and I wonder if he's willing to choke a whole sandwich down just to make her happy. He's a saint.

"Save some room for the ice cream," I toss over my shoulder as I walk to the door. Akoni gives me a grateful look as Rio sighs and follows. It's time for me to play some mind games and psychoanalyze the psychiatrist.

Dr. Grady and I end up sitting on a natural rock ledge nestled in a small dune. The waves gently lap the beach as we lap up our ice cream.

"I'm glad we found the time to get together," Dr. Grady says, shifting to get a little more comfortable. "It's a perfect beach day."

"It is," I agree, holding my ice cream away from me as the chocolate fudge pop drips down the sides of the stick.

"Here," she hands me a napkin. "I always have extra."

"That's very mom-like," I say with a smile. *Or dad-like.* My smile fades as I mentally amend.

"I don't have any kids of my own," she tells me. "But I'm a very lucky aunt. My sister has a five-year-old girl named Madison. I love her to death."

"It must be hard being away from them."

Her face tightens and her eyes grow shuttered.

"Yes," is all she says.

We sit in silence for a moment, finishing our ice cream.

"So!" She says brightly, as if remembering why she brought me here. "Tell me every little thing. How's Climate Club? How are things with your mom? Did I hear you're working with Dr. Walters now?"

"Climate Champions is still just me and Rio. We're going to volunteer for a few hours next week at the turtle sanctuary on the nature preserve."

"That'll be fun."

"And things with Mom and Evan are about the same, I guess. I work part-time with Evan now and that's okay."

"Just okay?" Her eyes hold mine and I remember why I'm here. Time to do some prodding.

"Actually, it's been really interesting to find out more about the company." I try to sound casual. "Not that Evan can tell me a lot of what he does, specifically, but it's good to get a general feel for it. I can pick up things here and there and it seems like the company is working really hard to help people."

"Yes, that's been our primary focus," she says carefully.

"I would imagine you've done work to aid them in their research."

"Yes, I have."

"I'd love to know more." Throughout our entire conversation, our eyes have been locked and I don't think either of us has so much as blinked. "What can you tell me about the work you do?"

"That depends," she considers her words before answering. "What can you tell me about the soldiers you see in your dreams?"

Well. That was direct.

"I chose this place for a reason," she tells me. "There aren't any video cameras out here and we're far enough down the beach that no one can hear us. This conversation is completely off the record."

"Okay," I say evenly. "What do you need to know about the soldiers—exactly? And why?"

"I need to know details. Do you interact with them? Can you give me names? It's important."

"Why?"

"Let's just say I'm really, really curious."

"Is Evan curious? Or my mom?"

She tenses, then looks around, trying not to look like she's looking around. Then she lowers her voice so I can barely hear her over the rolling waves on the beach.

"They don't know everything we've discussed. But I do need to know if you've mentioned the content of your dreams to either of them."

"I never tell them anything personal."

Her eyes soften at that, then she nods. "Understood. I'm also not in the habit of sharing anything personal with either of them. And I will never betray your confidence by sharing anything from our session beyond vague generalities with your mother. Ever."

That makes me feel better, but it also sets off warning bells. She doesn't trust Evan—who does? But my mother? This is interesting—but not in a good way.

"Well?" she asks. "What can you tell me?"

I hold her eyes as I recite the names. "Shadow. Beast. Chef. Gears. Rookie. And Sarge."

"You interact with Sarge?" She grabs my arm. "All right, you need to tell me everything." She looks over her shoulder and so do I. Nobody's watching.

"Everything?"

"All cards on the table. If we're going to help each other—if we're going to help *them*," she qualifies. "I need to know what you know."

"You want to help them? To get them out?"

"I have been trying to get them out from the minute everything started to go wrong," she says, and there is no mistaking the guilt and anguish in her voice. "I can't let the company do this to anyone else—but we have to be careful. The people they're dealing with—"

"Like Armando?"

Dr. Grady shudders at the name. "Yes. And he's only the beginning of what this program could evolve into. So work with me, please. You may be the key to figuring this out."

She trusted me enough to have this conversation off the record. And I need to know what she knows. Information for information. Despite my dislike of her prying into my life, she was just doing her job and she really did try to help me. Maybe she still does. I might regret this, but I'm going with my gut. I'm going to take a leap of faith and trust her.

"I think I was exposed to one of my father's early nanite experiments," I tell her. "That's why I can see them and talk to them. I managed to trigger White Protocol, but it didn't end the program."

She sucks in a breath. "How do you know about White Protocol?"

I speak quietly, even though the wind coming off the ocean makes it hard for us to hear each other when we're sitting side-by-side. I'm not taking any chances.

I tell her what I know of it—explaining how I got into Evan's files, but I don't implicate Akoni or Rio. She looks shocked and dismayed but she doesn't stop me as I fill her in on everything I've learned outside the program and in.

"You know nearly as much as I do," she tells me finally, "but I can fill in a few of the gaps. Some of us here don't agree with the direction that Evan is taking the company. His security lockdown was more than just increased surveillance of our emails. He has some very powerful people interested in the Eventide program—particularly in its military applications. For training," she pauses, swallows hard. "And for interrogation use. We don't agree with that. The people he's making these agreements with are—well, like I said, they're not good people."

"Armando and the guys I've seen strolling around the compound," I say. "They even look like the bad guys."

"Special security forces." She uses her fingers to make air quotes. "Here to protect their interests during contract negotiations. Stay away from them, J.J. Your age and your mother's name won't be enough to protect you."

I try not to let that get me too rattled—unsuccessfully.

"So why haven't any of you come forward?" I demand.

"There are only a few of us willing to speak out. It's gone further than you realize. Threats have been made against our families here on the island and back at home. One of us even had a family member abducted."

My eyes go wide. "Dr. Ruiz."

She pales, her lips tightening. "Dr. Ruiz was going to shut the entire program down. He didn't want to see it fall into the wrong hands. Evan wasn't going to stand for that. He had big money on the line, and his external partners—" She loads the word with several pounds of disdain. "They've already sunk a lot of seed money into this. Evan told us if we didn't play ball, it's likely we—or our families—would be made to pay. We thought he was bluffing. And then they took Mateo Ruiz."

"Evan had him put into Eventide," I say.

She nods. "At Armando's suggestion. To keep Dr. Ruiz under control and to force him and his team to work on a way around the Citadel virus."

"The virus my father put there." I grimace.

She reaches out and puts her hand over mine. We're both sticky from melting ice cream.

"He did the right thing. Several of us kept contact with him, and he tried to warn us about Evan and what he's capable of. Evan is very careful about covering his tracks and shifting money around. None of us could find anything concrete to get him with. Your father effectively stymied the program very early on, leaving it incapable of recording and transmitting data. The Citadel virus rendered it useless."

"He sabotaged his own research," I finish.

Dr. Grady shakes her head. "Your father never wrote in the extreme combat scenarios. That came from Evan and his development team. Then Evan—who was never a great developer himself—played with the code and had no luck disabling the Citadel virus. He hired some foreign hacker who had plenty of experience doing shady work. They made it worse, and that sent Sarge off the rails."

"Are you talking about the shakes?" She looks confused, so I clarify. "They get this—sickness. It makes them shake all over and frizzes their brain out for several minutes. Scribe and Wizard had it before they died for good, and now Chef is showing signs. But I haven't seen Sarge dealing with it. He still seems pretty solid. Does it affect their bodies in the pods? Can you see it happening to them?"

She stares at me for a long moment before she answers.

"Your father originally wrote a critical program interface that included some back doors in the code only he would know about," she explains. "He never trusted Evan. He used one of those back doors to get in and hijack the program. Evan responded by tinkering with a particular artificial intelligence interface in an effort to disable the virus. That AI was known as the Simulated Authority, Research, and Gamification Entity. Otherwise known as S.A.R.G.E."

"Sarge is an AI? My *dad* created Sarge?" I practically
shriek it, then clap my hand over my mouth as we both glance
around again. I feel like I just took a punch to the gut. I can't
breathe. *Sarge wasn't real.*

"No." I shake my head. "No, that can't be right. Sarge is
like a father to us all. To me." My eyes fill with tears and I
blink them back.

"Your father designed Sarge," she says gently. "Sarge
originally had a lot of your dad in his makeup and demeanor.
Patience, empathy, humor, curiosity—then it all went wrong."

It makes sense, in a crazy way. Sarge had become a father
figure to me—he shared so many qualities with my own
father. Of course, he did. Dad wrote him.

"Your father designed Sarge to be an interactive
monitoring program," Dr. Grady explains. "It engages with the
subjects via their nanites to pull out information on their
mental health and physical well-being during the run of the
simulated scenarios—everything from coping skills and
positive outlook to vital signs, serotonin, and adrenaline
levels. It can interface and adjust throughout the course of
the program, stimulating short-term memory and a long list
of cognitive functions as necessary. It's very sophisticated,
but not meant to do what it is doing now."

"Because Evan had to screw with it," I add, with a good
deal of disgust.

"At first, Evan altered the Sarge program to try and get the subjects to shut down the virus themselves from the inside," she continues.

"That explains why he tried to kill me and switched everyone into Red Protocol to attack me—he thought I was another virus."

"He's attacking you?" Her hand grips mine again.

"Not anymore—not since I triggered White Protocol. None of them know he's an AI. He certainly hasn't mentioned it. He's the reason they're trapped in there?"

Dr. Grady nods. "A glitch in the program, triggered by the modifications that were made while they tried to root out the Citadel virus. Sarge just keeps re-running scenarios. He treats them as training exercises to prep the squad for defeating the Citadel virus."

"Is he giving them the shakes?"

"The shakes are brought on by progressive neural strain," she says quietly. "The longer they all stay in, the more unlikely it is we can reverse it. It will eventually kill them all."

My hand comes unconsciously to my mouth as the horror of it sinks in. They're all in real danger. Not simulated, not virtual, not just in their brain. They're all going to die. I slide my fingers up to my forehead, as if I can feel the nanites circling in my brain.

"Am I—" I don't know if I can finish what I'm asking.

"Are you compromised, as well?"

I nod, and my mouth is suddenly dry as a bone.

"Possibly." Her eyes meet mine. "Probably. You should recover if we can get you off the island and away from the signals that trigger your nanites. Otherwise . . ."

That falls like a stone, weighting the air between us. My mind races, thinking, thinking, thinking.

"Can you get to Dr. Ruiz?"

"They have him locked up in the lab wing. I'm one of the few that gets to speak with him. There's an armed guard at his door." She rubs her palms across her knees. "Manuel and I have a standing meeting to discuss his latest findings on a weekly basis. We mock up mental health assessments and progress reports to show to Armando—to make it look like the program is on track despite the issues. We've been telling him for months that we're extending the experiment to get more information and confirm research methodology."

"Is there any way you can talk to Dr. Ruiz without the guard there?" I ask. "I'm sure he'd like to know his son is aware and reasonably okay."

"I can't talk about it—but I may be able to slip him a note in with the paperwork if I'm careful."

"He's healthy?" I ask. "They haven't hurt him?"

She shakes her head gravely. "Not yet. And despite his involvement in the program and his own child in jeopardy, he's no closer to getting them out than I am."

I'm not related to any of my squad, but we've become a kind of family all the same. It's eating me—and Dr. Grady—alive that we can't free them. I can't begin to imagine what it would be like to have a child trapped in that mind-bending slaughterhouse, wasting their lives in a pod until their brain couldn't function anymore. It's horrific, and torture seems too mild a word for it.

"From the time the Citadel virus infiltrated the system," Dr. Grady continues, "we've been unable to pull anything but basic biometric data. We have no idea what's really going on in there. Erik Andersson's death—"

"That's Boomer, right?"

"Yes. Completely undiagnosed medical condition. Dr. Ruiz tried to end the program right then and there, call in more experts from the outside, but Evan fought him. It's only going to get worse as the longer they're in there."

We—they—are running out of time. We have to beat the Citadel on the inside, and then be ready to trigger the pods from the outside. And we have to do it soon.

"Is the pod bay guarded?" I ask.

"Nothing beyond a normal security patrol," she replies. "But there's someone at the monitoring station twenty-four-seven, and the cameras feed into the station in the security office."

I get an idea—a frightening, dangerous, possibly insane idea. "Hold on," I say to her. I turn and look down the beach and spot Rio's hot pink tiara with the sparkling kitty-cat ears and Akoni's lanky frame easily even from a distance. I knew she'd talk him into ice cream. I pull out my phone, send my text, and watch as Rio receives it.

"I think we should all take a walk down the beach," I say to Dr. Grady. *"Far* down the beach."

28

"**This is certifiably insane**," I breathe as Rio, Akoni and I peer from the bushes together.

"What are you talking about?" Rio exclaims. "We are Operation Chimu Trio Masterforce and this is wicked cool!"

"No, she is right," Akoni agrees. "This is insane. But it is also my brother's best chance for getting out of there."

"She's late," I nervously rub my hands down my black pants. We're all dressed in black, even Rio. I had to loan her a shirt because she didn't have anything without color accents or glitter. In a few moments, Dr. Grady is going to help us break into the pod bay in the lab. We spent over two hours yesterday in our secret cave down on the beach putting this all together.

Once Dr. Grady realized how deep both Rio and Akoni were into this along with me, she started getting cold feet. She kept exclaiming that we were all minors, and maybe it would be best if we just find a way to get a message to someone in authority.

None of us would back down.

It has to be tonight. Every member of my squad has a target on their back, generated randomly by a computer program that's determined to deliver results no matter the cost. And I don't know how much longer Chef and Shadow—or the rest of them—can last. I haven't shared any of my doubts with Akoni—he's got enough to worry about. And I refuse to think about what this might end up doing to my own neurological health.

The door to the research building slowly opens and Rio is already in motion. Akoni looks at me with a shrug and he and I follow close behind her. We've already taken care of redirecting the security camera on this door. Rio was able to give us a printout of all the camera locations we would be passing. According to her, Evan scrimped when it came to building construction. The security logs often show cameras needing realignment and pointing at walls or ground.

"None of the wooden floors in the buildings are reinforced properly," Rio said matter-of-factly. "Everything vibrates when a truck drives by or just from people walking heavy. The security teams always have to readjust because the cameras slip down in their mountings. Nobody's going to think a thing about it if these cameras are out of whack. They'll just put it on the list for the day crew to take care of."

"You understand what you're supposed to do?" Dr. Grady asks Akoni and Rio.

"Rio and I will be keeping watch out here. We will text you if anyone is coming."

"I still say we should go in the pods with J.J.," Rio says, crossing her arms.

"I'm not putting nanites in your brain," Dr. Grady says, shaking her head.

I nod my head in agreement. "I can do this."

"You totally can," Rio says. "I just really want to fight drones in a mega maze."

"Be careful," Akoni says, putting a hand on my shoulder. "I'm counting on you, J.J."

No pressure.

"Let's go," Grady says, and we move quickly through the door. "I've taken care of the cameras along this hallway," she tells me.

We pause in front of the door marked QUARANTINE: SECURE AREA—BADGE ACCESS ONLY. Dr. Grady knocks twice, then badges in.

"Mike?"

Her voice is soft, but I can still hear her as she stands in the doorway.

"Hey Doc—what are you doing here this late?" says a man's voice.

"Walters has me working overtime compiling reports for another big contract pitch."

"Asshole. Such a God complex," he commiserates, and I smile in agreement. Then I hear him groan.

"Mike, what's the matter?" Dr. Grady asks innocently. "Are you okay?"

"Feel like crap," Mike answers her back. "Not sure what's going on."

"You look terrible," I hear her say as the door shuts quietly behind her. More words, but muffled—I can't make them out. I'm startled by the sound of the doorknob beginning to turn, and duck around the corner just in time.

"Take as long as you need," Dr. Grady says consolingly as Mike steps into the hallway. "I'm going to be a while. I've got a lot of data and I need to cross-reference it multiple ways."

"You sure you don't mind?" He asks. "I think I'm coming down with something."

"There's a bug going around," she tells him.

"It figures," he groans. "I'm so tired I can barely drag my ass through the door."

"Just go on home," Dr. Grady says. "I'm going to be here at least a couple of hours. Who do you report to? Juanita?"

"Yeah," he answers and then groans again.

"I'll give Juanita a call for you," Dr. Grady offers.

"Thanks. I really mean it."

"No big deal. Hope you feel better."

"Me, too."

He staggers off down the hallway, heading toward the door. I count to ten, but by the time I hit eight, Dr. Grady is reaching around the door and motioning for me to come in.

"Will he be okay?"

"It's just a mild dose of sleep aid that I added to the coffee pot in the kitchen. He drinks a lot of it to stay awake on the overnight shift. He'll be fine by morning. I'll just let his boss know I didn't want to disturb her, so I covered his shift. That gives us a little over six hours before the day shift and you have to be out of here."

"My mother thinks I'm sleeping at Rio's. She's got my phone so she can text back or run interference if Mom calls."

"I just need to access the control panel." She moves up to a raised platform as I look around the room. Eight pods. Three empty. And in the other five, my squad. My friends. Real, living human beings. I stare down at them, watching their chests rise and fall with each breath, wondering what horror they're living through despite the peaceful exterior.

"You're sure you can get me into the Citadel?" I ask.

She's typing rapidly on a touchscreen. "This should work," she says. "We can program any scenario to run, but since the Citadel is a virus and not a program scenario, it operates during a certain rest cycle we call stasis mode. I'm pretty sure if I target just before that, you should be able to slip right in."

I move through the spaces between the pods until I find him. Rookie's hair is longer than it is in the scenarios. I want to open the pod and run my fingers through it. He's paler, with a scruff of a beard. All of them have longer hair, and it's more than a little disconcerting to see all the facial hair—evidence that this has been a long process. Too long.

"There," she says. "That should do it. I can't abruptly end a scenario, but I can ease them out of it. They should be into or very close to stasis mode by the time I get you connected. Climb in." She hurries down to join me in the pod area.

Choosing the empty pod next to Rookie, I study his face one more time. I never did ask him about that scar near his mouth. I make a mental note to do so someday. Suddenly, he jerks and it startles me.

"Why is he twitching? I ask, alarmed.

"It's just the muscle stimulators," Dr. Grady answers. "To prevent atrophy. They've all been in these pods a long time. Too long."

As I start to lie down, Dr. Grady's hand on my shoulder stops me.

"J.J.—your mother is Evan's right hand. This could be bad for her. This could mean prison for her. I know you don't have the best relationship, but you need to think hard about this," she warns me. "You can turn back now. The few of us who object to all of this will not stop trying to get all of them out safely."

"It's too big of a gamble." I shake my head. "It has to be soon. Tonight."

She takes a deep breath and pulls me in for a hug. Then she begins attaching electrodes.

"I'll get them prepped—removing the intubation, catheters, etc.—so they'll be ready to make a quick exit when the neural interface disconnects. Be careful," she warns, as she fastens the electrodes to my head. "I'm only hooking up the neural connectors. I can't predict what Sarge will do when you're hard-wired into the system."

"The squad and I have a plan to get through the Citadel, and that's what he wants, right? It's a long shot, but it just might work." *It has to work,* I think. *It has to.*

"Good luck," she says, and the pod door closes. I have a moment of claustrophobia, and then my eyes close, and I spiral into gray nothingness.

Standing in the rubble, I see them at the end of the street near the foot of the clocktower. It looks like they're scavenging, searching for fallen weapons, ammunition, checking the houses for food and also to make sure no one is in there hiding. It's quiet, so Dr. Grady managed to target the end of the scenario.

"Hey." I call out. They all turn to greet me.

"Any word?" Gears asks as he saunters over.

Shadow drops down from the tank she'd been standing on. "Have you learned anything further that can help us?"

They all look at me expectantly—even Sarge. I can't help the icy shiver that snakes down my spine. Suddenly, I'm not so sure this is a good idea. What will he do if I out him to the others? Kill me again? Will they even believe me?

"Sparkles?" Rookie moves closer, reading my body language. "What's wrong?"

They all gather around me but Chef isn't among them.

"Chef?" I'm afraid to ask.

"Here." His voice calls out weakly and I see him sitting against a wall nearby. My relief must show because he slowly gets to his feet and joins us. He looks exhausted.

"Out with it," Sarge says. "What's wrong?"

I pause still looking at Chef. My stomach is churning. How do I even put all I've learned into words?

"It is about me," Chef says grimly. "About the shakes."

"No," I reassure him. Then I bite my lip. "Well, kind of. You're right—they're happening because of the extended neurological strain."

"And that's what killed Boomer? And Scribe and Wizard?" Beast asks.

"Boomer's death was an unrelated heart defect. Wizard and Scribe were taken out by Black Protocol." My eyes move to Sarge. He's looking at me intently.

"Go on," he gestures at me.

I find myself oddly reluctant to say it. Like saying it makes it true, and I am absolutely gutted that it is.

"Sarge isn't real. He's an AI program." I blurt it out because I really don't know how to ease into it. They all look at me blankly at first, then turn slowly to look at Sarge.

"Bullshit." Beast spits out the word.

"The other night when we were talking around the fire about home and our families," Shadow says. "You told us you didn't want to talk about it. I thought it was just difficult for you. But it's not, is it?"

"No way!" Gears shakes his head in disbelief. "He's been with us from the beginning."

Chef is eyeing Sarge warily now. "We originally designed an AI to observe and interact within the program, but on a therapeutic basis. Not a soldier—more of a counselor figure embedded in each session. When White Protocol engaged and our memories returned, I recalled it—but since everything had gone so wrong, I assumed the program never engaged."

"Sarge was hijacked by a side project Evan was working on," I tell them. "To utilize the nanites in other ways. Evan had been looking into militarizing the program, and the AI was corrupted when they tried to remove the virus by switching over to the military sub-routines. With data downloads being blocked by the virus, it essentially trapped you all in an endless loop, with Sarge embedded as one of the squad."

"Wait—" Rookie sticks his hands out and shakes his head as if to clear it. "Wait. You're telling me he's a computer program? He's not one of us?"

"I *am* one of you," Sarge says tersely. "Don't let her derail you from our objective here. We need to get through the Citadel. That's the priority."

"It's always about the mission objective, isn't it?" I look at the rest of them. "Singular focus. Rerouting you when you get off course. Convincing you to kill me when he thought I was another virus infiltrating the program."

Rookie's head whips to Sarge. "You told us—"

"He told us she was a threat," Shadow says.

"I was willing to indulge her in the beginning even though I had no data on her because Rookie arrived the same way," Sarge says. "But he assimilated quickly and had valuable skills that aided us in our objectives. Sparkles was intent on interfering with her prying questions so I made the call to eliminate the threat. She didn't respond to Black Protocol, so I engaged Red Protocol—"

"And weaponized us against her," Shadow finishes. Beast steps toward Sarge, but she pulls him back. "You can't kill him," she reminds him. "Not really."

"I can hurt him a lot," he growls.

"She's right. You can't truly kill him." There's no easy way for me to tell them this, either. "But he can kill you. He killed Scribe. And Wizard."

Shadow's face drains of color, and Beast and Gears spit out the same swear word. Chef grabs my arm.

"The neural degeneration did not kill them?"

"Wizard was definitely impaired," I say quietly. "But the decision to terminate—to engage Black Protocol—came from Sarge. After the trauma she suffered compounded her neurological issues, he decided she was hindering you from completing mission objectives. Just like he did for Scribe."

Gears still looks like he doesn't want to believe it. I can't blame him. I don't want to either.

"That can't be true." He looks at Sarge, bewildered. "Is it?"

Sarge's eyes scan the rest of the squad. "I have the power to permanently remove anyone who interferes with mission objectives, as necessary." There's no hint of the warm, caring leader we've all relied on to hold us together. His voice is emotionless.

"Son of a bitch!"

Beast is a blur of motion, tackling Sarge to the ground, but before he can start pummeling, Sarge throws him off. He's up and lunging for me in a heartbeat but Shadow and Rookie both move to get between us.

"Wait!" My hand goes up, trying to stop Sarge before he can retaliate—or worse. "My father designed you. I'm going to bet there's enough of his original programming in there that you will listen to me and work with us. I know you want to defeat the Citadel." I gesture at the others. "So do we."

Sarge stares at me. Blinks. "Your father is Michael Ashford?"

"Yes." I nod. "And I know how he thinks. I might be able to help us get out—end the scenarios. We already have the plan in place to use my med bag in the Citadel."

He eyes me shrewdly. "You're confident that you can complete the mission objective and gain access to the information contained in the pyramid?"

"I think we've got a decent chance. If not this time, then maybe on the next run of the scenario," I tell him, even though I'm nowhere near sure. I'm also not about to tell him that I'm going to do everything in my power to keep him from joining us if we make it into that pyramid. The key to disabling the program is encrypted in there somewhere. Evan and Armando can't be allowed get their hands on the key—with it they could reset and restart the Eventide program.

"Completion of the Citadel scenario is imperative," Sarge states firmly.

"We understand," I assure him. "I entered right before the stasis cycle, so the Citadel should be next."

His eyebrows raise. "Is that right?"

"Yeah," I reply. "There's a way to program—"

I don't finish the sentence. Sarge lifts his automatic rifle and sprays us with bullets, emptying the clip until every one of us is dead.

29

IN A HEARTBEAT, WE'RE under the triple-mooned sky.

"This mission has to succeed," Sarge barks out even though we've barely assimilated our cold-blooded murders and the change in scenery.

"Hey asshole," Gears snarls. "We understand. You didn't need to mow us down."

"If the urgency was truly understood, we would have accomplished the objective by now," Sarge snaps. Then he shifts his gaze slowly over the rest of the group. "Maybe some additional motivation is needed."

My blood freezes at the complete lack of humanity in his eyes. Did I actually hope my Dad was in there, somewhere? He looks like a machine now. A cold, calculating war machine.

"What motivation?" Shadow demands.

"Black Protocol." Sarge smiles as though he's just been handed a state-of-the-art weapon—and I suppose he has.

"Killing us off won't get your objective accomplished," Rookie says.

"It's counterproductive," Shadow points out. "We may need several runs at the Citadel before we get it right."

"You've had more than enough time and we now have a solid plan." Sarge speaks conversationally, as if he's talking about the weather or his next meal. "You've all gotten jaded. Desensitized. Complacent. Let's see how much you accomplish when your lives are truly on the line. Any death in this scenario will now be the permanent kind."

The walls of the maze stand before us in the shadow of the great pyramid, and the sound of approaching drones comes from behind us. I open my mouth to join the cries and epithets of the others, but there's no time to lose. Swinging my med bag off my shoulder, I rip the zipper open and toss the contents on the ground in front of me.

There are three different types of scalpels, and two types of tweezers. I give them all to Gears. Shadow yanks one of the larger scalpels out of his hands and pockets it. I cram the scissors in my own pocket.

"Aspirin powder!" I call out as I toss it to the ground. Shadow scoops it up.

I yank out the bicarbonate of soda, peroxide, rubbing alcohol, and saline, passing them to Chef. Then I dump the rest of the contents of the bag on the ground.

Sarge picks up the empty bag, unzipping it on all three sides so that it now lays flat. He wraps his arm around one of the rubber-banded straps inside.

"These scalpels might be handy," Gears exclaims. "If we can capture a drone, I may be able to rewire it."

"Portable defibrillator!" Beast calls out.

"Anywhere we can use that in the maze?" Sarge asks.

"Maybe the section with the electric-charged walls," says Gears. "But we can just avoid those instead."

"Let's keep it," Chef says.

"You never know—we may need it," Shadow agrees.

Everyone has divided up the supplies, and among what's left on the ground are some Ace bandages and gauze, which I cram into my jacket pockets.

"Everybody know what to do?" Sarge asks. There are several yesses and head nods as we all take our supplies.

Beast looks down at the few remaining items and scoops up a handful of ammonia inhalants, breaking a half-dozen of them before he buries his nose in them, breathing deeply. His eyebrows shoot up into his hairline and his eyes water as he coughs violently.

"Let's rock this," he says in a hoarse voice, wiping his eyes. He picks up a large metal splint and shoves it down the waistband of his pants.

Then we run.

"Fibonacci!" Chef shouts, as the first of the drones arrive. He calls out the numbers, all of us falling in line behind him.

"One! One! Two! Three! Five! Eight! Thirteen! Twenty-one! Thirty-four!"

We nearly make it through when a drone shot hits the tiles and sends Rookie and Beast flying. Beast stands up, shaking his head against the ringing in his ears, clouting himself on the temple with a fist as if to correct it.

Rookie staggers to his feet a moment later and I let out a whoosh of relieved breath. He gives me a thumbs-up and on we go.

A drone blast hits the wall to my left, ricocheting and slamming into the wall on the right. A chunk of marble flies, hitting me in the ankle. I stumble, but Shadow is right there to catch me, steadying me as she pushes me forward.

"Winged him!" Beast exclaims as a drone careens and spins wildly. He leaps into the air what has to be four or five feet off the ground and yanks it down. Gears rushes to it.

"I need cover!" Gears shouts, and a moment later, he's disassembling the drone. He pops a back panel off the drone with a scalpel and goes to work.

We all form a protective circle around him, firing at the oncoming drones so he can finish.

"Good to go!" Gears says. "All I have to do is press the end of this wire—" He shows us where. "To the flash panel to fire and we've got a laser cannon."

He grabs the small wing-like stabilizer on the left of the drone, turning it sideways. Then he puts his hand into the back panel.

"Let's do it," he says.

"Move out!" Sarge snaps the order, and we all move forward, following his lead. The drone fire is coming hard and heavy and we're all dodging, leaping, and rolling between our shots. Gears is firing back, taking down a good majority of them with his newly improvised drone blaster. Then a volley of shots rocks the passageway so hard I actually wonder if my eardrums have ruptured. When the smoke clears, I push forward, kicking away the rubble at my feet—only I hit something soft.

Shadow. Blood pours from her ears and nose, and her leg is bent at an impossible angle.

There isn't time for bedside manner. I kneel next to her, slapping her face lightly. "Shadow!" She's breathing, but unconscious.

"Keep moving," Sarge orders. "Leave her."

"We can't!" I cry out. There's a break in drones at the moment—the next wave hasn't been dispatched, but we still have most of a maze in front of us.

"We're not leaving anybody behind. Sparkles, cover me!" Beast scoops Shadow up in his arms, and we're all running behind him as he follows Sarge.

"Darts!"

Sarge's voice rings out as the darts fly, but the med bag holds true. He was holding it before him like a shield, and every one of them impacted the bag and bounced right off.

"It worked!" he says. "Keep going!" He waves us all through and we run past only to barrel into each other again as Chef stops cold, clutching a bleeding hand.

"Wire!" he calls out. I dig in Shadow's pocket and hand out the packets of aspirin powder. We each take one, ripping them open and dump them into Chef's hand. With each one, he blows the powder toward the waiting wires. It does its job, sticking to and revealing each thin line.

I grab the scissors out of my pocket and begin cutting, and Chef digs the scalpel out of Shadow's jacket pocket to help me. Most of us are through the passageway as the next wave of drones arrives.

"We need to make better time!" Sarge shouts. "Stay on your toes and pick up the pace!"

The drones are relentless, circling, diving, blasting, and surrounding us.

"There's too many of them!" Beast shouts, and as if to prove his point, one of them opens up on him. He dodges to the side but not before a shot grazes his arm. He drops Shadow with a roar, stumbling. Rookie and Gears are on him, reaching out to help him and pick up Shadow. Beast waves them off, throwing her over his good shoulder as I cover them.

"Slime!" Chef calls out a moment later as Sarge goes down, and then he's followed by the rest of us as we roll through the muck, pushing and pulling Shadow's limp body along. Once we're through, I dig out the gauze pads and we wipe off our hands and shoes as best we can.

"Up!" Rookie shouts at me as drone fire explodes around us. He all but throws me out of the way and takes a large chunk of marble to the back of his neck along with a laser graze to his shoulder.

"I'm all right," he insists, waving me off as he stumbles but keeps firing.

I don't like the blood pouring down onto his collar, but stopping to tend to his wound is not an option, so I run—right into a disorienting nightmare.

This entire section is a large, mind-bending optical illusion. The pattern on the floors and walls tricks the brain into thinking we're on waves, or steep slopes, the walls pushing in or pulling away, that the floor moving. It's making me nauseous and dizzy, but I keep running until we reach a maze of mirrors.

Everyone in the squad is reflected around me multiple times. We're all turning and looking at each other in confusion, calling out. Nobody knows where anybody is because everyone is everywhere.

"Hold on!" I yell. I turn to Rookie, who's right behind me. "Take this," I say, tying off one end of an Ace bandage to the loop of his belt. "Follow it." I begin walking forward, unrolling the bandage with one hand as the laser sight of my gun stays on the right-side mirrored wall. As I pass each team member, they grasp the bandage, following behind me. When that bandage runs out, I tie it to another and keep on rolling. Eventually, by passing them or by calling out to them to get them over to me, I have everyone in tow.

"Wait!" Sarge says as we exit the mirrors. "Everybody get down. Gears has an idea. Be ready to run on my signal."

We all crouch as the next wave of drones advances. They drop down into the mirror maze looking for us. Gears waits until they're positioned along the final run of mirrors—a long corridor with the mirrors set diagonally across from each other all along the passage. Once all four drones are down inside, Gears uses the captured drone to blast away, sending laser fire ricocheting from side to side down the mirrors, amplifying it, slamming into the drones and eliminating them all in one shot. He and Beast fist bump as Beast kicks the nearest dead drone.

"Now that's what I'm talking about!" he shouts.

"Celebrate later," Sarge barks.

Still in the lead, I step forward, trailing the loose end of my ace bandage behind me.

A soft click is the only warning I hear before the floor drops beneath me into a steep angle, sending me sliding down toward a dark pit of God only knows what.

The bandage goes taut and my arm jerks painfully in its socket. I look up and Rookie is at the edge of the pit, feet braced, holding the other end.

Gears has one arm around his waist. Beast steps forward and grabs the bandage, pulling as I climb back up out of the pit, panting heavily as I realize the sound coming from the darkness is that of whirring blades. Lots of whirring blades.

Beast reaches down for my free hand as I hit the edge.

"You good?" He asks.

I let out a shaky breath. "Not good. But I can move."

"Thatta girl," he says patting me on the back. "Gears, you on that drone?"

Gears tosses it to the side with a disgusted sound. "Looks like it's fried after that last round."

"You've still got a gun. Use it." Sarge motions us forward.

"Shadow?" I ask.

"Still breathing," Beast says, looking down at her.

"Leave her." Sarge states it like an order. To hell with that.

"No." The word is firm, and it's said, shouted, or snarled by every one of us.

"We're not leaving her," I tell him firmly. "You want me to get into that pyramid? Well, I won't go without her."

Sarge gives a curt nod and moves past me.

"Keep an eye on him," I whisper to the others. "I don't trust him."

"He's not a him," Beast growls. "He's an *it.* And *it* better watch its ass."

"We can't let him into the pyramid," I tell them in a low voice, glancing ahead to be sure Sarge isn't hearing this. "They can't get the access code to disarm the virus, they may be able to re-enable the program."

"No," Chef agrees, "We cannot let that happen."

"I'll take care of him," Rookie says, tapping his gun. "I can slow him down, at least."

We move forward as fast as we dare, tossing gathered chunks of marble ahead of us, hoping to trigger any oncoming traps. It works, for a while.

"Acid!" Gears calls out.

"Drones!" Rookie calls back, as a fresh wave approaches from behind us.

"All right—the timing has to be perfect for this," Chef reminds us. "Step only on the neutralized spots."

He grabs the scissors from me and cuts off the tip of the saline bottle before he pours in the bicarbonate of soda, placing a hand on top of it as he shakes it to mix. Then he pours a small amount onto the thin layer of acid. It hisses and bubbles, and he cautiously reaches out and touches it with a finger. We all hold our breath as nothing happens.

"It's good," he says. "But we need to move fast."

He steps carefully on the small spot of neutralized acid and pours another small circle diagonally from it—then another and another, as he walks forward on his toes, creating a pathway for each of us to follow.

I'm very, very glad he did it in a zigzag pattern because the drones are on us before he's done crossing. We're all running on our toes to follow him.

There are a couple of hisses and curse words as some of us fall a little outside the lines. Gears and Beast both have holes burned in their shoes, and Beast is sporting a particularly nasty blister on one side of his foot.

"Next time we use my feet as the guide," he snarls at Chef.

"Let's make sure there is no next time," Sarge snaps. "Move!"

We all turn to provide cover fire for Rookie as he makes his run. He misjudges as well and lands without a sole on his left shoe, hopping and cursing.

We're almost there! The pyramid is so close I have to tilt my head back to see it in its entirety. We turn the corner and there's one last corridor before the doorway.

Beast lets out a roar of frustration. Then Gears curses, long and fluidly, putting together combinations of swear words I've never heard before.

"It's the spinner," Sarge says. "What have we got for this?"

"Me." Beast sets Shadow down and limps forward with the metal splint—the one meant for broken legs. He may only have one working arm, but it's the size of a tree trunk. He bends the splint in half and rams it into the small area between the spinning wheel and the wall, jamming it tight. The wheel screeches to a halt, making a low insistent humming noise as it fights to break free.

"Make it quick—it may not hold for long!" Sarge yells as they all take off running across the now stationary circle, with Beast dragging Shadow through.

"Go!" I yell at Rookie, "I've got your six." I pull up my rifle, firing at an oncoming drone.

He starts to protest but I shut him down.

"I'm the one who can run this thing if it breaks free. You go first!"

He gives me a worried look and runs across, with me right behind him. The splint starts to dislodge just as we pass midpoint, and I grab blindly, my fingers sinking into his hair as I wrench him forward and throw him off at the others. I leap, and end up next to him in a heap, my wounded and now twisted ankle barking in protest.

Rookie rubs his head comically and gives me a disgruntled look before he pushes to his feet. We all look up at the pyramid.

"Hell yeah!" Beast exclaims. "We did it!"

"We're not in yet," Sarge reminds him. "Gears, get on that door!"

Gears rushes forward, scalpel in hand. "I need scissors!" He calls over his shoulder at me. I dig them out, hand them to him, and then turn with the others to provide cover fire.

This wave of drones is larger. Instead of the normal three or four, I count at least a dozen, maybe more. It's hard to tell while they're all flying and looping in erratic formations trying to keep us from targeting them as they zero in on us. We split into two groups, trying to draw their fire on either side. My gasping breaths freeze in my throat as I see the wave of drones on the horizon coming toward us. Dozens more.

"Gears!" Sarge shouts.

"Any second!" He shouts back. "Al . . . most . . . there . . ."

A blast of drone fire hits the wall beside him, and he's thrown to the ground. Chef rushes forward, his hand slapping out the fire that singes the shoulder of Gears' uniform. He's conscious, but he's reeling, and blood is pouring into his eyes from a wound on his forehead.

"Wrap the red wire . . . around the green one," he pants. "Then strip them and touch them to—to the metal plate. Left of the circuit board."

Chef runs forward to complete the actions as Gears gasps them out again.

With a loud tone, the heavy door slides up.

"In!" Sarge shouts.

Rookie and Chef drag Gears through the opening with Beast and Shadow following. Blood paints a path behind them. I run back to give cover fire, and to make sure Sarge stays behind us. He sees me coming, and knows what I'm about. He lunges, trying to get past me.

"Out of my way," he snaps as he swings his rifle toward me. "This mission is going to be completed. I am coming in."

"Like hell you are," I say, getting in his way.

Rookie moves in beside me and shoots the rifle right out of Sarge's hand, sending him staggering. Then he opens fire. Nothing. The shots impact Sarge, pushing him further back, but they're not killing him.

More drones have arrived, along with Beast, who shoves me toward the doorway as shots ricochet all around me. I glance over my shoulder, and Sarge isn't far behind, moving toward the pyramid with nearly manic determination.

If we let him in, he'll be able to control everything again and I know—I know—none of these people will ever leave here until Evan can find a way to wipe their memories completely. God only knows what that will do to them. And I'm the only one Sarge can't truly kill. He needs me.

Ducking around Beast, I rush at Sarge. Using the hold that Shadow taught me and a sweep of my leg, I bring him down. He's strong, grappling with me as I fight with everything I have to keep him back.

"J.J.! Get over here!" Rookie screams at me, still firing at the drones.

A blast from a drone strikes the access panel, blowing it apart. Sarge throws me off and as he stands, I use both feet to kick his knees, hard. He goes down and Beast is there hauling me up, practically throwing me toward the entrance.

"We have to close the door!" Rookie screams as Beast joins him and they hold back Sarge and the drones with their fire. Everything is chaos.

My nose suddenly stings at the strong smell of rubbing alcohol as Rookie hauls me through the doorway. Chef is kneeling in the doorway, pouring out the last of the alcohol bottle. He tosses it over his shoulder and then he sets something down in the center of the liquid—the large lithium battery from the defibrillator.

"Go!" he exclaims as we run past. He takes his gun and unloads it into Sarge as he tries to enter right behind me, knocking him back again, but not far.

"Chef!" I start to run forward, but Beast pulls me back.

"Move back! Duck and cover!" Chef shouts. His eyes meet mine for a long, charged moment. "Get everybody home," he says. "And tell my brother I love him very much."

Then he aims his rifle down and fires directly into the battery. It explodes with a pop, into the pool of rubbing alcohol. The second explosion is nearly simultaneous and hollows out my ears, blasting the door frame into rubble. The heavy door and a part of the ceiling fall, sealing the entrance to the pyramid shut. Over the sound of tumbling rock, I hear Sarge roar in fury and defeat.

I fall to my knees, choking and blinded by flying dust. It takes several moments to clear it from my mouth, my nose, and my eyes. Chef! He's completely buried!

I dig like mad to free him. My sobs cut the air and I feel Rookie's hands on my back, on my shoulders, pulling at me. I fall back, spitting and coughing to clear out my mouth and lungs. Beast stares at the widening pool of blood seeping out from under the rubble. He shakes his head.

There is no med kit now, no bandages. Nothing can save Chef. If we don't get through this soon, there may not be a Gears anymore, either. Or Shadow.

What am I going to say to Akoni? How am I going to be able to tell him this?

Beast puts a hand on my shoulder.

"Mourn later," he tells me. "We haven't won yet. And now we're the only ones who can finish this."

I take a deep, shuddering breath, and nod. He steps back and Rookie reaches out a thumb to wipe the tears and grime out of my eyes as he helps me to my feet.

We were expecting more booby traps, but this is nothing but a very large room, cavernous and empty save for a glowing neon door set in the opposite wall.

"I don't like this," Rookie says.

"Too quiet," Beast agrees.

"Nowhere to go but forward," I tell them.

I look over at Beast, who's crouched next to Shadow, ripping his shirt into pieces and wrapping them around Gears's head. "Keep pressure on that wound," I tell him.

Beast nods, rifle at the ready, eyes scanning the room for any hidden danger.

Rookie and I walk toward the door, rifles sweeping in a circle all around us. I tip my head back to look up at the ceiling, sure that something is going to come swooping down and take us out, but we still appear to be alone.

"I don't see any sort of access panel," Rookie says, looking the door over. "And Gears is in no shape to help us even if we do locate something like that."

We examine the area around the door, Rookie prodding the floor in front of the doorway with his gun, then the toe of his shoe. Nothing. No clicks, no whirring blades, no shooting darts, no bubbling acid.

There's no doorknob, not even a hinge to show which side of the door opens. He puts a hand out to touch it. A light flares briefly, but it's only a light, and the door doesn't move.

"Wait." I step forward. "Let me. I'm the wild card, here. Maybe whatever is keeping you out won't work on me."

"I've got your six. And be careful," Rookie says. "I've got a hot date tonight." He gives me a crooked grin.

"Get a room," Beast calls out from behind us. I choke on a laugh, grateful to have it break the tension. Then I take a breath and put my hand on the door.

There's a sudden lack of noise, as if someone put a jar over my head. The room disappears, along with everyone else.

I'm standing in my living room in Chicago, facing the kitchen. A man turns from the refrigerator to look at me and breaks into a wide grin.

"Hey there, Bug!" he says.

30

HIS SMILE GOES ALL the way up into his eyes, crinkling them at the edges. He stands there looking at me with one hand shoved into the pocket of his wrinkled khaki pants, his beloved face just under the mop of unruly brown hair and just above the neck of his favorite t-shirt. It features a winged horse with a light saber-toting cat on its back—I gave it to him for Father's Day one year. It's like I just woke up in my bed six months ago on a Saturday morning and stepped out of my room to find him starting breakfast in the kitchen.

"Dad?" I say it hesitantly, because despite my leaping and thundering heart, I know this isn't real. I know I am dreaming. But he looks so real. Oh God, he looks so real.

"It's okay, Bug," he says. "I know you weren't expecting this. But it's okay."

"I—I don't understand."

"You've gotten through all the preliminary levels of the security protocols I placed on these files. And you got past Sarge, which is even more impressive. I'm so proud of you."

His words make me feel funny inside, even though I know this isn't really him talking. Is it?

"Are you trapped in here, too?" I ask hesitantly.

"Not trapped," he says. "Placed. Wormed my way in. I created my own A.I.—starring yours truly—" He gives a short bow. "Within the Citadel virus to keep Sarge at bay."

"And are you the reason I've been able to visit this place in my dreams?"

"Not directly. It appears you've been exposed to the nanite prototypes, which got you in the door, along with your physical proximity and propensity for lucid dreaming. Once I figured out you were here, I enabled gateway access when you made it to the pyramid."

"You knew I was here?"

"Yep." He smiles widely. "I triggered the memory of your visit to my lab in your dream and sent it back-to-back with the Citadel scenario, hoping you'd figure it out, and you did." The pride in his voice pulls tears to my eyes.

I didn't, really, but I'm here now. He gestures over to the couch in the living room, and we sit.

"I know you created the Citadel," I tell him. "You think I would have picked up on it sooner."

"The pyramid was straight out of Stargate," he says with a grin. "It was easy enough to manage once I got wind of Evan's activities. I'd set up a few security back doors when I wrote the code. Call it a hunch, but I had a feeling Evan wasn't the most trustworthy guy."

"You were right on that one."

"I built a pretty good case against the company. I planned to go public with what I knew as soon as I had everything assembled. Then the island went into lockdown. The insiders who were working with me went silent."

"Evan suspected you were onto them. Threats were made to some of the employees."

"That's when I decided it was my mission to keep Eventide from ever being successful as a military tool. It was risky. I'm going to guess that with the lack of recent updates, I'm in jail or I'm not around to prosecute anymore."

My eyes fill with tears. "You're not in jail."

Understanding dawns on his face.

"Aw, Bug," he says, reaching for me. "I'm sorry."

I know he's only a simulation. I know he's only in my mind. But I wrap my arms around him, and I hold him. I swear he smells like Old Spice aftershave. My tears soak his shoulder.

"I'm sorry," he says again.

Eventually, I pull back, wiping the tears from my cheeks with the backs of my hands.

"You knew you were going to die?"

His eyebrows go up. "No, of course not. But things were turning ugly at Codonexus, and they knew that when I left the company, I took with me some very promising work we did early on. They've been after me about it for a while. I denied it of course, told them everything I'd done in that direction had failed and I scrapped the files out of pure frustration."

"They knew better," I said. "A good scientist keeps a data trail. Failed data is as important as working data, and you left a few gaps."

He taps the end of my nose with his finger. "Still sharp as a tack, Bug. Yes, of course they knew I was lying. But legally, there was nothing they could do since they couldn't prove it and the missing data never surfaced anywhere else. They tried to hire me back at one point. Offered me ridiculous sums of money. Big, fat dollar signs. Evan even told me he could get you into Princeton or Yale for a free ride. I told him you'd get there by yourself, the big jerk."

"What is this place?" I ask, looking around.

"This is it," Dad says, stretching his arms out wide. "The final security protocol. Once you get through this, you'll only need to access my safety deposit box at Northern Trust Bank in Chicago. There's a note with all the same clues I'm giving you here, and a laptop encrypted with the same password. It has all the documentation I've amassed on Evan and Codonexus, and all the research I kept out of Evan's reach."

"So now we all go free?"

"Yup. Getting past this level ends the program and sets the squad free."

"And Evan can't re-enable it?"

"Not unless you give them the code—they can't access any of the data regarding went on inside here. One more hurdle and you're all out."

"What do I do?"

"It's two letters and three symbols followed by a series of numbers—and you're the only one that would be able to figure it out. You have all the clues you need in this conversation, so it'll be obvious."

He points to a red door that suddenly shimmers into existence on the opposite wall from where we sit.

"Right through there," he says. "Input the password and it's a done deal."

"And what happens to you?" I ask. "After I walk through the door?"

"It disengages me, too. Sorry, Bug."

I want to stay sitting on this couch, with him, his hand holding mine. I want to feel his shoulder rubbing up against my shoulder. We can sit here and watch cheesy old Sci-Fi TV with a bowl of popcorn, catching kernels in our mouths, and laughing over bad special effects from the pre-CGI days. I wonder how long I could stretch that out.

But I know Gears and Shadow are on borrowed time, and there may be a slim chance that Chef is hanging on. Akoni, Rio, and Dr. Grady are in danger as well, out in the real world. They all took great risks to put me exactly where I am right now. I can't let them all down.

I have to say goodbye—something I didn't get to do in real life. Why does it somehow feel like this is worse?

"Daddy—" My voice cracks and I can't finish.

He reaches over and cups my face gently in his hands. "You and I lived a great life together. Now your life will go on. And you know what I always say about life."

Tears clog my voice as I make a poof gesture with my fingers and answer. "Terms and conditions apply."

He taps my node with a finger, his eyes twinkling. "You get to carry me forward now. And you are everything I want to leave to the world. My brightest, best gift to humanity."

"Dad—" the dam breaks and I grab him again, my arms around him so tight that if he were real, I'd be hurting him.

He holds me just as fiercely as I sob. We rock for a minute, holding each other, until I take a deep shuddering breath and force myself to pull away and get to my feet.

"Remember who you are, J.J. You can do this." He gives me a nod of encouragement. I walk forward and grip the doorknob in my hand, turning for one last look.

"I love you," I say, even though I know he isn't truly hearing me. I have to say it all the same.

He smiles at me and raises two fingers. "You and me, Bug. Me and you."

I raise two fingers in return and open the final door.

31

I **STEP INTO THE** room, turning back for one more glimpse through the doorway, but there is no door anymore. This room is covered in consoles crammed with keyboards, dials, and touch screens covering every inch of space below the display screens on the walls. I walk to the closest set of consoles. They all appear to be active, the screens above scrolling through various lines of code, flashing and revolving graphs, spreadsheets, and columns of data.

I'm supposed to input a password. Where? Dad made it sound like this was going to be easy, but if this is the final security protocol, logic tells me it should be more difficult than anything else.

My senses are on high alert. Just because Sarge is blocked from getting in here doesn't mean I'm safe. What if he breaks through, bringing in drones that slaughter my squad? For all I know the walls are going to start closing in.

Stop it, J.J. Focus.

I slowly inch along, stepping side to side, surveying the consoles in front of me. I need to input the password on one of these keyboards or touch screens.

But what is the password?

Information flashes on the screens in front of me, but none of it looks familiar.

I need to go about this scientifically. The data on the left-hand side of the screen—the spreadsheet data—looks like biometrics and projections. I look at the other three walls to see if the medical data is consigned to spreadsheets on those displays as well, but it's not. It appears in bar graphs on another wall, and the spreadsheets on the third wall show statistical probabilities of a series of projected outcomes in various nanite configurations.

So much data. I wonder if it's supposed to be a distraction, keeping me busy trying to figure out which stream of data is important. It's making my head hurt.

Is it in the code? I know nothing about writing code. Computer science was never really my thing. But Dad would know that. He said this would be obvious. This is *not* obvious.

I begin walking more quickly around the room, glancing down. *Think like Dad.* Is every console the same? Sometimes when you're conducting experiments, all you're looking for are anomalies. What's different?

I keep walking, frantically trailing my fingertips along the edges of each console. Keypads. Dials. Touch screens. A circle with a knob in the center. I keep walking. Keypads. Dials. Touch screens. Keypads. Dials.

Wait. There was only one circle.

I turn around and go back, looking again at the circle set into the console. At the center is a large, rounded knob with a keyboard directly beneath. The knob has a red triangle sitting at the nine o'clock position. Above the knob at twelve o'clock on the circle and set into the console is a very small pair of wings. Pegasus wings.

I reach out and turn the knob so the triangle points at the wings. Suddenly all of the screens flash yellow for a moment then go back to showing their various modes of data. The room begins to hum and the top right corner of every screen—to my horror—begins to show a countdown clock.

Sixty seconds. Fifty-nine. Fifty-eight. I have less than a minute to figure this out!

Obvious to me. Obvious to me. Do the letters and symbols repeat? Are the numbers my birth date? No, they'd have tried that. The phone number of our favorite pizza place? How many numbers? He didn't say, did he?

I replay our conversation in my mind. Two letters, three symbols, and a series of numbers. Panic floods through me and I fight to keep my focus.

Forty-eight seconds.

We were just in our house in Chicago. The initials might be my home state of Illinois—IL.

They tried to hire me back at one point, Dad said. *Offered me ridiculous sums of money.*

Three dollar signs, maybe? I let out a frustrated stream of air through my teeth. Now what about the number?

I take a deep breath and type IL, then three dollar signs and our zip code. I press "Enter" on the keyboard.

Every one of the screens turns red, and then they show one black X, along with that countdown clock which shows me I have thirty-five precious seconds left.

Come on! It's obvious! He said it was obvious!

I stare down at the dial and realize that the triangle is not just a triangle. It's footed at the bottom almost like a capital letter A without the center bar. And there's a dot over the top.

Stargate. We used to watch Stargate together—it was my dad's favorite show. They used to dial the Stargate to travel to other planets and it had alien symbols all over it. You dialed the symbols like dialing a telephone number. This symbol—the triangle with the dot over it—it's the symbol for Earth.

Seven symbols to dial a Stargate. So, the number section is seven symbols long. Dates won't work. Or my social security number. Too obvious.

I've given you all the clues you need, he said. I will my mind to replay every word of what he just said to me, but that black X is staring me in the face and there's no time, no time—

Twenty-three seconds. Think. Think!

It has to be seven numbers. It's Stargate. Dad and I watched it together all the time. It was our favorite! I stare intently at the knob. At the wings over it.

Realization dawns on me. Stargate was Dad's favorite, but the spinoff—Stargate *Atlantis*—was mine, because it takes place in the Pegasus Galaxy. You need an eight-symbol dialing sequence to travel to another galaxy.

The date I won the $25,000 scholarship for young women in STEM! When I told Dad, he picked me up and swung me around. I told him it was one of the best days of my life. He said any best day of my life was the best day of his life, too.

I take a deep breath, flex my fingers, and type in IL—$$$—and the date and press Enter. Red screens, then one more ominous black X.

Ten seconds. The screens begin flashing and a claxon sounds, jarring my nerves and loud enough to vibrate through my skull. My heart is pounding frantically.

What are the damn numbers? I close my eyes, replaying our conversation.

What do I always say about life?

"Terms and conditions apply," I whisper.

Remember who you are, J.J., he said.

It can't be that easy.

I type in J.J., then three asterisks. Then I reach for the dial and spin the numbers, singing along as I do.

Eight-Six-Seven-Five-Three-Oh-Niiiine.

Six seconds and I need the final number. I think of his beloved, smiling face and I know.

You and me

Me and you

Nobody rocks it

Like we do

Just us two!

I dial the number two exactly when the countdown reaches the same number, and press Enter.

Then the room goes black.

32

Consciousness pulls me to the surface and as my head clears, I hear a faint click. Air rushes in, and bright light assaults my eyes, making me raise a hand to block it out as I squint. I'm lying on my back, and the pod is around me. The lid is open, and I am free.

Joy, blinding and ecstatic, rips through me. I tear off the electrodes, swing my legs over the side and leap out, stumbling. Before I can run for the red EVAC button on the other pods, a voice calls out from somewhere behind me.

"Not so fast, *chica.*"

I turn slowly, and my eyes first land on Akoni and Rio—who looks pale and stricken. Next to them are my mother and

Evan, and beside them is Armando, with a gun in his hand trained on my friends. Dr. Grady is nowhere in sight.

"Step away from the pod," Armando says in that same silky tone. "You and I need to talk."

Nausea grips my stomach and terror squeezes my throat, making it difficult to speak. I finally manage one word.

"Mom?"

My wide, frantic eyes land on her, sure she'll do something, say something. Evan is spineless, but she—

"Do as he says, J.J."

Her words are quiet but firm, and her eyes are steady as they meet mine.

"What?" I cannot believe she's all right with this.

"J.J." Mom steps forward, speaking calmly—far too calmly for this situation. "Give Armando the password and then you need to come with me."

"I'm not going anywhere without my squad," I tell her, wishing I sounded more brave and less shaky. "Or my friends. And the only one I'm talking to is the police."

"You're not talking to anyone but us." Evan moves to her side. "Just give us the passcode."

"Please hold your breath while you wait for that," I snap.

"The information is in her brain, si?" Armando's grip tightens on the gun. "Put her back in the pod and pull the password out of her head."

"It doesn't work like that," my mother interjects hastily. "Just give me some time to talk to her—"

"We gave you time." Armando's words snap like a whip. "Time and time and time, with no results for our money. Now one of you has paid dearly for those delays. How many more must there be?"

My mother winces at that statement, and Rio sucks in a sharp breath. Akoni's jaw hardens and his eyes shift to the entry of the lab, where a large pool of red then smears to a series of red streaks all the way to the door, as if something—or someone—bloody had been dragged through it. Cold fingers claw out from the pit of my stomach. Armando is the reason there is no Dr. Grady here.

He addresses my mother. "You will get the passcode. Or she will tell me the passcode. And you will not like that."

"That might be the quickest option," Evan says tightly.

"Evan!" Mom's voice is sharp. "Let's all just calm down and talk about this. She's a *child*."

"She's eighteen. An adult now." Evan reminds her, and from the gleam in his eye, it's clear he agrees with Armando. "And of course, I'm concerned about your daughter. But she's going to be smart about this and not cause any trouble. Isn't that right, J.J.?"

"You're not concerned about me. Your bank account is at stake," I clarify for him. "I don't give a shit. You've tortured these people for months. And you would have kept on doing it if my father hadn't found a way to stop you."

"If your father hadn't found a way to steal from me," Evans seethes.

"You really think your company would have survived what he was planning to share about you?" My eyes harden and my mouth compresses into a thin line. "That's why you had him killed, isn't it?"

"J.J.," my mother holds out a hand as if to calm me down. "That was investigated and declared an accident."

"It was damn convenient," Evan says coolly, and I notice the way his eyes shift to Armando, whose eyes lock with my mother's before his lips curl into the slightest bit of a smile. Her returned look of warning is like a boot to the face. Searing pain and rage rip through me, clenching my fists and sending my heart pounding.

"Mom?" I stumble back a few steps. "You couldn't. You *didn't.* Tell me you didn't!" I beg. Her silence is deafening. Evan, of course, loves to talk.

"Come on, J.J." He flashes that infuriating shit-eating grin. "You can't just throw around accusations like that."

"He knew you too well—knew what you were up to—and you were getting desperate. How much did you stand to lose here Evan?" I ask.

"Millions, potentially," Evan replies with a casual shrug. "And some of that money could really benefit a young woman with her entire life ahead of her—and her two friends, who can encourage her to make the right choices and know how to keep their mouths shut. This company is on the cusp of some very important contracts with some very interested parties—parties like Armando. Contracts that will make us a power player in this emerging market. It's incredibly lucrative and all of us—including the three of you—could be set for life." He turns to gesture to Rio and Akoni.

"The college of your choice, the careers of your choice," he goes on. "You could all sit back on healthy bank accounts, spend your life traveling the world and enjoying a different party every night. A life of your choosing. Think about it!"

"What about them?" I ask, gesturing at the pods.

"Give me the code," Armando says reasonably, "and they will stay under until my associates can debrief them properly at a secure location. We'll discharge them afterward."

Ice flood my veins. I didn't miss the deliberate choice of the word *discharge.* I've seen his associates. He's going to discharge them like he discharged Dr. Grady. And I know it.

"Money will not repair the harm you have visited upon my brother," Akoni says in a low, furious voice.

"I want to get off this rock," Rio says flippantly. "But I don't need your filthy hush money."

"Do you think we will stay silent?" Akoni presses. "We will be speaking to the authorities and to the media."

"None of us are backing down," I tell them. "How long do you plan to keep us here? Or do you plan to kill us all?"

"If we all just keep our heads—" My mother says soothingly. Then she turns to Armando. "Grady said J.J. carries the prototype nanites. That's really what we need here. We need more than the password to unlock Eventide—we have to rebuild it from the ground up."

"Get the nanites out of her blood or her flesh—whatever you need to do." Armando tips his chin at my mother. "I will have a helicopter here within the hour."

Mom shakes her head. "It—it's not that simple. The nanites are programmed to migrate to the hippocampus and amygdala, the areas of the brain that hold situational and emotional memory. We'll need a top surgeon, otherwise we could do a lot of damage—"

Armando swings the gun to me and I look right down the barrel. For once I'm actually thankful for every wretched scenario I've been through because I'm not afraid. I've been wounded and killed so many times that staring at a gun is no longer a heart-pounding event.

"Go ahead," I tell him. "Pull the trigger. Murder me in front of my mother. I'm sure that'll go over well. And you definitely won't get what you want."

"Evan." My mother's voice is low, tense. "This isn't what we discussed."

Evan's face goes red and he's flailing his arms like a crazy man. "I'm not going to stand by and let this spoiled little brat with her self-important morality complex destroy everything we have worked to build! I gave you time to get her in line," he snarls at her. "Apparently, it was wasted time."

"Enough." Armando sounds bored, but his eyes are calculating as they slide to me. "Give him the code," he tells me, and then he centers the gun on my mother. I stand frozen as Armando starts counting. Will I let him pull that trigger?

"Uno . . ."

I stare at my mother's shocked face, then at the gun. Then my gaze shifts over Armando's shoulder to Rio, who is slowly inching behind the control panel.

"Don't let this go too far," I plead with Evan. "You don't want to do this."

"Dos . . ." Armando keeps counting.

"It won't go that far," Evan says, eyeing Armando and the gun nervously. "Because you're going to tell us what we need to hear. Aren't you, J.J.?"

I look at Armando's cold eyes, at that gun, at my mother, and search frantically for something to say to stall—to stop all of it. I shove my hands out in front of me.

"Wait!"

Three things happen within a heartbeat. First, Rio hits the large, red EVAC button on the console. Then the lids on all the pods unlock, and my mother's scream splits the air as a gunshot rings out. She crumples to the floor.

"Mom!" The word tears from my throat. Despite all that she's done, I dive for her. Her hands claw at me as she sinks to the ground, ripping my locket off as she falls.

"Get away from her," Armando motions with the gun. "Get over there with the others. And you—" He points at Rio. "Try anything else and you're next!"

Armando keeps the gun trained on Rio and Akoni as he digs his phone out of his pocket and hits a button. A voice answers immediately.

"Esteban?" Armando says. "In here. And bring Alonzo." He ends the call, his eyes still firmly glued on the squad.

"You." Armando points his chin at Evan. "Let them in."

"B-But—" Evan is clearly shaken, his horrified eyes locked on my mother.

"Now!"

"Of course. Of course." He rushes over to the door, and Armando's goons must have been waiting right outside because they step in as soon as the door is open. He signals them to move over and train their guns on the pods.

Mom is still conscious. The bullet went through her shoulder, but it's high up enough that she should be all right if I can get the bleeding stopped. I ignore Armando and clamp my hand over the wound. His eyes are riveted on the opening pods, and I can hear the sound of consciousness returning to the occupants. The squad is starting to sit up, stretching and still disoriented. Beast rips his neuro sensors off and climbs out a little clumsily.

"What's going on?"

The voice is Rookie's, and he's pulling himself out of his pod. His eyes search the room until they find me. Then he and Beast notice Armando with his gun and start forward at the same time.

"Don't move unless you want a bullet in your head," Armando warns. "Now get over there with the other two. All of you." He jerks his head toward Rio and Akoni, and his men move forward to herd everyone to one side. Shadow is up now, and Gears is right behind her. Akoni is very still, his eyes glued on the final pod where Chef lies unmoving.

My squad and I are still in tune with each other, still scanning the scene for any weapon or an opportunity we can take in this scenario. We've faced danger together so many times, it's become second nature. Mom makes a whimpering sound and I glance down to see my locket, speckled with blood and lying next to her on the ground. Sliding my hand over it, I meet Shadow's eyes.

She gives me a barely perceptible nod, and Beast rolls his shoulders, readying himself as they all move to stand by Rio and Akoni. Gears looks at Shadow, then me, and I slowly push to my feet with the bloody locket clenched in my hand. Rookie and I lock eyes and his voice plays in my head.

Line it up. Don't second-guess. Take the shot.

My arm whips out and Armando catches the motion out of the corner of his eye. He pivots toward me, pulling the gun around as the locket flies from my hand, striking him hard in his left eye.

Gears shouts at Akoni and Rio to get down and I dive as Armando's shot goes wide, ricocheting off the wall. He only gets one in before Beast barrels into him and they go down. Shadow whips a hard kick to the chest of one goon, knocking him off his feet, and Gears slams a punch to the jaw of the other before wrenching his gun away, sending it skidding across the floor to Rookie, who grabs it up. Armando staggers to his feet.

"I know how to use this," Rookie levels the gun on him. "You know I do."

He waves Armando over to where Shadow and Gears are holding guns on the other two.

"Not so fast." Beasts's voice is a growl from behind me. "He thought he could slink away." He drags Evan by the collar and throws him to the floor at Armando's feet. Evan shrieks like a child.

We all stand there panting, riding the adrenaline rush until Rio's enthusiastic clapping breaks the mood.

"Yes! Chimu Trio Masterforce!" she squeals.

Akoni's mood is very different as he walks to his brother's pod. I move toward him, my chest aching, watching Chef's too-still form with growing anguish.

My hand settles on Akoni's shoulder, and then Chef's whole body arches as he sucks in a deep breath. His eyes flutter as Akoni lets out a whoop, reaching into the pod, arms circling and lifting his brother.

Chef—Kalu—sits up, holding Akoni tight, tears streaming unashamedly down his face. Somehow, Chef was still hanging on under all that rubble, and I got him out in time. My relief nearly sends me to my knees. Akoni's eyes meet mine over his brother's shoulder.

"Thank you," he says, his voice hoarse. "Thank you all."

It only takes a few moments to brief the squad on the situation and I watch with pleasure as Beast hauls a visibly shaking Evan to his feet.

"Somewhere on him is a key to a room at the end of the hall," Akoni tells him. "You will find Dr. Manuel Ruiz inside. Release him."

"Yeah, you can lock these lowlifes in there," Rio offers. "And it's okay if their faces meet a few walls along the way."

"We've got them," Gears says, taking the badge key from Evan's lab coat and gesturing to Shadow. Together they herd Evan, Armando and his thugs through the door.

"My mother needs medical attention," I say. "There's a first-aid kit on that wall."

Rookie passes it over to me and I bandage mom tightly, grateful again for these last months of on-the-job field training, as hellish as it's been.

"I'm sorry, J.J. I'm so sorry." Mom's voice is choked with pain. "I don't know how it all went so—so horribly wrong."

"We'll talk about it later," I say tightly, though I'm not sure I'll ever be able to speak to her again. I pull her mobile phone from her pocket and toss it to Rio. "Call security and the infirmary. They should be here soon."

My mother's sorrowful eyes follow me as I get to my feet, only to be lifted from behind by a giant pair of tattooed arms.

"Beast! I exclaim, laughing as he nearly breaks my ribs.

"You're really something," Beast says, ruffling my hair. "Did they have you fighting a Minotaur behind that door? Or were you dodging more drones?"

I smile up at him despite the slice of anguish across my heart. "I was hanging with my dad."

Rio finishes her call and is watching my reunion with wide eyes and an enormous grin. I throw my arms around her.

"Oh my God, we did it!" I say, relief flooding through me.

"Are you bad-ass or what?" She crows, mimicking my throw. "You were like *shloop!* And then his eye was like exploding and damn! *So* bad-ass!"

I turn with my arm still around her and motion to Akoni. "Guys? This is my other team: Rio and Akoni. None of this would have happened without them."

The squad steps forward to shake their hands, clapping them on the back, hugging and thanking them both repeatedly. Beast swings Rio around as she giggles madly, and Akoni offers his phone to anyone who wants to contact their family.

"What do we do with those men?" Chef asks.

"I'm happy to shoot that bastard Walters," Beast offers.

"I would agree with you," Akoni says. "But his death will not tell us the names of everyone who was involved in this, or which countries were planning to buy this technology. We only have some of the web. We need to see how far it stretches."

"There are no formal police on the island," Rio says. "But security will call the mainland—they'll send a boat."

"It just so happens we have our own specialized security force," I say smugly. "We'll let them keep guard until the authorities get here."

As they make their plans, a hand rests on my shoulder and I turn my head, looking closely at every single angle and plane of his face, at that scar by his mouth. He looks the same but more real somehow.

"J.J." He says my name like it's part of a magical incantation. And it feels like it.

"Mateo." I seal the spell with his name on my lips.

"You did it," he says, stroking my jaw with his thumb as his hand cups my face.

My hand comes up as my fingers twine with his. "*We* did it. All of us."

I start to hug him, but he suddenly goes still as his eyes focus somewhere behind me. His father stands in the doorway, along with Shadow and Gears. He's pale and his eyes are frantic as he searches the room. I give Mateo's hand a squeeze.

"Go," I say. "We'll find our time later."

He drops a soft kiss on my forehead. "It's a date."

Then he crosses the room in four long strides, his father meeting him halfway as they hug each other fiercely.

My legs leave the ground as Beast comes up behind me and hoists me up onto his shoulders like I'm a rockstar. The rest of the team hoots and claps, demanding that he put me down so they can hug me too. Then I'm engulfed by them all, holding them close, seeing them for who they really are in this bright new world we're all finally in together.

Time to go back to our real life. I'm not sure how we're defining it—everything is too chaotic right now. It's too much to deal with between the Citadel, my dad, Evan, my mom, Dr. Grady . . . I'm overwhelmed and shaking with a mix of pain, weariness and elation.

When Beast sets me down, I drop to my knees, bury my face in my hands, and cry. And cry. And cry.

My squads—both of them—surround me. Their hands are on my back, my hair, their arms around me, and their words of support are a balm to my tattered soul.

And as always, they've all got my six.

33

IT'S BEEN ELEVEN DAYS since the return to the real world. The island has been in a state of upheaval. The Chilean government has shut the company down while it investigates, and the place is swarming with not only government agents but also agents from Interpol and even the CIA.

Most of the workers have been released and given assistance in transporting themselves and their families back to their countries of origin. The key management of the company is being detained for further questioning and possible criminal charges. My mother is among them.

She's recuperating well, but not talking much to them. She did ask the authorities to assure me that this will all be cleared up—like we're magically going to be a family afterward. I'm not sure how far her involvement goes in all of this, and in the death of my father and part of me doesn't ever want to know. So I don't respond to her. I imagine the next time I see her will be in a courtroom.

And now it falls on me to pack up all of our belongings. I'm sorting through everything at the house right now, packing my mother's things into one set of boxes pushed carefully against the living room wall. My things are in my room, and it should go quickly considering I never unpacked a lot of it in the first place. I'm just putting tape across one of the boxes when I hear a knock on the door.

"Dude," Rio says as she walks in and tosses her neon green backpack on the couch, not bothering to wait for me to open the door for her. "Did you go through Dr. Walters' stuff before they took it? I bet he's got some nice things."

"I'm sure he does," I reply, giving Akoni a wave as he follows behind her through the door. "Evan's things—and some of my mother's stuff—were already carted away by the authorities doing the investigation."

"Everything is considered evidence now," Akoni says. "From what little I have been able to glean from the interviews they had with me and the talk around the island, Evan is going to be locked away for a very long time." He looks over at me. "I haven't heard anything regarding your mother yet," he finishes apologetically.

I give him a dismissive wave and return to packing. He takes the hint and doesn't remark further.

"Those interviews were looong," Rio grumbles. "Like they took hours or something. How many times can you tell someone the same story?"

"I doubt we're finished," I remind her. "Even after we've all gone our separate ways they're going to need to follow up. And then I'm sure there will be a trial."

"At least we'll all see each other again, right? I mean—" Her voice breaks a little and she blinks back tears. "It would be really bad if we never saw each other again."

Akoni puts an arm around her. "I'm going to miss you, too. Both of you."

"Where are you going?" I ask him. "Back to Nigeria?"

"Only for a short time," he answers. "Kalu has gotten in touch with his university, and he will be starting classes again after he's taken some time. I will be staying with him, near Washington DC. I hope to be starting classes as well, at a future date."

"At least you two will be in the same country," Rio sobs, dashing the tears from her cheeks. "We're going back to Japan. Since our school here was online, my parents say I can finish the semester from there."

"That's what I'm doing, too," I tell her. "Mr. Silva is helping me get everything organized before I leave so that I can complete the rest of it on my own through the online portal."

"You're eighteen now," Akoni says. "You can go anywhere you'd like. Kalu wanted me to let you know that you are welcome wherever we go."

"You can come live with us," Rio offers. "At least I say you can. My parents are still kind of pissed over losing their jobs and me having a gun waved in my face. But they'll warm up to you eventually."

It feels weird to laugh over that, but I do anyway.

"Thanks, but I've got a plan. Beast lives in California with his family, near Sacramento. He's got a guest room and offered it to me until college starts. I applied for an early admission decision at UC Berkeley, and that came through last week."

"But we'll still have an ocean between us." Rio says, sniffling. Then her face lights up. "But I'm on track to graduate a semester early. Cal State East Bay isn't far from Berkeley—and it's got a great environmental studies program that I was considering."

"Maybe once your parents calm down, you could come for a visit and tour the college." I look over at Akoni. "Both of you are welcome to visit anytime. I'm going to miss you. A lot."

"I never thought I'd be sad to leave this rock," Rio wails, throwing her arms around both of us.

"Sorry to interrupt." Mateo's voice comes from the doorway.

I reach behind me to the table for a tissue to hand to Rio before I use one to hastily wipe my own tears away.

"How are you doing?" Akoni asks him. "I know it is very difficult adjusting."

"It's strange," Mateo admits. "I have to keep reminding myself that this is reality now. The government has brought in counselors to work with us, and they're also giving us referrals for services that can help us further—wherever it is we're going."

"And where is it that you're going?" I ask softly.

I haven't seen him much since he got out. Between all of the interviews with law enforcement, the packing, and trying to figure out the logistics of moving away, things have been a little hectic.

Before he can answer me, Rio blows her nose loudly and then shoves the wet tissue down into the front pocket of her red denim overalls.

"I think it's time for ice cream," she says to Akoni. "That one guy in the village has the best mango flavor."

"That is on the beach near the place that sells meat pies, isn't it?" he asks.

"Yes, but O-M-G do not eat the meat pies!" she exclaims. "That dude has ants the size of my hair clips. And all that crusty stuff in his nose."

Akoni links his arm with hers. "I will avoid that place." He looks over at me. "We will speak again before you leave."

"I'll be over tonight," Rio says. 'We still have two seasons of Stargate to get through before you go."

"I'll have the popcorn ready," I promise her as they make their way past Mateo and out the door.

"So." I say.

"So." He parrots, walking over to stand in front of me.

"Where are you going?

"Nowhere, for a while," he answers. "My father is too involved with the company liquidation. He's not being indicted or anything, but his testimony is critical, and he's able to grant them access to a lot of information. We're going to be on the island for at least another few weeks and then my father has a couple of job offers that have already been made—one from the company that your father used to work for in Chicago."

"So that's where you're going to end up? Chicago?"

"He is." Mateo smiles, tucking an errant piece of my hair behind my ear. "I've got college to think about. According to the school, I qualify for graduation. I missed the deadline for early admission decisions, but my SAT scores were pretty good. And I still have a scholarship offer waiting from the archery team at Stanford that—along with my grades—pretty much guarantees my acceptance. They need team members."

"Seriously?" I can't help my delighted smile.

"They have one of the top archery teams in the country," he says. "They have half a dozen Olympic team members in their alumni."

"That's good to know," I say, playing with the hem on his tee shirt. "But is it too soon? Maybe you should take some time. Take it easy for awhile."

"I talked to my counselor about it. We both think it's good for me to get back to my life again."

"I just worry about you."

"I know. And Stanford has a strong computer science program, which, by the way, is what I want to be doing."

"You're a developer nerd?" I raise my eyebrow. "You look *nothing* like a developer nerd."

He leans over and his voice sends a shiver down my spine as he whispers in my ear.

"I have tiny robots in my brain."

"Me too," I whisper back.

He turns his head, hesitating as his lips hover over mine.

"I can't believe you're really real," he breathes. "Part of me still wonders if this is just another scenario."

"I'm real." I promise.

"Maybe I'd better test this out—just to be sure."

There's a light in his eyes that stops my breath, and his lips touch mine gently, as if he really is testing, really making sure. Then he's kissing me like he has all the time in the world, like he plans to kiss me for a good, long while.

My hands move across his chest, feeling the warmth of skin and muscles beneath his tee shirt, moving up over his shoulders and into his hair as the kiss deepens. I can't get close enough, and a little sound breaks from my throat as his hands travel down over my hips, gripping me and pulling me in tighter.

"Dudes. *Ew.*"

Rio's voice breaks in, shattering our moment.

"This is reality, all right," I say with a sigh.

"I forgot my backpack," she tells us, scooping it up. "But as long as you're finished, you might as well get ice cream."

I look over at Akoni, who cringes and shrugs apologetically from the doorway.

"It's been a long time since I had ice cream," Mateo says with a wistful sigh.

"Okay," I give in. "Ice cream does sound good."

Rio flounces to the door, and we move to follow. Mateo leans down, his words low and only for me.

"We're not finished."

I give him a wicked smile. "Not even close."

34

Darkness surrounds me.

I breathe for a moment, getting my bearings and letting my eyes adjust. I am dreaming again. My entire body tenses at what is sure to be some sort of residual nightmare. A rustling sound from behind sends me whirling around, arms up to defend or attack if I need to.

Relief swamps me, followed by a wave of disbelief as my eyes become accustomed to the darkness and a shape begins to come clear.

"Hey there, Bug!" he says. "I've got the popcorn ready."

"Dad?"

He moves toward me, carrying a large bowl of popcorn. "I've got Stargate: Atlantis queued up and ready to go. Grab the Cokes and M&M's and follow me."

I do ask he asks, still too dumbfounded to speak. He plops down on the couch and I do the same as he sets the popcorn bowl between us and grabs the TV remote.

"Maybe I should have left the lights on," he says. "I can't see the buttons on the remote."

"Gimme." I take it from his hand, switching on the DVD player. The opening credits roll.

"Thanks. Now where is my couch pillow?"

"This is a dream." I blurt it out, but it comes out like more of a question than a statement.

He turns his head and in the dim light from the TV I can see his wide grin. "Sorta."

"Sorta?"

"Let's just say I slipped in through the back door. You didn't honestly think I was gone for good, did you?"

"Yeah." I swallow hard, blinking back the tears. "I did."

"That's because you thought our goodbye at the Citadel was just a goodbye." He crams a handful of popcorn in his mouth and talks around it. "It was goodbye with an *asterisk*."

"Terms and conditions apply." My voice is thin, being squeezed out through the lump in my throat.

"That's my girl." He reaches out and playfully taps the end of my nose. "I'll be popping in here and there, if that's okay."

"It's okay. More than okay."

He takes my hand. "You and me, Bug."

I look down at his fingers twined with mine and the knowledge that I'll be happy in my dreams sends a fierce, bright wave of joy coursing through me as I answer.

"Me and you."

ACKNOWLEDGEMENTS

First and foremost, I'd like to thank my daughter for a good part of my inspiration. Night terrors are awful, and she's battled them since the age of two which means for most of her childhood and a good part of her young adult years, I had a front row seat. She's pushed through with grace and resilience, forging a good life despite her brain trying to eat her alive some nights. I am fiercely, fiercely proud of her.

Next, I need to thank my amazing son. He's put up with dinner occasionally being late, mom staying up to the crack of dawn, incessant tappity-tapping and curse words filtering in from the other room, and rarely offers a word of complaint. Best of all, whenever he introduces me to someone it's always: "This is my mom. She's a writer." Whenever I don't feel like a writer (or at least much of one), I remind myself that my kid doesn't doubt it for a moment.

Next on the list would be my indomitable editor, Lina Matthews. You've guided my hand, listened to my rants, untwisted my brain, and helped me put together a coherent, and hopefully entertaining manuscript. Thank you is hardly sufficient, but I'll say it, or shout it, or sing it anyway.

Thanks is also due to the team at Gaze Publishing for their belief in me and my not-quite-your-usual-sci-fi-thriller of a story. The art department hit a home run with my fantastic cover, and the publicity team has been pushing, emphasizing, and throwing spotlights everywhere it can. They've been tireless, and taught me so much.

The final thank you goes to you, dear reader. Thanks for buying, thanks for reading, thanks for supporting me and liking my posts, reels and stories. Thanks for giving me a reason not to give up when it gets rough. I appreciate every one of you so much.

ABOUT THE AUTHOR

L.E. DeLano comes equipped with a "useless" Theatre degree that has opened doors for her in numerous ways. Though mostly raised in New Mexico, she now makes her home in Amish country, Pennsylvania. In her spare time, she eats too much refined sugar and tries to thwart her cat's plans for world domination. This has been unsuccessful on every level.

L.E.'s 2021 Novel, BLUE, was named the 2021 SPARK Award winner by The Society of Children's Book Writers and Illustrators (SCBWI), was the 2021/22 Gold Medal Winner in Young Adult Fiction in the Reader Views Reviewer's Choice Awards, and was chosen Teen Book of the Year by Reader Views Kids. Her debut YA novel, TRAVELER, was selected as a Keystone to Reading Secondary Book Award finalist by the Keystone State Reading Association (KSRA).

OTHER BOOKS BY L.E. DELANO

BLUE

TRAVELER

DREAMER

BLOW YOUR MIND, WRITE YOUR BOOK

Find L.E. Online at:

LEDeLano.com

Instagram   @ le_delano

X: @ LE_DeLano

Tumblr: @ledelano

Facebook: @authorledelano